Dory's heart was pounding as she stepped out of the bathroom

"Good morning," Jim said brightly—too brightly.

"Good morning yourself," She was surprised to see him sitting already dressed on the rumpled bed.

Now what? This had been her first sexual encounter as an unmarried woman. What were the rules? Last night they'd come together like two starved and lonely people, each of them too badly in need of love to worry about the consequences.

"Uh, you're an early riser," he remarked inanely. *What on earth do I say to her?*

They looked at each other in silence and then both blurted at the same time:

"Dory, about last night..."

"Jim, about last night..."

It was so ludicrous that after the first startled instant, they began to laugh. Jim came over and hugged her, and suddenly Dory knew everything was going to be all right.

ABOUT THE AUTHOR

Jane Silverwood created her hero after reading about the plight of returning hostages. "These people have undergone a terrible ordeal," she relates. "They have a hard time coping with life—never mind love." A former teacher, this sensitive author has written more than thirty novels. Fans will be happy to know Jane is working on an intriguing Superromance trilogy called The Byrnside Inheritance. Watch for it!

Books by Jane Silverwood

HARLEQUIN SUPERROMANCE
282–THE TENDER TRAP
314–BEYOND MERE WORDS

HARLEQUIN TEMPTATION
46–VOYAGE OF THE HEART
93–SLOW MELT
117–A PERMANENT ARRANGEMENT

Don't miss any of our special offers. Write to us at the following address for information on our newest releases.

Harlequin Reader Service
901 Fuhrmann Blvd., P.O. Box 1397, Buffalo, NY 14240
Canadian address: P.O. Box 603,
Fort Erie, Ont. L2A 5X3

Handle with Care

JANE SILVERWOOD

Harlequin Books

TORONTO • NEW YORK • LONDON
AMSTERDAM • PARIS • SYDNEY • HAMBURG
STOCKHOLM • ATHENS • TOKYO • MILAN

Published October 1989

First printing August 1989

ISBN 0-373-70375-9

CHAPTER ONE

"You're three minutes late and your fans are getting restless."

Dory Barker ran a hand through her soft blond curls. "I know, I know. Thank God our town house is at the top of a hill. That's how I had to start up the Plum."

Brenda, the administrator for the adult noncredit program, grinned. She knew Dory was referring to her aging maroon station wagon.

In too much of a rush to linger by the front desk, Dory hurried through the lobby to the stairs. As she took the steps at a run and then turned left into the tiled corridor that led to the pottery workroom, she reviewed her plans for her class. Though this was the beginning of a fresh eight-week session, she'd read through the class list and knew that most of her students would be familiar faces. Since her divorce two years ago, Dory had been teaching ceramics for the community college's noncredit program. It didn't pay much, but she enjoyed it and had developed a loyal following.

Just at the threshold of the workshop Dory paused to glance around. About fifteen adults of all ages, mostly women, but a few men, lounged at the long stained tables.

"Hi. How are you? Sorry I'm late." Dory waved and then hastened toward a bentwood clothes tree to hang up her well-worn corduroy jacket and oversize canvas purse.

Cool air just above the waistband of her jeans warned that her pink cotton sweatshirt had ridden up. After she tugged the errant top down low over her neat hips, she turned to survey her class a little more carefully. Yes, there was the plump young woman who claimed that this weekly night out from her three preschoolers was the only thing that saved her sanity. Next to her the flirtatious dentist who'd been attending since last spring winked broadly. Just behind him the lady who loved to make brightly glazed pottery figures for her large brood of grandchildren beamed and gave Dory the high sign.

Dory grinned back, but as her gaze shifted to the far corner of the room and her blue eyes encountered an unfamiliar pair of dark brown ones, her smile slipped slightly. Now who was that, she wondered. She knew she'd never seen him around before.

Suddenly, with that burned-charcoal gaze fixed on her, Dory felt prickly with self-consciousness. Wondering slightly at her reaction, she shot the man another curious glance. Though he had an attractive, strong-featured face, the loose denim shirt and slacks he wore only emphasized the fact that he was far too gaunt. If she'd ever seen a man it would be a pleasure to cook a good square meal for, it was he. Had he been ill, she wondered.

Not wanting to stare, she dragged her gaze away and dug out her class list. When she read through it, she discovered that the stranger responded to the name James Gordon. Had she heard that somewhere before? Nothing came to mind, so she shrugged and said, "Let's get underway, shall we?"

Amid the chorus of enthusiastic yeses, she pointed at the barrel in the center of the room. "Most of you know where to find the clay. And most of you already have projects underway. If the four newcomers will follow me to table number one, I'll get them started with a lesson on how to wedge."

After passing out hunks of clay to James Gordon and the three other new students, Dory began her wedging demonstration.

"One of the great things about ceramics," she explained as she broke her own lump into halves and then folded the two pieces into each other, "is that it's very therapeutic. You get to take out a lot of your aggressions." She hurled the gray mound down on the table, where it landed with a satisfying thump, then picked it up and repeated the action, this time so firmly that the wood surface quivered.

"What's that supposed to accomplish?" queried Linda, a pleasant-looking middle-aged woman who was taking the class with her freckle-faced teenage daughter, Janice.

"I'm wondering the same thing," chimed in Ben, a cheerful little man who'd already announced he'd signed up for ceramics because he wanted to give all his friends an ugly ashtray for Christmas.

"It knocks out air bubbles, improves the consistency and malleability." As she spoke, Dory's small, deft hands worked rhythmically, kneading, folding and then slamming. Now and then she glanced at the faces of the four adults watching her. Though James Gordon was silent, she was more conscious of him and his dark scrutiny than of anyone else in the room.

Again she found herself wondering about him. How old was he? With those harsh lines around his mouth and the gray sprinkling his close-cropped hair it was hard to tell. But surely he couldn't be much older than she was, which put him somewhere just past thirty. And what was he doing here in her class? Somehow he didn't seem like the sort of person who would be interested in pottery—too intense. It was easier to picture him whipping an opponent in an aggressive game of tennis or manhandling a sports car through

hairpin turns on a race course than to visualize him being
content making a pot.

And what was there about him that she found so darn
compelling, Dory asked herself. He was too thin to be called
handsome. Still, there was something about his face, with
its high cheekbones and cleanly carved, aquiline features,
that riveted her. And she wasn't the only female in the room
responding to him, Dory suddenly realised. Young Janice
was glancing at him with undisguised interest.

Dory stopped wedging and said with an encouraging
smile, "Now it's your turn to try. Let's see the four of you
knock your clay around a little bit."

Roly-poly Ben attacked his with gusto. Laughing, Linda
and Janice looked at each other and then, hesitantly at first,
began imitating Dory's movements, kneading and slamming.

James also imitated Dory's movements, but without
much enthusiasm. Frowning slightly, she looked down at his
hands—remarkably attractive, long-fingered and sensitive
hands. Then she shook her head. "No, James, you're being
much too gentle. Believe me, you can't hurt clay. It doesn't
feel pain like the rest of us." Now why had she said *that*, she
asked herself.

"She's right, buddy," Ben interjected jovially, "it's not
really some bozo's throat you've got your fingers on, but it
doesn't hurt to pretend." As he spoke, he demonstrated by
twisting his elongated roll of clay as if it were a neck he was
trying to wring, an exaggerated expression of glee on his
face. "Gkkkk! This is the last truck driver who cut in front
of me."

Janice giggled and shook her straw-colored ponytail.
"I'm pretending this is my little brother, Glen," she declared, giving her clay a thump and then squashing it on the
table. "Sometimes I'd like to bash his brains in."

"Now, Janice," her mother chastened. "Is that a nice way to talk about your brother?"

"I don't care! Glen is such a twerp. He drove me nuts today with that stupid game of his." She gave the clay another resounding thwack.

For a moment James Gordon gazed across the table at her and Ben. Then, his expression closed and his dark eyes hooded, he put his clay down and stepped back from the table.

Janice and Linda stopped their own work to turn and stare.

"Sorry, this isn't my thing I'm afraid," he muttered.

Dory's jaw dropped. "But we've only just . . ."

"I think maybe I'd better go now." He went to the sink and rinsed off his hands. Then he scooped up his light jacket and stalked out of the room.

"Well, for crying out loud!" Ben exclaimed when the door closed behind the younger man. "What a sorehead. Doesn't the guy have any sense of humor?"

"And I thought he was a fox," Janice mumbled.

"I wonder what's wrong with him," Linda questioned. "Was it something we said?"

Staring at the door through which he'd just disappeared, Dory shook her head. "I don't know," she murmured. "Maybe he wasn't feeling well."

BY EIGHT-FIFTY-FIVE the next morning, Dory had banished the scene at the college and the disturbing stranger from her thoughts. As she rushed out the front door, fishing for her keys while trying to push her free hand through a coat sleeve, she prayed that the car wouldn't give her trouble. Luck was with her and the engine caught on the third try. "Thank you, Plum," she murmured, and patted the worn vinyl dashboard.

A few minutes later Dory pulled up in front of a rambling brick building, the modern new clinic where she worked part-time as a receptionist for a group of medical specialists.

"I can't understand you working there," Dory's best friend and former next-door neighbor, Lydia Prentice, had exclaimed when Dory had first taken the position. "Isn't Neal's law office right across the street?"

"Yes," Dory had admitted. In fact, it was from Neal's secretary that she'd heard about the opening for a receptionist at the clinic.

"Considering what that guy did to you, walking out after a kid and ten years of marriage, I should think you'd want to see as little as possible of him!"

Dory had shrugged. "Divorce or no divorce, Neal is Beth's father. I can't avoid the man completely. Besides, I don't see any more of him because of where I work than I would otherwise. I'm not sitting at the window watching his comings and goings, you know."

Lydia had rolled her expressive eyes. "Maybe not, but I wouldn't be surprised if he put his secretary up to telling you about that job so he could conveniently keep tabs on you."

At that fanciful notion Dory had only smiled. "I enjoy my work, Liddy. Later I have plans to try for something more ambitious. But right now, while I'm going back to school and with Beth such a handful, part-time receptionist is about all I can handle."

Which is certainly the truth, Dory thought as she hung her trench coat up in the closet, then turned to check through the mail and fill the coffeepot. Within minutes of her arrival, coffee was perking, the telephones were ringing and she was fielding questions and arranging appointments.

"Does Dr. Lucas have a cancellation this week?" a distraught-sounding voice on the other end of the line asked.

"This afternoon at three," Dory answered after checking the schedule.

"Oh, thank God. I really need to talk to him."

"We'll see you at three, then." Dory shook her head. Sam Lucas was a psychiatrist, and judging from his crowded schedule, she had to conclude that still waters ran deep in her quiet little suburban community.

"The prettiest receptionist in the building is also the hardest worker, I see."

Dory looked up from where she'd been penciling in the new appointment and saw Sam ambling toward her across the small lobby.

"Thanks for the compliment, but I'm not going to be the only one working hard today. Wait until you see your appointment schedule."

Sam Lucas was a slight middle-aged man with a grizzled mustache and a fatherly air. From the first he'd been a kind and considerate boss and Dory had come to regard him as a friend. Now he perched on the edge of her desk and glanced down at the appointment book. "Who've I got?"

Dory scanned the lines under the date. "There's Mr. Sutton at ten, then Mr. and Mrs. Levine. You've got Mrs. Preston at one." Dory's finger continued down the list. "Lorraine made the rest of these appointments," she said, referring to the other part-time receptionist, who spelled her two days a week. Suddenly Dory's finger paused and she glanced questioningly up at her boss. "J. Gordon?"

Dr. Lucas nodded. "James Gordon. Which reminds me, I'd better warn you he might show up at that ceramics thing you teach. I hope you don't mind that I recommended it to him."

Dory conjured up an image of the man who'd walked out on her class the night before. "Of course I don't mind. But who's James Gordon and why did you recommend ceramics to him?"

Sam cocked his head. "I'm surprised you don't recognize the name. The guy has been in all the local papers."

"I haven't had a chance to read the papers much lately." Beth had a way of making newspapers disappear before Dory got to them. And when she did have a spare minute to sit down and study the *Post*, very often it was so full of holes where Beth had clipped articles for school projects that reading it was like trying to make sense of Swiss cheese.

"Just a minute, I think I have one of the articles on Gordon in my office. I'll get it and let you see for yourself."

A moment later Dr. Lucas came back and placed an open copy of the local newspaper under her nose. "Kidnap victim ransomed from captors in Afghanistan after brother dies tragically," the headline read.

"Oh, my God!" Suddenly what had happened the night before made sense. No wonder James Gordon was touchy on the subject of brothers. Dory stared at the large black-and-white photo dominating one half of the page. It showed two men gazing directly into the camera. The one she didn't recognize had a handsome boyish face and a sensitive mouth. The older and taller of the two was the dark-eyed man in her class. But what a difference! Instead of the tense person who'd captured her attention and hurt Janice's feelings, the picture showed a relaxed, affable man smiling as if he were king of the world.

"What happened to him?" she exclaimed. Then, glancing up and seeing her employer's puzzled expression, she put the article down and described her previous night's encounter with the man in question.

Dr. Lucas shook his head. "I'm not surprised Gordon reacted the way he did. He's very prickly right now and has a lot to work through. This hostage business . . ." He shook his head again. "I suggested your class to him because I thought an undemanding physical activity like that might help. Sorry if he made you or your students uncomfortable."

"Oh, he didn't. I mean, really, that doesn't matter."

Sam rubbed his jaw. "Well, if you don't mind, I think I'll encourage him to go back to it. I do think it might help."

"Of course. But what happened to him?" Dory repeated her question.

"You'll find out when you read the article, but I'll tell you some of it. Gordon is a pediatrician and his brother, Tom, was an orthopedic surgeon, a brilliant one by all accounts. They were working as volunteers in a field hospital near the Afghanistan border, when they were kidnapped and held for ransom by outlaw tribesmen."

"Outlaws?"

Sam nodded. "Apparently outlaws are as much a danger to American medical personnel in that part of the world as the Russian military. Anyhow, after the outlaws separated James from his brother, Tom's appendix burst, and for lack of proper medical care he died. When they finally told James what had happened, he was so beside himself with grief and rage that he attacked his captors. They treated him pretty badly, beat him and almost starved him to death before his family was able to put up the ransom. His sister lives in Columbia, so he came back here to convalesce."

As she listened to the horrifying account, Dory stared down at the photo. Now she understood some of what she'd seen in James Gordon's dark eyes. No wonder he was "prickly."

The phone rang and Dr. Lucas turned away to pour himself a cup of coffee. Then, while Dory took the call, he saluted and went into his office to await his first appointment.

A moment later, Dory replaced the receiver and made a notation for Dr. Arndquist, the urologist. As she folded the small piece of paper, she glanced at the newspaper on her desk. Smoothing the page, she began to read the article about James Gordon.

She was less than halfway through the piece, when Dr. Lucas's first patient strolled in. After that the morning accelerated like a downhill toboggan. Between answering calls, typing letters and soothing and directing patients, Dory had no more time for reading.

She had just returned to the office from a snatched lunch at a local deli, when the outer door opened and James Gordon walked into the waiting room. Though she'd known about his appointment, Dory was so startled to see him again that she almost dropped the envelope she'd been sealing. Several of the people who were in the red-and-purple chairs that lined the wall glanced up from their magazines and stared at him curiously. He was that kind of man, Dory thought as she watched him approach her desk. There was a quality about him, a fierce dignity, that arrested the attention.

"May I help you?" she said when he stood directly in front of her.

"I have an appointment with Dr. Lucas."

"Yes. If you care to take a seat, he'll be with you in just a few minutes." Unconsciously she clasped her hands. Should she say something to him about the ceramics class?

"I'm sorry about what happened last night," he said abruptly.

"Oh, it was nothing. I'm just sorry you missed the rest of the lesson." She tried to look friendly and interested in a neutral sort of way.

"My walking out had nothing to do with you. You're a very good teacher. I was impressed."

"Why...thank you."

Without another word, he turned on his heel and took a seat. Dory stared after him, but when he picked up a magazine and began leafing through it, she dropped her gaze back down to her desk. The newspaper story with his picture was still lying open under the pile of mail she'd been sorting through. Had he noticed, she wondered, and felt herself flush. But when she stole a glance in his direction, he seemed to be absorbed in his reading material, his face quite expressionless.

She could certainly see the resemblance between what he was now and what he had been, she reflected. The strong, regular features and aggressive jaw were still there. But his face had a much different cast from that of the good-humored, ruggedly handsome man in the feature. He looked as if he hadn't smiled in months and his long dark lashes shuttered eyes that were hard and wary. *Poor guy,* Dory thought, and wished there were some way she could hold out a friendly hand and express sympathy. But his closed expression and the rigid set of his shoulders made it clear that he didn't want sympathy.

A moment later Sam buzzed to let Dory know he was ready for his next patient.

"Dr. Lucas will see you now," she told James Gordon.

With only a brief glance in her direction, he put down his magazine and strode into Sam's office. Dory stared at the closed door, reviewing the procedure Sam would take Mr. Gordon through. Would they discuss what had happened in her ceramics class, she wondered. Dory shrugged. What was it to her, anyway?

"HELLO, JAMES. I'm happy to see you."

"Wish I could say the same, Doc. But we both know it

wouldn't be true.'' Jim sat down opposite Sam Lucas and stretched out his long legs.

"How have things been going for you?''

"Pretty fair,'' Jim responded. "My sessions with the physical therapist have been coming along. He says I'm ready to start swimming and working with weights at the health club.''

"That sounds good.''

Jim nodded. "Considering that a couple months back I could barely get out of bed, it is good.'' He recrossed his ankles. "Another positive thing, I had a talk with my old chief of staff at the medical plan. He tells me I can go back to work for him anytime I want.''

"That's wonderful news. He must have a high regard for you.'' Sam smiled. "I know you're anxious to start practicing medicine again.''

"Yes, but not because I'm the male version of Florence Nightingale. The simple fact is that I need to start doing something useful with my time, and I need to start making money. My sister and her husband mortgaged themselves to the eyeballs to borrow my ransom, and I need to pay them back.''

"I notice how often you used the word 'need' in that statement. You feel very strongly about working and paying your sister, don't you?''

"Yes,'' Jim said simply. "I've always paid my debts.''

Dr. Lucas cleared his throat and Jim guessed at what the next question would probably be. Since he'd taken courses in psychoanalytic theory and technique in med school, he had a pretty clear idea of what the psychiatrist was trying to accomplish. *Why am I waiting for him to him to make the first move? Why don't I just tell him what I want to talk about?*

"Do you feel you're ready to start working again?" Lucas asked.

"I thought so. In fact, I was feeling pretty good about the prospect. Then something happened last night that forced me to reconsider." Jim steepled his hands over his knee. "Maybe you already know about it. Maybe your receptionist already told you that I behaved rather badly in her ceramics class."

Lucas responded calmly. "Dory did say you'd walked out after another student made a thoughtless remark."

"Yes." Jim sighed. "Afterward I felt like an idiot. The poor girl didn't mean anything by it. It was the sort of thing sisters say about kid brothers all the time. My reaction was way out of line and probably upset her. That's the last thing I want to do. When I go back to working with kids, I want to heal them, not scare them or upset them."

"Why do you think you reacted so strongly?" Lucas asked.

Jim's mouth tightened. Then he leaned back, resting his head against the cushioned top of the chair so that he could gaze up at the ceiling. "I don't need a degree in psychiatry to answer that question. It's because I feel guilty. I feel personally responsible for what happened to Tom."

"You know that you aren't, don't you?"

"I know it on an intellectual level. But here—" keeping his gaze fixed on the ceiling, Jim raised his hand and touched the left side of his chest "—here I'm not so certain. If I'd shown more foresight, if I'd been a little more diplomatic in my dealings with the men who took us prisoner..." He dropped his hand. "Hearing that girl talk about how she'd like to bash her brother's brains in ..." I used to say things like that about Tom when we were kids. He used to follow me around, you know. He was always borrowing my stuff, nosing into my games, bugging me about one thing or another. And there were times when I . . ." He paused again, seemingly at a loss for words. Finally he met the psychiatrist's concerned gaze squarely. "Anyway, I'm sorry about walking out on your receptionist's class."

"You're planning on going back, aren't you?"

Jim's dark eyebrows lifted. "Hardly."

"Maybe you should reconsider. After all, your emotional wounds are only just beginning to heal. It's not surprising that you reacted the way you did to that young girl's remark. What's important is how you handle the situation now. Don't slink away with your tail between your legs. You paid your tuition for that class, didn't you? You should go back."

"Why? I acted like a fool. Probably everyone in the class thinks I'm a nut case. Maybe I should try something else. Basket weaving would serve the same purpose, wouldn't it?"

"That's not the point. You have to get back into the real world, Jim. You shouldn't rush the process, but you shouldn't run away from it, either. Dory's class is ideal. You liked her, didn't you?"

"Sure. What's not to like? She's a pretty little blonde and smiles a lot." Suddenly Jim shot Dr. Lucas a suspicious look. "You're not trying to fix me up with her, are you?"

Emphatically Lucas shook his head. "Definitely not! Dory has enough problems in her life. What she requires right now is a man who can take care of her emotional needs, and you're too busy picking up the pieces of your life to shoulder anything like that. I just think it will do you good to be involved in an undemanding activity and associate with people who are nice. And God knows, Dory Barker is one heck of a nice lady."

CHAPTER TWO

"WELL, HERE WE ARE AGAIN. Just two sleepy mothers too darn dumb to stay in bed," Lydia Prentice said, paraphrasing the old song.

"We have to stop meeting like this," Dory agreed, responding to Lydia's impish grin with a chuckle.

It was six o'clock in the morning, and outside the first gray streaks of dawn were just beginning to thread the September sky. Inside the ice rink Dory and Lydia huddled on metal folding chairs, sipping cups of coffee and gazing out through the Plexiglas windows at their offspring. Beth and Lydia's Gracie, along with eighteen other youngsters of various ages and sizes, were patching, working on variations of the figure eight in order to pass one of the figure and freestyle tests that make up a skater's lexicon.

"You know what they say about a sailboat race—being a spectator at one is about as interesting as watching grass grow?"

"Yes," Dory answered, "and I know what you're about to tell me. Watching someone work on school figures is even more boring. Do you realize we've been getting up before the crack of dawn four mornings a week for four years now?"

Lydia nodded. "It all started after the girls went to that ice show together. Remember?"

Dory rolled her eyes. "I remember it well. Little did we know what we were getting into."

"Yes. From the first they saw themselves as budding little ice princesses. Within a couple of months they were both begging for private lessons. And after that, if you'll excuse the pun, the thing just snowballed."

"That's the word for it," Dory agreed.

"Beth has really bloomed," Lydia commented diplomatically. "If I hadn't seen her for a year, I'd hardly recognize her."

Dory eyed her daughter, a worried frown tugging at her forehead. She knew what Lydia really meant. At twelve Beth had been a skinny little girl, as agile and light bodied as a cricket. Like her father, who had the metabolism of a hummingbird, she'd been able to eat as much ice cream for dessert as she desired, then get up the next morning to put away a breakfast of waffles and bacon without showing the slightest effect. Now that she was going through puberty, however, she had a tendency to store fat. She hadn't yet accommodated to her new womanly metabolism, and it showed.

"Neal is starting to complain about Beth's weight," Dory confided. "He doesn't understand how tough it is for some girls to adjust when their bodies start to change. I remember when I was that age. The kids used to make fun of me."

Dory shook her head and two bright spots of anger appeared in her cheeks. She was recalling a phone conversation she'd had with her ex-husband three days earlier. "It's time you did something about Beth," he'd informed her. "She's beginning to look ridiculous in a skating dress."

"Well, you'd certainly never know you ever had a weight problem now," Lydia remarked. She eyed Dory's trim figure enviously. "Ever since I've known you, you've looked like a swimsuit model."

Dory laughed. "And ever since you've known me I've been living on salads and cottage cheese."

"Yes, darn you. If only I had your willpower—slaving over gourmet meals for your family and eating like a rabbit yourself. Bob's always holding you up to me as an example. You could have knocked us both over with a feather when Neal walked out. I mean, you were the perfect wife—pretty, a good cook, a good mother."

"Not such a great housekeeper, though, and never quite the flawless hostess."

"You're a great hostess. Speaking of which, I suppose you know what I'm dying to ask," Lydia said.

Dory took a sip of her cooling coffee. "I can guess."

"So, what did you think of Greg?"

"I thought dinner was lovely, last night, and Bob's friend seemed very pleasant."

Lydia rolled her dark eyes. "But no sale."

"I didn't know you were trying to make a sale."

"Dory, don't play dumb. You know what I mean. I was hoping you and Greg might hit it off. I know he liked you. So far, all the men I've introduced you to have liked you. You're the one who's hard to please."

As Dory gazed at her well-meaning friend, a hint of exasperation flashed in her large blue eyes. In the past year Lydia had repeatedly lured her back to the old neighborhood on the pretext of dinner or a party and then sprung a series of unattached males. Last night Dory had innocently imagined she was dropping by to eat pizza and see the Prentices' vacation slides of Barbados. Instead of palm trees and sandy beaches, she'd been treated to a five-course dinner and a recently divorced old school friend of Lydia's husband, who looked almost as embarrassed as she'd felt. She'd done her best to put him at ease, and it hadn't been long before he'd begun to relax and tell her all about his job as a stock analyst. She'd listened politely, but she couldn't honestly say she was interested in seeing him again.

"Lydia," Dory began diplomatically, "I appreciate your efforts—really, I do. But I'm not looking for another man right now."

"I know you're not. That's just the trouble. You should be." Lydia peered at her suspiciously. "You're not still hung up on Neal, are you?"

"No, I'm not."

"Because he's certainly not pining for you."

"I know that, too. Why is it so hard for you to believe I like my life the way it is?"

"Because you're not the kind of woman who was meant to live alone."

Through the window Dory looked out at Beth. "I'm not alone."

"You know what I mean. You're the kind of woman God created to make some man divinely happy, and anything less is a waste."

Dory started to laugh. "Why are women always supposed to do all the work? What about me? Isn't there some Mr. Wonderful out there who was created to make me divinely happy?"

Illogically, the thought brought James Gordon to Dory's mind. It was funny how some people, people you didn't even know, intrigued you, while with others it was out of sight, out of mind.

Dory had been thinking of James Gordon off and on for the past two weeks. She'd been disappointed, though not surprised, when he hadn't returned to her class. She'd looked for him at the office, but he'd scheduled his appointments during the hours Lorraine was there. Several times she'd been tempted to question Sam about him, but had decided against that. It wasn't her place to get nosy about her boss's patients. *Forget the man,* she told herself now. *He's nothing to you, and he's certainly not Mr. Wonderful.*

"JIM, I WISH you'd reconsider." Margaret Curak perched on the only chair in her brother's empty new apartment and watched as he pulled a cup out of a haphazardly packed box.

"Good try, Maggie," he said, "but no sale."

"Be sensible. You know you're not ready to live by yourself yet. How are you going to eat decently? Why look at you! Turn sideways and you're the invisible man. I bet you haven't gained more than ten pounds."

"It's not as bad as that. I'm a doctor so I know a thing or two about nutrition. I also know how to operate a microwave. Besides, it's dangerous to put weight back on too quickly. Hard on the heart." His eyes warmed as he reached down to stroke the fat marmalade tabby who'd ambled across the floor to rub against his leg. "Are you sure you want to leave Cleo with me? There's not much for her here."

"Are you kidding? She'd be heartbroken if you left her behind. She can take or leave Les and me, but she's fallen in love with you."

Jim's gaze followed the cat as she prowled to the far corner, then leaped up to arrange herself on a sunny windowsill. "Funny, when we were kids Tom was always the one our pets fell for," he murmured. "Remember how Daisy used to follow him around? That old hound dog worshiped him."

Brother and sister looked at each other. They were twins, but they could hardly have resembled each other less—James with his lean saturnine looks and Maggie with her bright red hair and matronly figure. Finally she said, "I know you're still grieving over Tom. Me, too." As she clasped her hands in her lap, her golden brown eyes reflected her sorrow. "And I know you feel all torn up and guilty. But you have to let go of that. What happened isn't your fault."

"Isn't it?"

"No, Jim." Firmly Maggie shook her head. "Tom was the idealistic one, the one who was always out on a limb over some cause. In some ways he was just too good for this world."

"Maggie..." Jim began, but she held up a hand.

"Okay, I loved him, but I never really understood him. I do know he would have gone to Afghanistan alone if he hadn't succeeded in talking you into volunteering with him. You even admitted you went along partly to keep an eye on him and make sure he didn't get into trouble."

"Did a wonderful job of it, didn't I?"

At the bitterness and pain in her brother's voice, Margaret sighed. "Listen, I know you're as irritable as a porcupine with fleas and living with Les and me was getting on your nerves. We're not in such great shape ourselves these days. But I hate to think of you all alone in this empty, depressing little apartment. Les does, too, believe me."

Jim smiled wryly. "Meadowlark Management would be insulted if they could hear you. Their brochure describes this place as 'suburban living at its finest.'" He walked over to the window, where he stood gazing out at the parking lot and frail young trees lining the quiet street just beyond. *Summer's gone,* he thought. *Pretty soon those trees will be bare.* Aloud he said, "I'm sorry if I'm worrying you, but these days there's a lot of stuff in my head that no one but me should have to deal with."

For a moment Maggie was silent. "What does your therapist say?"

"Not much. Mostly he just listens. That's what psychiatrists do, you know. Actually, I like Lucas, because unlike some shrinks who want you to pay them for falling asleep while you talk about your childhood, he does occasionally make a good suggestion or impart a bit of interesting information." Over his shoulder, Jim glanced back at his sister. "Ever hear of the Stockholm syndrome?"

"The Stockholm syndrome. Sounds like a movie title. Anything to do with beautiful blond porn stars?" she joked lamely.

"Hardly. Try again."

She frowned. "Okay, I think I have run into the term. Is it some sort of psychological defense that occurs in a hostage-captor situation?"

"I see you've been doing your homework, reading up on my problems."

"Only because I love you and I'm worried about you."

He nodded resignedly. "All right. The Stockholm syndrome was named after the Swedish hostage incident in which it was first recognized. Lucas told me about it. According to him, there are stages I have to work through to recover from my grief and sense of victimization. You'll be interested to hear I've already gotten past stages one and two."

"Refresh my memory. What are those?"

He turned back to the window. "Shock, disbelief, then fear, compulsive talking. Sound familiar?"

Maggie rubbed her palms together and said seriously, "I hardly recognized you when you first came back. It wasn't just that you were in such bad shape physically. You didn't act like the Jim I knew."

"That's because I *wasn't* the Jim you knew. Who knows, maybe I never will be again. But I'm past most of that."

"Glad to hear it. Dare I ask what stage you're in now?"

Jim laughed dryly. "Stage three is a bag of goodies consisting of traumatic depression, self-recrimination, apathy, nightmares and irritability." He turned to face her. "I need to be by myself for a while, Maggie. I need to be alone."

An hour later Maggie left. After Jim closed the door behind his sister, he went into the kitchen to get himself a beer. "Alone at last," he mumbled as he sat down in the stained old brown velvet wing chair that Maggie had insisted he take with him.

The chair was the only real piece of furniture in the small apartment he'd rented for himself. Other than his stereo equipment, the mattress in the bedroom, a six pack of beer in the refrigerator and the few articles of clothing still crushed into wrinkled clumps in his duffel bag, the place was empty.

Reaching down, he lifted his half-full beer can and took a swig. After he swallowed, he muttered in a mock Swedish accent, "I vant to be alone."

The words seemed to echo in the barren room. Only they weren't true. Alone wasn't what he really wished for. No, what he really wanted was for none of this nightmare to have happened and for Tom to still be alive and for his life not to have collapsed like a paper house in a windstorm. His gaze drifted to the sliding glass door, which badly needed a curtain. Only that meant getting the right measurements and then going out to some sort of store and picking one out and paying for it. And then you had to put the damn thing up. Would he ever again have the energy or the desire to accomplish all that?

Maybe it hadn't been such a good idea to move out on Maggie, Jim found himself thinking. Maybe she was right and he wasn't ready for this yet. Why had he been in such an all fired rush to get into his own place, he wondered. But as his mind drifted over the events of the past couple of weeks, he knew. The interview with Clayman about going back to work, the progress he was making with the physical therapist, his talks with Lucas—they all added up to something. The time had come to make a move.

At that moment Cleo abandoned her spot on the windowsill and leaped up on his lap, where she arranged herself into a purring doughnut. "I'm not so alone after all, am I, old girl?" Jim stroked the cat's ears and looked down at her affectionately. A shaft of sunlight caught her fur, turning the lighter stripes into the color of melted butter—a shade very close to that of Sam Lucas's receptionist's curly blond hair, Jim suddenly found himself thinking.

All week he had been considering Lucas's suggestion that he go back to her pottery class. But the disastrous wedging scene kept appearing in his mind. The teacher had looked so shocked. What was her name? Dory? Cute name, just right for a cuddly little blonde with baby-blue eyes.

As he pictured her, the corners of his mouth lifted slightly. He knew the type—cheerleader in high school, fraternity sweetheart, happy homemaker with the regulation 2.5 well-scrubbed kids.

No, that had never been his type. He'd always liked his women leggy, complicated and challenging—like Lauren. So it had been a surprise when he'd met the cute blonde's guileless blue gaze and felt an undeniable tug of attraction. Maybe it was the femaleness of her, the gentle warmth she gave off like an almost visible aura. Some women were like that. If you were feeling weak, you took one look at them and wanted to wrap your arms around them and pillow your head against their breasts.

He remembered clearly the moment Dory had first walked into the room and, with her back to the class, taken off her coat. Her sweatshirt had been pushed up, revealing a pale strip of white skin above her waistband. What was so touching about that brief instant of vulnerability? Why did he keep wondering what it would be like to explore that patch of skin with the pad of his thumb?

Scowling, Jim finished off the beer, gently removed Cleo from his lap, then stood and checked his watch. Almost six. The class didn't start until seven-thirty. That gave him an hour and a half to cook himself a hamburger while he made a decision.

"HI, EVERYBODY. What a night! It looks as if there's going to be quite some fog later on," Dory commented as she hurried into her class. She stopped short. James Gordon was sitting at the back table. So he'd returned, she thought with a small jolt of surprise.

Trying not to stare, Dory turned away to hang up her coat, then spent the next five minutes answering the questions of the small knot of students gathered around her. But all the time she was intensely aware of him sitting there.

After she'd made sure that all her other students were started on their individual projects, she walked over to his table and gave him a friendly smile. "We missed you."

He shot her a dry look that made her flush slightly. "Somehow I doubt that. But Dr. Lucas talked me into coming back, so here I am."

"Believe me, I'm very happy to see you. But I'm afraid you have some catching up to do."

"I realize that. As I recall, I was just picking up the rudiments of wedging."

Instead of commenting, Dory crossed over to the bin and returned a moment later with a lump of clay, which she placed in front of James. "Want to start on this?"

"Sure. Why not?"

A little apprehensively she watched as he picked up the clay, broke it in two then began folding the pieces into each other. His hands didn't lack strength, she observed. She glanced up at his face, noting his impassive expression. He had himself tightly under control.

"It really doesn't matter how you manhandle it, you know."

"You've been talking to Dr. Lucas about me, haven't you?"

Startled by the directness of the question, Dory took a step backward. "He did mention he'd recommended my class. But other than that—"

"Other than that, you've probably seen one of the half-dozen or so articles about me that have come out in all the newspapers, and my life's an open book."

"Nobody's life is an open book."

They stared at each other for a long moment. To Dory's surprise, he was the first to look away. "You're right. And I'm behaving stupidly. I really am sorry about my conduct last time. What can I do to make up for it?"

"There's nothing to make up for. Really. But if you want a happy teacher, you'll relax and start enjoying yourself."

He looked down at the clay. "What is there to enjoy about this stuff?"

"Everything. Here, let me show you." She took the material out of his hands and began working it herself. "I think people like potting because it's so simple. I mean, the elements of it are about as basic as you can get—earth, air, water and fire. To do it, you don't need a fancy education or a high IQ, or even talent."

"What do you need?"

She could feel him regarding her curiously. "Just a willingness to forget everything but the feel of the clay in your hands." As she spoke, Dory began to roll the gray material and then pull it apart. "This batch has good plasticity. I can tell that as I work with it. After you work clay awhile, you begin to get a sense of what can be done with it."

"Maybe you do. I don't."

"That's what you're here to learn, isn't it?" She handed the clay back to him.

He tossed it from one hand to the other. "Now what?"

"Now I'm going to teach you about coil construction."

"What's that?"

Dory broke off a piece and began to roll it into a rope. "A very simple way in which pots and drinking vessels were fashioned thousands of years ago and that still works just fine." She cut out a flat circle, then pressed the coil around it, pinching the edges to bond the pieces. When a second coil was in place, she had produced what looked like a shallow bowl. She crushed her crude production back into a lump and returned it to the table. "Now you try it."

"I feel like a little kid," Jim remarked as he began to roll out his own coil.

"That's one of the charms of potting. It's okay to do something simple just for the fun of it. And if you make a mistake, you can always start over. As she spoke, she reached out to smooth down an edge of the coil Jim was pressing into place. He reached to do the same thing, and their fingers brushed. At the contact, Dory had to fight the urge to pull her hand away. But if Jim noticed, he showed no sign.

Instead he responded to what she'd said. "Good therapy?" he remarked, shooting her a faintly amused smile. "Obviously that's why Lucas recommended ceramics to me."

"It's always been good for me, and I've been doing it for years."

"But you don't need therapy as much as yours truly here."

Dory cocked her head. "Now how can you possibly know that?"

Once more their gazes met. "You're right again," he said soberly, a hint of curiosity gleaming in his dark eyes. "I can't."

Why did I say that? Dory asked herself as she turned away to go to another table. *Am I trying to intrigue him? Make myself out to be a woman with hidden depths and unspoken sorrows?*

She was beginning to be more than a little disturbed by her reaction to James Gordon. After her performance a moment earlier she could no longer tell herself she just felt sorry for the man. It was far more complicated. Something about him attracted her on a purely sexual level. What's more, that chemistry had been there from the moment she'd first laid eyes on him.

Over her shoulder, she shot him a brief, worried glance. He was bent over his table, hard at work, his dark brows drawn together in deep concentration. Everything about him was so intense. *Maybe that's what appeals to me,* she thought. *He's like a brooding hero in a Gothic novel, and I'm an incurable romantic.* Recognizing the fact didn't make Dory particularly happy. If there was anything she'd learned to be suspicious of it was romantic fantasy. Years ago the illusions she'd woven around Neal had gotten her into deep trouble. Fortunately she was now a lot older and a lot wiser.

For the rest of the two-hour class, Dory busied herself helping out at the other tables. From time to time she glanced in James Gordon's direction, but he seemed perfectly content with the coil jar he was meticulously building.

At the end of the second hour she announced it was time to close down for another week, and after the students had cleaned their work spaces and wrapped their projects in damp cloth and plastic for storage, she was left alone to finish tidying up.

Indulge a Little
Give a Lot

With proofs-of-purchase plus
postage and handling

Indulge yourself with these irresistible gifts and at the same
time help raise up to $100,000 for **Big Brothers/Big Sisters
Programs and Services** in the United States and Canada.

Indulge a Little
Give a Lot

Wonderful, luxurious free gifts can be yours with proofs-of-purchase from specially marked Harlequin or Silhouette books plus postage and handling. And for every specially marked "Indulge A Little" Harlequin or Silhouette book purchased during October, November and December Harlequin/Silhouette will donate 5¢ toward **Big Brothers/Big Sisters Programs and Services** in the United States and Canada for a maximum contribution of $100,000.

Gifts include a beautiful porcelain collector's doll that brings to life the look and feel of the Old South (consumer value $65.00), European-formulated soaps in a handsome, natural willow basket (consumer value, individually packaged, $25.00), a wonderful lace sachet filled with potpourri (consumer value $12.00) and fragrantly scented satin-and-lace hangers (consumer value, package of two, $5.00).

See advertisement on last page for proof-of-purchase and offer certificate.

That took no more than half an hour. Still, by the time Dory left the college it was past ten o'clock at night. With so few people around at that late hour, the long walk to the parking lot always made her a trifle nervous. There'd been a mugging on campus the year before, and since then she'd taken to carrying a can of Mace in her handbag. She was relieved when she unlocked the Plum's door and slid in behind the wheel. This time, however, her relief didn't last long. When she turned the key in the ignition there was a sick grinding noise and then nothing at all.

"Oh, God, not tonight!" Dory muttered under her breath, and turned the key again. But her prayers went unanswered. The car was deader than an abandoned conch shell. *I should have taken it in for service weeks ago,* she thought, running a distracted hand across her forehead. Nervously she peered out the window. There were no more than a dozen automobiles in the parking lot, but lights still shone out of the windows of the main building. Even if the office wasn't open, she would be able to call a service station from a pay phone.

Unhappily Dory climbed out of the car and hurried from the parking lot. It was damp and a chill fog hung in the air. As she listened to the faint slap of her rubber-soled sneakers against the pavement, she tucked her head down and pulled the collar of her blazer around her neck. Then all at once she looked up, aware of other footsteps approaching her. Dory peered through the gloom, but all she could make out was a tall, masculine shape. She hurried into the light cast by a street lamp and pulled her can of Mace out of her bag, stuck it in her pocket and, with one finger on the nozzle, waited, unwilling to brave the foggy darkness until she'd gotten a better look at who was out there.

"You look scared. Is something wrong?"

Dory's shoulders sagged with relief. She recognized that voice and now, as he came into the light, the face that went with it. It was James Gordon.

"Nothing wrong," she said a little breathlessly. "It's just that it's so late at night and no one's around."

"Were you afraid of me?"

"No. No, of course not." She looked up at him, noticing that his hair was wet, as if he'd just taken a shower. His skin looked damp, too. "It's just that—" Briefly she told him about her car and the mugging.

"You mean you were all set to Mace me?" He laughed. "That's all I need." Then he sobered and studied her thoughtfully. "Actually, it's really not such a good idea for you to be wandering around alone this late at night. Why don't you ask your students to stay and help with the cleaning? Then everyone could leave at once."

"Oh, I hate to do that."

"Why? I'm sure they'd be glad to. I'd be glad to." He touched her lightly on the shoulder. "C'mon, let's have a look at your car. I'm no mechanic, but maybe I can get the thing started for you."

At the brief contact, Dory stiffened slightly. But then she shook off the ridiculous reaction, smiled and thanked him for the offer of help. As she matched steps with him back to the parking lot, she said, "Why are you still here?" She glanced up at his dark hair where tiny beads of water seemed to catch the moonlight.

"Swimming," he answered. "The pool is open until ten-thirty, you know. I thought I'd catch a few laps before I went home."

"Do you swim a lot?"

"Not since high school, but my therapist tells me it's an excellent way to rebuild muscle, and I find it relaxing—a good thing to do before I try getting some sleep."

"Oh, I see." His remark raised all kinds of questions in Dory's mind. How physically weakened was he by his hostage experience? Did nightmares make sleep difficult for him? It must be something like that or he wouldn't be seeing Sam.

When they got to the car Jim's diagnosis was quick and discouraging. "I'm afraid it's the solenoid," he said after trying Dory's key.

"The what?"

"The solenoid. There's not much to do except replace it. How about I drop you by a service station?"

"Oh, would you? I'd appreciate that."

"No sweat."

He helped her into a small, economy-model car, which he explained he'd picked up cheap in the want ads a couple of weeks earlier. There was an all-night service station half a mile from the college. He waited while Dory made arrangements for her car to be towed back and repaired. When it was taken care of, he gave her a lift back to her town house.

"I don't know how to thank you," she said as he pulled to a step in front of her door. "You've really been a lifesaver."

"Hardly."

"I'm very grateful for your help. Is there anything I can do in return?"

For a moment he was silent, regarding her quizzically through the shadowy interior of the car. "Actually, you've already done it."

"Done what?" She cocked her head. "I don't know what you mean."

"Oh..." He tapped his finger against the steering wheel. "It's hard to explain. I'm taking your class for several reasons. One is that I need to rejoin the human race—you know, start behaving like a normal person again. When you've been in isolation for as long as I was, that's not such an easy thing."

"I can imagine."

"No, I don't think you can, and I hope you never do. But anyhow, I've enjoyed just talking to you tonight, doing something for you—though it certainly wasn't much. That probably meant a lot more to me than it did to you."

Dory was touched. And she understood what he was trying to say. She cleared her throat. "I was wondering if you'd like to have dinner with my daughter and me some-time next week. I can't invite you for this week because there's an exam in a college course I'm taking and I have to study for it."

"You're a busy lady."

"Yes, well, dinner wouldn't be anything fancy. We don't often entertain. But you'd be very welcome."

He hesitated so long that she felt her cheeks begin to heat. She was sure he was taking her invitation the wrong way and meant to refuse.

"Yes," he finally said. "Yes, I'd like that very much. Just name the day."

CHAPTER THREE

BETH RAN UP the cement steps and flung open the front door. "Oh, hi," she said when she spotted her mother holding a book in one hand and standing to one side of the living room window. "What were you doing there?"

"Just watching your father drop you off."

Dory put down the fine arts text she'd been making notes in and smiled at her daughter. "How was your weekend?"

"Great, just great! We had such fun! Saturday night Dad took Deanna and me to see *HMS Pinafore* at the Kennedy Center. Oh, Mom, it was so good! And then we went to the old Ebbitt Grill for dinner. It's this really fancy place down near the White House."

"I've heard of it. Come on into the kitchen and tell me about it. I've got dinner all ready for us."

While Dory crossed the small living room toward the hall, Beth followed behind chattering. "Then Saturday morning Deanna took me shopping at Harborplace. She bought me this sweater." Beth thrust out her chest. "It's handmade, with angora at the neckline. Wait until you see the skirt that goes with it!"

"Who's Deanna?" Dory had already guessed, but she figured she might as well ask.

"She's Dad's new girlfriend."

"Oh?" Dory began to set the round oak table.

"You should see her. She's a tall gorgeous brunette. She looks just like Victoria Principal, who used to be on *Dallas*."

"I can imagine." Since their separation Neal hadn't allowed himself to be seen in public with any woman who wasn't at least good-looking enough to qualify for the Miss America pageant.

"And she's a lawyer, just like Dad."

"Only a lawyer? Not a brain surgeon?"

"What?" Beth gave her mother a startled look.

"Nothing. It's nice that she's a lawyer. They must have a lot in common." *More than we ever did,* Dory thought as she opened the refrigerator to take out the salad she'd prepared earlier that afternoon. As her hands closed around the chilled ceramic bowl, she pictured Neal and this new female paragon. In her mind's eye they were setting off for a romantic weekend in his cream-colored Mercedes convertible.

Was she jealous, Dory asked herself. She straightened and, while the refrigerator door swung closed behind her, stood testing her feelings.

No, as far as she could tell, her emotions didn't include jealousy. Irritation, perhaps—but not jealousy. Briefly she considered telling Beth about the dinner invitation she'd extended to James Gordon. But she decided to wait on that. Right now Beth was so full of her father and his new girlfriend, and Dory didn't want her to misinterpret what was merely a neighborly gesture on her part. Dory set the bowl in the center of the table and took out the bran muffins warming in the oven.

"What's that?" Beth asked, peering suspiciously at the salad.

"It's all kinds of good things—cottage cheese, spinach, broccoli, cauliflower, green peppers, grated carrots, garbanzo beans, sunflower seeds."

"Yuck!"

Dory put her hands on her hips. "Now, Beth, you know we've discussed this. You agreed that you wanted to start eating healthy."

"Yeah, but not that healthy!" Moaning, the teenager reached for a bran muffin. "I hope we have something decent for dessert." When Dory didn't answer, Beth gave her a suspicious look. "It's not those disgusting fruit bars you made last time, is it?"

"We have Jell-O and fresh strawberries."

Beth rolled her eyes. "There's never anything worth eating around here anymore. It's not like it used to be when Daddy was at home."

Thank God, Dory would have liked to say. "What did you have for dessert when Daddy took you out?"

"Two pieces of chocolate cheesecake," Beth threw out. Her eyes, the same shade of blue as her mother's, sparkled with a martial light.

With a groan, Dory calculated the calories. "Oh, Beth!"

"I know, I know. But I'll make up for it. Honest." Beth sat down at the table. "I'll starve myself on this luv-er-ly salad."

Dory watched her daughter slather a half-inch layer of butter on a muffin. Oh, well, she thought. So she's put on a little baby fat. She'll outgrow it.

The next morning Neal called Dory at work. "Beth said she had a wonderful weekend with you," Dory told him politely.

"Good. I'm glad she enjoyed herself."

After they exchanged a few more guarded remarks, Dory heard him take a deep breath, always a sign that he was about to drop a verbal bombshell. What now, she wondered. She pictured him in shirt sleeves, with his expensively shod feet crossed at the ankles on his impressive mahogany desk. The sun from the showy skylight overhead probably glinted off his razor-cut dark blond hair.

"As long as I've got you on the line, there's something I've been meaning to discuss with you."

"Oh?" Dory said warily. "What's that? Remember, I'm in the office. I don't really have time for an involved discussion."

"This won't take long. It's about Beth's weight. I think it's time you did something about it."

Dory turned her head to stare across the street, her eyes dark with irritation. "Like what?"

"Like taking her off those French fries and milk shakes she binges on."

"Neal, as I've already told you, I'm trying. And what about the two desserts you let her have when she went out with you?"

"An occasional treat isn't going to make anybody fat. It's the steady diet of greasy junk food that's doing it."

"What am I supposed to do, tie her up in bed? Keep in mind it's the big allowance you give her that she likes to blow at French Fry Heaven."

"Then it's time you taught her something about money management. I'm not interested in having a blimp for a daughter. She's going to her first South Atlantic competition next month, remember? If she gains any more weight, she'll look ridiculous in a skating dress."

Several angry retorts competed in Dory's head. But before she got to fire any of them off, Neal added, "Since you're so busy, I'll hang up now. Just give some thought to putting Beth on a diet."

As THE ESCALATOR brought Jim down to the fountain level of the mall, he smiled over the heads of the other shoppers at his sister.

"Have you been standing around long?" he asked as he approached her.

"Just a few minutes. You know you really should do something about your wardrobe."

"I should?" Nonplussed, he glanced down at himself. "Is there something wrong with what I'm wearing? Spots, rips, broken zippers?"

She laughed at the way he mockingly checked himself over. "No, it's not that you're indecent. But look at those pants. They don't fit right anymore. You should buy yourself something new."

"Why?" His expression was genuinely puzzled. "In a couple of months I'll have gained back most of the weight I lost and then my old clothes will fit me again."

She took his arm and began guiding him down the concourse. "And in the meantime you're walking around looking like a ragpicker. Now that you're starting back to work you need to consider your appearance."

"I don't see why." He shot her a mischievous grin. "That's one good thing about being a doctor, you know. You get to cover yourself up with a white coat."

"You really feel ready to go back to work?"

"Yes, I do. In fact, now that I've made the decision, I'm looking forward to it. I think, as they say, that getting back in harness may be just what the doctor ordered. Now tell me why you wanted me to meet you here. What's the mysterious surprise?"

"I don't know, but it's the third thing on my agenda."

"Agenda? What agenda? What are you talking about?"

"I was thinking about you last night and I always think better with a pen in my hand, so I jotted some things down."

Jim rolled his eyes. "You and your lists, Maggie. You used to drive us crazy with that when we were kids."

"Laugh all you want, lists are the way to get a handle on things. Anyway, here it is." She produced a folded piece of paper from her large black leather purse and handed it to Jim. "I've been reading about Stockholm syndrome. I think you're in the next-to-final stage now, the stage in which you start rebuilding." She tapped the list. "This is a sort of step-by-step blueprint."

"Why do I get the feeling I'm being managed?" Jim said as he unfolded the paper and scanned it. "Number one," he read, "find apartment. I've already done that."

"Yes."

"Number two, go back to work. I'm about to do that. Hallelujah, so far I'm right on schedule."

"So far, so good. But now we get to the tough part." She watched his face expectantly.

"Number three, select and purchase items for apartment at area malls and shopping centers—a. curtains, b. pictures for wall, c. furniture, d. linens." Jim frowned.

"You haven't done any of that yet, have you?"

"No," he admitted.

"In fact, other than going to the grocery store, this is the first time you've been out shopping at all, isn't it?"

Jim grimaced. "I told you. I don't like these damn contemporary temples to mammon." He indicated the chrome-and-marble structure around them, with its glossy store-fronts and mesmerized consumers. "I consider them a blot on the face of the landscape."

"Yes, but they're a fact of life, so it's time you got used to them and learned to enjoy what they have to offer. And that's why we're here," she explained cheerfully. "I'm going to help you with number three on my list. I'm going to buy you a housewarming gift. How about a nice picture for one of those bare walls?'' she suggested as she steered him into a print gallery.

"Maggie, I'm not sure I can explain the reason, but I don't think I'm ready to pick out pictures yet."

"Try. Just look around. Maybe you'll see something that appeals to you."

"Okay, but I doubt it."

While he strolled down the aisles of the store, stopping to gaze bemusedly at posters showing ballet shoes, city scenes, cats and drawings of outsize fruit, Jim continued to read through the list. "Number four, gain weight and work on physical fitness. I'm already doing that. I've joined a health club and I'm swimming regularly."

"I don't think you're doing so well at the weight-gaining part, though." She eyed his sagging slacks. "Would you like to come to dinner tomorrow night?" she asked when he paused in front of a misty painting of a river at dawn.

"No. I have another dinner invitation for that night."

"Oh?" Maggie was startled. "Who invited you?"

"My ceramics teacher."

"Really? That's nice." Maggie stepped closer. "What's she like?"

"Very nice, and terrific with clay."

"You know what I mean."

He chuckled when he caught his sister's stern expression and shook his head. "Okay, she's my age and divorced. But don't get any ideas. Dory Barker is just a nice lady taking pity on a lonely guy."

Maggie frowned. "Jim?"

"Hmmm?" He'd returned his attention to the river scene.

"I'm sure you know this better than I do, but you're very vulnerable right now."

"Vulnerable? You make me sound like a tearful virgin."

"Hardly, but I think you know what I'm trying to say. You're just finding your feet again after a terrible experience. It would be easy for you . . ."

"Easy for me to fall into the snare of some calculating vixen?" He snorted. "Maggie, relax. Dory Barker is nothing like that."

"You like her, so I'm sure she isn't. But if you feel you're ready to get back into the social swim, I know several very attractive unattached women who'd be only too happy—"

"Maggie, take it easy!" He glanced down at the sheet of paper in his hand. "According to what you've written here, meeting eligible women doesn't come until I've gotten through five, six, seven, and eight—buying clothes, joining clubs, taking up a hobby and networking with male acquaintances."

"I know but—"

Suppressing the smile that twitched at the corners of his mouth, Jim said, "This is just a simple dinner invitation. I accepted it because I thought getting out and behaving like a human being would be a step in the right direction. And I only mentioned it to you because I believed you'd be pleased."

"I am pleased. Really I am. It's just—"

"I know. It's just that you're worried about me. Humpty Dumpty had a great fall, and all the king's horses and all the king's men— Your brother's going to be okay, Maggie. He's gluing himself together again and getting back on the wall. Pretty soon you won't even be able to tell how badly he fell off."

When he turned and started to walk out of the store, she caught at his arm. "Jim, you were looking at that river picture. Did you like it? Would you like me to get it for you?"

He shook his head. "No, thanks but I'm not ready to pick out a picture for my living room. I think we'd better start with something a little more basic."

Jim tried to discourage her from buying him a house-warming gift, but Maggie insisted. Finally they went to a bath boutique, where she purchased a stack of fluffy designer towels.

"Now at least you'll have something decent to dry yourself off with," she said as they left the store and she checked her watch to see if she was going to make her dental appointment on time.

"Yes, that's very important," he teased.

"Well, it is." She gave him a peck on the cheek. "Things are definitely improving. You'll see, pretty soon you'll feel just like your old self again. Now goodbye—I have to run."

"Goodbye, and thanks for the towels."

After she was gone, he stood for a moment while people from the escalator swirled around him. It made him feel slightly panicky. Large open spaces teeming with crowds of noisy people affected him that way. A month ago he doubted if he could have endured being in a place like this at all. Now he was proud he'd been able to hide that panicky reaction from Maggie, who could usually read him like a book.

Nevertheless he felt anxious to leave. As soon as there was a break in the steady stream of people he stepped on the escalator. Yes, he assured himself as he rode up, things were definitely improving. These past couple of weeks alone in the apartment hadn't been easy, but he'd made it through them okay. And now that he was slated to resume work and a regular schedule, he felt better able to face each new sunrise.

He hadn't admitted it to Maggie, but accepting that dinner invitation from Dory Barker had helped in some strange way. It was ten days now since it had been issued. Instead of gazing down a long endless tunnel during that time, he'd been looking at a bright spot in the near distance. And then, as he'd lined up a few of the other things he wanted to get started on, he'd been able to fix on several bright spots. Funny how those made life seem more worth tackling.

After stepping off the escalator, Jim directed his steps back out toward the parking lot. As he strode along, however, his attention was suddenly captured by a couple who'd just walked out of a store and were sauntering along the concourse ahead of him. The woman was small and slender, with a head of golden curls. The man, wearing an expensive tweed jacket, was tall, dark and well built. He put his arm around the woman's shoulders and she leaned into him as they laughed softly together, sharing a private joke.

Jim stiffened. Was that Dory Barker with a man who was obviously her lover? He hadn't thought about her having a boyfriend. But why shouldn't she? It would be the most natural thing in the world.

Unconsciously Jim gritted his teeth. He'd told his sister that Dory was nothing more to him than a nice lady, but the reactions he was now experiencing made hash of that casual disclaimer. He felt angry, jealous. Illogically he found himself wanting to push the man's arm off Dory's slender shoulder. Then they turned so that Jim could see them in profile. The woman wasn't Dory at all, just a pretty blonde with hair the same bright color.

Shaken, Jim stopped and faced a storefront. Pretending to study the window display, he stuck his hands in his pockets while he martialed his thoughts. His fingers encountered the folded paper on which his sister had written her list. *Maybe I should make a list of my own,* he thought. *Maybe I should think about where to put my attraction to my ceramics teacher. Does it go after joining clubs, or can I move it under hobbies?*

Suddenly he caught a glimpse of himself in one of the storefront's mirrored columns. Was that skinny, rather disheveled-looking guy the sort of man a beautiful woman like Dory Barker might be drawn to? Frowning, he hitched up his slacks. Instantly they slid back down on his hips. Maybe Maggie hadn't been so wrong about his clothes. Up until this minute he hadn't given his appearance any thought. Longingly he glanced toward the revolving glass doors that opened onto the parking lot. He really did want to get out of this place. On the other hand, he hated to show up at Dory's house tomorrow night looking like a scarecrow.

"May I help you, sir," a salesman inquired as Jim took a deep calming breath, turned into the entrance and paused in front of a colorful rack of ties.

"Yes. I need a couple of pairs of pants—and three or four shirts, and—" he thought a moment "—maybe a new sport coat."

BETH FROWNED. "Who is this guy, anyway?"

"I told you, honey. He's just a man in my ceramics class."

"But I don't see why you had to invite him for dinner. You hardly ever invite anyone for dinner. The last person was Aunt Katie when she came for Easter."

"Mr. Gordon helped me out when my car died last week, so I owe him a favor. And he seems rather lonely."

"Maybe Daddy gets lonely, too."

Dory gave her daughter an assessing look. "Do you honestly think that's true?"

Beth dropped her gaze. "No," she mumbled grudgingly. "No, I guess it's not."

"Only last weekend you couldn't stop raving about your father's new girlfriend."

"Well, Deanna Ingram really is wonderful," Beth defended herself. "She's gorgeous and smart and she makes a lot of money at her career. And she and Daddy have a lot of fun together."

"Then how can you imagine that your father is so lonely he'd like to come here for dinner?"

Beth plopped into a kitchen chair. She stared down at her knees. Inside the pink-and-black flannel check shirt she wore her shoulders slumped. "I guess he wouldn't."

"Honey," Dory began carefully, "I know what you really want is for Daddy and me to get back together. It's natural you should feel that way, and I'm not blaming you for it. But it isn't going to happen. I'm afraid you're just going to have to accept that."

"I know." Beth slumped farther. "I guess I've known for a long time, but it just makes me feel so..." She didn't complete the sentence, but the expression in her eyes said it all.

"Oh, honey!" Dory dropped down beside her and put her arms around the young girl's shoulders. "I'm sorry—I really am. But it's not so bad, is it? You see your father on the weekends. Actually, you do a lot more with him than you used to."

"Now I do."

"Now you do? What do you mean?"

"Who knows how much longer that will last."

Dory sat back so that she could look into Beth's face. "What are you talking about?" She cocked her head. "Are you afraid your father is going to stop wanting to see you?"

"He might, now that he has Deanna," Beth mumbled without meeting her mother's eyes.

"What a crazy thing to say! I thought you liked her, for gosh sakes."

"I do, only—" Tears began to trickle down Beth's cheeks. "Oh, Mom, she makes me feel so dumb."

"Dumb? Beth!"

"No way can I ever be smart and foxy like her. I'm just not."

"Oh, sweetheart!" Dory wrapped her arms around her daughter's stiff body and hugged her to her breast. "You're as foxy as they come."

"Sure."

"Beth, you're a wonderful girl. I'll always love you, and so will your father. Nothing and no one is going to change that. Not ever! Do you believe that?"

"I guess."

"Well, believe it. Now," she went on as Beth dried her tears, then sniffed into a tissue, "about dinner tonight."

"What about it?"

"Mr. Gordon isn't a boyfriend for me or anything. He's just a nice man who needs a little fattening up."

Beth let out a watery giggle. "Is he so skinny?"

"He's pretty skinny."

"Okay, then I guess you didn't invite him because you're hot for his body."

Dory's eyes widened. "No," she said emphatically, "that was not the reason. But I wouldn't mind seeing him put away a decent meal."

"Yeah, well you've been cooking all day."

"Not *all* day."

"Just about."

"Well, right now I could use a little help. How about it?"

Beth shrugged. "Yeah, sure, I guess. I mean, what do you want me to do?"

Dory got to her feet and turned back toward the kitchen counter. "Okay," she said after checking her recipe for *Bavarois Clermont* and then handing Beth the electric mixer, "would you please whip the cream in that chilled bowl until it forms stiff peaks?"

The teenager began to work on the cream. Over the whirr of the mixer, Dory peeked in at the turkey roasting in the oven, then went into the dining area to set the table. As she put out her best china, crystal and silver, she fretted over what Beth had just said.

Surely there wasn't any danger of Neal losing interest in her. Dory knew how much Beth adored her father and how important these glamorous outings with him were to her. On the occasions when he had to cancel, she was devastated. If he ever started to cancel on a regular basis, it would be a disaster.

Putting the worrisome notion from her mind, Dory stood back to survey the table. The blue-and-white flowered china against the dark blue tablecloth looked nice, she thought. And the crystal, which hadn't been used in almost a year, sparkled attractively under the chandelier.

When she went back into the kitchen, she found Beth licking her fingers.

"That's a no-no," Dory chided. "The cook doesn't eat the dessert until it's ready to serve."

"Then what's the fun of being the cook?"

"Good question. I've wondered the same thing on many occasions." Dory took the bowl away from Beth and tested the stiff white peaks. "Just right."

"Do you realize how long it's been since you fixed a yummy dessert like this?" Beth commented as she watched her mother add the chestnuts.

"Ages, and it's a good thing. A mixture such as the one before us is death on female waistlines. Our job is going to be to push it on our guest and eat as little of it ourselves as possible."

When Beth made no comment, Dory said, "I'm going upstairs to dress. What about you?"

"What about me?" Beth took the dish out of her mother's hands and put it back into the refrigerator for the mold to firm.

As Beth made room for it on the shelf, Dory stood surveying her daughter's rounded backside. "Wouldn't you like to put on something besides jeans and an old flannel shirt?"

"No. Why should I? I mean, you said this guy wasn't anybody special."

Dory debated for a moment and then turned away. "Okay, well, I'll be back down in a minute."

"Sure. I'm going to watch some TV," Beth announced as she strode out to the living room.

Upstairs, Dory opened her closet and stood in front of it. "It's been a long time since I've bought anything new," she muttered as she rubbed her chin with her forefinger. Actually, she'd done almost no shopping for herself since the divorce—lack of time, lack of money and lack of interest. Quickly she checked through her dresses. They were all of good quality. Neal had insisted on that for when she entertained his clients. Still, they weren't quite this year's look.

She reached in and pulled out a fleece knit in a soft shade of peach. She knew that it was particularly flattering, but then so did Beth. If she wore it, Beth was bound to start drawing awkward conclusions. *Which is more important, my ego or Beth's equilibrium,* she asked herself. There were arguments on both sides. Nevertheless she put the dress back.

Then she stood frowning. Because she really did want to look good for James Gordon. Having him in her class had added a new element to her week. Instead of throwing on any old thing when she left the house to teach the last time, she'd selected her most flattering sweater to wear over her jeans. And when she'd walked into class she'd felt an undeniable little flutter of anticipation.

Since it had been actual years since she'd last entertained such feelings, she knew she would have been disappointed if he hadn't shown up. But he'd been there, dark and disturbing as he'd worked with quiet concentration on the pot he was building. It was silly, of course, and she didn't expect it to go anywhere. But James Gordon and her awareness of him had certainly made life a few shades more interesting.

Sighing, Dory reached for a pale yellow shirtdress. She wore it to work a lot. Beth wouldn't think she was trying for any special effects and feel threatened. Nevertheless Dory was particularly careful with her makeup. And when she went downstairs, she double-checked all her preparations, just to make sure nothing would go wrong. What was that old saying, she asked herself with a smile. A hostess should be like a duck on a lake—floating serenely on the surface, but paddling like mad underneath.

Then, as the clock crept toward the appointed hour, a new worry began to nag at her. What if he didn't show up? The man had been under a lot of stress and probably wasn't exactly Mr. Reliable. He might not even remember the invitation. It had been issued more than a week ago and she hadn't thought to remind him about it at the last class.

A cloud seemed to descend over Dory's shoulders. If he didn't come, what was she going to do with all this fancy food? How was she going to treat him the next time she saw him in her class or at the office? Hand him a doggie bag? It would all be so awkward. She should never have invited him in the first place. It had been a stupid thing to do.

"What's wrong with you, Mom?"

"Wrong with me? What do you mean?"

"You're pacing up and down in front of the window like you're about to have a kitten or something."

"Oh?" Dory sat down in front of the television and forced herself to be still while she pretended to watch the game show Beth had switched on.

Five minutes later a car pulled up in front of the town house. Steps sounded on the concrete porch and the doorbell rang.

"I guess that's your student."

As Dory got to her feet, she checked her watch. "Yes, right on time." She crossed the room at a consciously sedate pace and opened the front door.

There he was, smiling tentatively and holding a bottle of wine in one hand. "I didn't know what you'd be serving, so I brought white."

"It's turkey, so that's great." She accepted the wine and showed him in, thinking as she closed the door that every time she saw him he looked different—better. The sight of him tonight had given her a small shock of pleasure. For one thing, he was wearing clothes that fit—well-cut gray slacks, a pale blue shirt that appeared new and a heathery tweed sport coat. The outfit suited him, underlining his dark good looks. And though he was still gaunt, it was not nearly so obvious as it had been a few weeks back.

"Turkey, that's pretty fancy," he commented.

"I was in the mood to do something besides open cans and pry packages out of the freezer and stick then in the microwave. I hope you don't mind."

"Not at all." He turned toward Beth, his smile still tentative. "This must be your daughter."

"Yes. Beth, Dr. Gordon."

" 'Jim,' please."

The two eyed each other, Beth wary, Jim faintly amused. *Oh, dear,* Dory thought, *maybe I shouldn't leave them alone.* But just then a timer sounded in the kitchen and she had no choice.

"Beth, would you please offer Jim a drink while I start the gravy?"

"Sure."

With a last worried frown, Dory hurried toward the kitchen.

As Jim turned toward her, Beth straightened on the couch so that she could get a good look at him. From what her Mom had said, she had expected some anemic-looking jerk to show up. This Jim Gordon was a bit on the skinny side, but he didn't look anemic. In fact, he was seriously cute. He reminded her a little of Gary Purnell, the dark, sort of broody-looking junior all the girls in school were crazy for.

"My mom has some sherry and there's beer in the refrigerator," Beth said. "Do you want some of that?"

"No, thanks." Jim sat down on a chair slipcovered in a cheery blue-and-yellow floral and stretched out his long legs. "I'm fine." He looked around at the orderly, comfortable living room with a bemused expression.

"You sure about the drink?"

"Absolutely."

"Would you like me to turn off the TV?"

"No. What are you watching?"

"*The Dating Game*." Beth felt a little bit embarrassed and wished she'd been watching the news or something not quite so silly.

"Oh, how is it?"

She shrugged. "Really dumb. They have to pick each other by asking questions, but then usually when they actually see each other you can tell they think they picked the wrong one."

"Sounds like a slice of life."

Interested, Beth turned toward him. "Why's that?"

"Because when it comes to picking a date, or mate, most of us are operating in the dark no matter how smart we think we are."

"You're not married, are you?" she queried suspiciously. She didn't want her Mom cooking dinner for a married guy.

"No, but I was."

Beth took a moment to digest that. "Did you have any kids?"

He shook his head.

"I'm not going to have any, either."

"Oh, really?"

She didn't know why she'd told him that, but now that it was out, she nodded vigorously. "No, I'm never going to marry." She didn't add that she was sure she'd never marry because no one would ever ask her.

"It's hard to guess at the future," he responded gently. He pointed at the TV, where a pretty brunette was trying to decide among three eligible bachelors. "But I'm willing to bet she's going to go for the one with the beard."

A moment later Beth started to laugh. "You were right. How did you know?"

"I didn't. But he's the only guy too short for her, so it was a pretty safe gamble."

"Why?"

"Because that's life." Jim grinned. "A lot of the kicks we get out of it are from behind."

The young lady on the television set was just being presented to the bachelor of her choice. At the expression of consternation on her face, Beth started to laugh in earnest and Jim joined her.

"Dinner's just about ready." Dory came out of the kitchen and stopped short, her gaze alternating between the two people chuckling in the living room. *I guess I didn't need to worry,* she thought. They seemed to be getting along fine.

CHAPTER FOUR

"Ta-da," Beth said when Dory emerged from the kitchen bearing the turkey platter. "It looks really classy, Mom."

"Gorgeous," Jim seconded. He pulled out Dory's chair. "I hope you didn't go to all this trouble for me."

"Who else?" Beth mumbled. "Normally we live on salad and tuna fish."

Dory gave her daughter a stern look and then handed their guest the carving tools. "I hope you'll do the honors."

"Certainly." Jim picked up the carving knife with a flourish. "This is where my medical training comes in handy."

"Are you a doctor around here?" Beth questioned, reaching for the French bread.

When he told Beth where he practiced, she cocked her head. "Then how come I haven't seen you around? My mom takes me there sometimes."

"Dr. Gordon—Jim—has been out of the country," Dory quickly interjected. "He's just getting settled in Columbia."

Thinking about his sister's list, which had amused him enough so that he'd taped it to his refrigerator, Jim chuckled. "If you saw my apartment, you'd know how true that is." As they picked up their forks to start eating, he described his barren rooms with their curtainless windows.

"So how come you don't go out and buy stuff for them?" Beth wanted to know. "If I had my own apartment and some money. I'd rush out to a mall and go crazy."

"I don't doubt it," Dory commented dryly.

"Well, so would you, Mom. You used to love to shop."

Jim looked from one Barker to the other, noting how blue both their eyes were. Though Dory's cheeks were far less plump than her daughter's, they both had the same fresh complexions. He was amused by the way they subtly—and sometimes not so subtly—needled each other. It was a typical beleaguered-mother-teenage-daughter-coming-into-her-own relationship. "Maybe that's one of the differences between the sexes," he said aloud. "Shopping's never been one of my interests."

"I know what," Beth burst out. "Mom, you like to decorate. Why don't you pick out some curtains for Jim?"

Dory shot the faintly smiling man across from her an embarrassed look. "Well, I . . ."

"I'd be very grateful," he said quickly, jumping at the opportunity. Ever since walking into Dory's cozy town house, he'd been wondering how to go about seeing her again outside of class without actually asking for a date. "Of course, if you're too busy—"

"She's not too busy," Beth declared. "Mom, you can do it after you get me at the rink tomorrow. We can all go together. It'll be fun."

After glancing at Jim questioningly, Dory agreed and they spent the rest of dinner arranging times and comparing the merits of various shopping malls in the area. After dinner she brought out the dessert. Jim admired the rich molded confection, but when Dory went to serve him, he would only take a small amount. "I'm full. If I eat more than a tablespoonful of that I'll fall asleep at the wheel when I try to drive myself home tonight."

Maybe she had gone a little overboard, Dory admitted to herself. A simpler dessert would have made more sense. After handing Jim his nearly empty dish, she served Beth and herself a small portion, too, and was pleased when her daughter didn't demand more. However, that left most of the Bavarian Cream untouched. Dory made a note to get rid of it. Neither she nor Beth needed all those calories. Mrs. Barnes, the elderly widow who lived next door was fond of sweets and always grateful for any extra attention. Maybe she'd take it over to her in the morning.

Jim asked Beth what she was planning to do at the rink. "I'm a figure skater," she told him. "On Saturdays I have patch."

"And what's that?"

"Working on figures for the fourth test," Beth explained between mouthfuls of dessert.

Dory put down her spoon. "It's called patching because each skater is given a patch of ice to practice his or her figures on."

All through dessert and coffee, Jim listened with apparent fascination while Beth explained about the consuming interest of her young life. Actually, however, his thoughts kept straying to Dory. He liked the soft yellow color of the dress she wore. It brought out the gold of her hair. In fact, he mused, sitting across the table from her was a little like being in a room with a bowlful of daisies. There was such a fresh prettiness about her.

As he sipped his coffee, he couldn't keep his eyes off her. Their gazes snagged and they both smiled like people sharing a pleasant secret. Then, simultaneously realizing that something more compelling than a smile was passing between them, they both quickly looked away.

Sleep eluded Dory that night. As she lay in bed thoughts marched through her head like parading soldiers. She kept

reviewing the conversation at dinner and later. Images of
Jim flickered through her mind's eye. It was crazy how little things about a man attracted you. It was his mouth and
his hands that she liked best. He had beautifully cut lips,
firm and rather thin, yet with just the right hint of sensual-
ity. Her hands stirred on the bedclothes as she tried to
imagine shaping a likeness of his face into clay, sculpting the
broad brow, the high cheekbones, the angular contours of
the nose and chin.

This is ridiculous, she thought as she glanced at the clock
on the bedside table. It was after one. She had the house to
clean first thing tomorrow morning, and she was lying there
mooning like a teenager.

Suddenly a creak outside in the hall made her open her
eyes wide. She sat up and stared through the shadows. Was
that Beth wandering around at this hour? No, it was probably just the house settling. Nevertheless, a moment later
Dory threw back the covers and got out of bed.

The hall was empty and no light shone under Beth's bedroom door. Shrugging, Dory went downstairs, the thick
carpeting muffling her steps. In the kitchen she flicked on
the light and looked toward the stove. A cup of cocoa might
make her more inclined to sleep. She opened the refrigerator door and reached for the milk. But her hand stopped
short, hovering as if it were suspended on invisible strings.

The Bavarian Cream, which had occupied one quarter of
the middle shelf, was gone. Dory blinked and then closed the
refrigerator door and opened the dishwasher. The plate on
which the rich dessert had reposed was inside, rinsed and
scraped clean. "Oh, Beth," she said with a sigh.

UPSTAIRS ON HER BED Beth huddled in the darkness. *I can't
believe I ate the whole thing,* she thought as she put a tentative hand on her full stomach. She hadn't meant to eat the

entire Bavarian Cream. When she'd snuck downstairs half an hour earlier, she'd only intended to have a little piece. She'd been so careful about not eating too much for dinner that she'd still felt hungry. And she'd kept thinking about that yummy dessert going to waste in the refrigerator. Didn't she deserve another little serving? After all, she'd put almost as much work into it as her mother had.

But when she'd finished that small piece, it had tasted so good that she'd cut herself another—and then another. Soon there hadn't been much left, and that little bit had looked ridiculous sitting all by itself on the platter. So she'd eaten it, too. Now she wished she'd never snuck downstairs to the kitchen in the first place. Because she felt sick.

Oh, well, she thought as she stretched out carefully so as not to disturb her unhappy innards. *Tomorrow's another day. I'll start my diet tomorrow and be really good.*

THE NEXT AFTERNOON Jim picked Dory up and drove her to the rink. They arrived a few minutes early, so they stood in the warming room watching through the Plexiglas window as Peggy Schrion, Beth's teacher, finished her lesson.

"Those two certainly look awfully serious out there," Jim commented.

"In competitive amateur skating, figures *are* serious business," Dory answered.

Jim rocked back on his heels. "Last night Beth talked about this South Atlantic competition that she's going to. It's awfully important to her, isn't it?"

Dory nodded. "Maybe too important." She turned toward Jim, who was still looking out at the ice. The wind had ruffled his thick dark hair into wayward curls, and he wore the same ruggedly attractive tweed sport coat he'd had on the night before. "As you've probably gathered," Dory continued, fixing her gaze on his lean jaw, "Beth really loves the sport and she's a hard worker. She's put an awful lot into getting ready for South Atlantics, and I know she has dreams of placing in the top three and going on to Easterns, maybe even Nationals. But—''

"But you don't think she has a chance?''

"There's always a chance. Beth's very talented. It's just that so are the other girls she's going to go up against.'' Dory turned back toward the window, and saw that Beth was still working with fierce concentration. She wore a powder blue warm-up suit, an expensive Christmas present from her grandparents. When she'd received it the year before she'd loved the style and color, but it had been so large she'd had to put it away for a season. Now, only ten months later, it was tight.

Ruefully Dory thought about the Bavarian Cream. When she'd confronted Beth about it that morning, the girl had apologized. "I'm sorry. I don't know why I did something so gross. In the middle of the night I got hungry.''

That was no excuse, and Dory had been disturbed and disappointed. But what was she supposed to do—get out a bullwhip? There were kids Beth's age doing a lot worse things than sneaking desserts.

Jim gazed down at Dory. "All this is tough on you, isn't it? Tell me something, how did Beth become so hung up on skating in the first place?''

"I made the mistake of taking her to an ice show,'' Dory answered. Worriedly she considered the years of effort her daughter had put into developing her skill on ice and the fantasies and dreams she still cherished. When Beth had first started skating, Dory had been delighted to have her take such an interest in an activity. They'd tried ballet and piano and violin lessons, and none of them had clicked. Only skating had stirred a boundless enthusiasm in Beth.

After a while, however, the money and time the sport was eating up had begun to appall Dory. Also, as Beth started to compete, Dory had worried about where all this was leading. She'd tried to put on the brakes, but then Neal had stepped in. He'd liked the idea of having a daughter who was a figure skater, who could twirl and jump in beautiful costumes. She had, too, actually. The beauty of the sport was very appealing. Only now she'd begun to worry again. Up until recently Dory had been looking forward to the South Atlantic competition. After all, in theory it would be the culmination of countless hours of practice plus considerable money and inconvenience. Now she was beginning to dread it.

Her mood lightened somewhat when Beth came off the ice looking flushed and triumphant. "I got my brackets," she told Jim with a delighted grin.

He quirked an eyebrow. "Is that important?"

"Yes!" Beth declared emphatically. "Before they were scraped. But now I'm getting them right."

While Beth loosened her skates, Dory was suddenly conscious of the little flutter of excitement Jim's presence was creating in the crowded warming room. The other girls who'd come off the ice were shooting him bright-eyed glances and giggling among themselves.

Jim, apparently realizing what was going on and not altogether comfortable with it, went outside to wait until Beth and Dory were ready. When he was gone, Beth eyed her mother's outfit. "You look nice. Did you get dressed up because of Jim?"

Dory glanced down at her beige wool slacks, cashmere sweater and houndstooth check blazer. "This isn't dressed up. I wear this sweater and jacket to work all the time."

"Yeah, but you have on your good gold earrings, too. And usually on weekends you just slop around in jeans and a sweatshirt."

"Usually on weekends I'm potting or gardening or cleaning house," Dory responded carefully. "We are going to be taking Dr. Gordon shopping. Naturally I don't want to appear in public looking like a slob."

Beth stood and gave her mother an awkward little pat on the shoulder. "Mom, it's okay."

"What?"

"It's okay if you like him, y'know, I mean if you really like him. I think he's pretty cool, too." Beth suddenly looked embarrassed. "And why are you calling him 'Dr. Gordon'?" she added gruffly. "He said to call him 'Jim.'"

"That's true," Dory admitted while she digested her daughter's statement. Was she actually being given permission to be interested in a man who wasn't Beth's father? Glory be!

THEY TOOK Jim's car to a nearby shopping mall. When they walked through the swinging doors a blast of noise struck them in the face.

"What's going on?" Jim exclaimed, stopping short.

"An antique expo," Dory explained. "They have them every now and then. Dealers come in and set up displays all along the concourse. It really draws the crowds."

"Yeah," Beth commented. "The joint is jammed and there's no place to walk because of all the old furniture and tables full of junk standing around."

Dory's gaze was fixed on Jim's face. He looked tense, she thought, as if he wanted nothing better than to turn around and walk out. She realized immediately what was wrong. She'd rescued a dog from the pound once. After weeks in a cage he, too, had had a visceral reaction to noise and confusion. "If we're going to buy your curtains, we'll have to walk through these crowds, I'm afraid."

"Of course." After taking a deep breath, Jim started forward.

She hurried to catch up with him. "If you'd rather not, we could come another time."

"It's okay. Mall paranoia is something every patriotic American has to learn to overcome. Freeways, malls, boom boxes and deficit spending are now part of our national birthright."

Two minutes later they were on the second floor of one of the mall's big department stores, looking at the displays of ready-made curtains.

"What color do you like for your living room?" Dory asked Jim.

"I don't know."

She eyed him with concern. Though he was trying to hide the fact, she knew that fighting their way through the jumble of noisy shoppers and browsers had been a trial for him. He was obviously tense and uncomfortable. He'd stuffed his hands into his pockets as if he didn't know what to do with them and was rocking back and forth on his heels like a trapped tiger. Yes she also sensed it was very important to him to get through this.

"You don't know what color you like?" Beth exclaimed.

"I know which colors I don't like." Jim pointed at a pink-and-blue pattern, then a sickly yellow solid. "I don't like those."

"Who would? They're yucky!"

"How about this?" Dory pulled out a panel in a deep shade of garnet.

"Euuu," Beth commented. "It looks like dried blood."

Impassively Jim stared at it. "Dried blood is nowhere near that attractive."

"How about blue?" suggested Beth.

"Blue is a fine color, but maybe I should have something a little different." Jim's gaze swept back to Dory. "That's nice." With a nod of his head, he indicated her sweater.

It was a muted shade of green, which she had picked out because it seemed to add depth to her eyes. Suddenly, as he stood there studying it, she became conscious of the soft cashmere molding her upper body. She could feel the luxurious knit draping over her shoulders and clinging to her breasts. Quickly she turned back to the curtains. "There's a green over there," she said, pointing at a display next to the one where they were standing. "It's not quite the same shade, but it's close."

Jim walked over and, his hands still jammed firmly into his pockets, gazed down at the fabric. "That's fine. I'll take it."

I wouldn't say I've exactly earned my spurs as a decorating consultant, Dory reflected as she stood back and watched Jim make short work of buying the curtains. It was obvious he'd needed only a little moral encouragement to get this job done and that he was anxious to get back out into the open air.

But Beth had other ideas. On the way back through the antique expo, she suddenly let out a high-pitched squeal of delight. "Oh, look at that! Isn't that neat!"

She rushed over to a huge, ornate brass bed that had been placed next to an elaborate chandelier display a couple of carpenters were setting up. Dory shot Jim an apologetic glance. "I'm sorry. I know you're eager to escape from this scene."

"It's okay, really. It's quite a bed," he added after they'd paused to inspect the object of Beth's attention.

Dory stared at it, for the first time really seeing the thing in all its shiny yellow splendor. "Yes, indeed," she murmured.

The brass bed with its lacy filigree, painted china porcelain medallions and elaborate canopy was definitely a conversation piece—except that it seemed to have throttled both her and Jim. It had been fitted out with fancy sheets, little satin throw pillows and a turned-back pink moire comforter. To add to the bed's inviting look, a lacy white nightdress and man's pair of black silk pajamas had been arranged side by side next to a brass warming pan. The sleeve of the pajama top was wrapped around the slender waist of the skimpy nightgown.

Standing next to each other, Jim and Dory gazed at the suggestively bedecked mattress in a silence that was sudden, mutual and packed with censored thoughts.

"Oh, look," Beth cried, peering up under the canopy, "there's a mirror on its ceiling. What would you want a mirror on top of your bed for?"

"I can't imagine," Dory said, and felt herself flushing as she caught the sudden smile twitching at the corners of Jim Gordon's attractive mouth.

"May I help you?" A saleswoman who'd been directing the pair of carpenters nearby approached them.

"We've been admiring this bed. Can you tell me the price?" Jim asked.

"I'll have to check on that. As you can see, we're just getting set up. I haven't got all the price tags on yet."

As she turned away, the display under construction, a complicated framework on a pedestal, began to totter. "Watch it!" the workman directly behind Jim shouted as he rushed forward with his arms outstretched to steady it.

At the sharp crack of the man's voice, Jim dropped into a defensive posture and whirled around. His knees bent, ready to spring, and his hands balled into fists.

"Hey, buddy, take it easy," the other carpenter exclaimed. Admiration warred with alarm on his rough-hewn features as he gazed at Jim. "You an ex-marine or something? My brother's an ex-marine. He saw a lot of action in 'Nam and now he does that exact same thing every time he hears a loud noise." He shook his head. "A man never gets over combat, I guess."

"No, I guess not." Jim straightened. "Sorry."

"S'nothing." The man gestured at his co-worker. "Phil, it needs extra bracing."

Dory, who had watched this scene with concern, noticed the saleswoman eyeing her and Beth speculatively.

"Hey, did you see that?" Beth whispered. "Did Jim really used to be a marine like the man said? Honestly, he reacted like one of the guys in the karate movies."

"I think he acquired his skill from the school of hard knocks," Dory murmured.

"Shall we go?" Jim said.

"Don't you want to find out about the bed?" Beth asked.

He shook his head. "Right now all I want is to make it back out to the parking lot without causing a riot." He shot Dory a guarded smile. "Sorry about that."

"Nothing to be sorry for."

He gave a little shrug. "Thank you. Thank you for your help today."

"I didn't do much, just tagged along and made a couple of dumb suggestions."

"They weren't dumb, and having your company was just what I needed. Left to myself I might have lived with uncurtained windows for months."

Anxious to put him at ease, Dory laughed. "Yes, but now that you've bought your curtains, will you actually put them up? That's the hardest part, you know."

"True," he admitted with a lift of his eyebrows. "I'll do it if you and Beth come back to share a dish of ice cream with me and offer a little more moral encouragement."

"Sure we will," Beth said as she walked alongside them. "We want to see how they look on your windows, don't we, Mom?"

JIM GORDON'S APARTMENT was on the second floor of a large, centrally located complex of three-story brick buildings. They were clean and attractive, the grass and bushes planted at symmetrical intervals around them neatly clipped. The feeling Dory got as they parked in front of them, however, was sterile and impersonal.

That feeling was underlined when Jim unlocked his door and then stood to one side. "Step into my parlor. I'm afraid it's not going to win any awards in *House Beautiful*," he added a moment later as his two guests stood gazing around them.

"Boy," Beth exclaimed. "You weren't kidding last night, were you?" She pointed at the barren walls and empty corners. "You really don't have any furniture."

"I have that." He indicated the wing chair, where a marmalade cat reclined. The animal regarded them warily.

"One chair, that's all?"

"Well, there's now a television in the corner. And I've got a table for the kitchen. Hey, what can I say? I wasn't cut out to be a decorator."

As Beth and Jim bantered, Dory looked around thoughtfully. The place was very clean, the rug spotless. There were no dirty dishes in sight, and the magazines and newspapers against one wall were stacked neatly. Still, she was puzzled and deeply disturbed by the lack of furnishings. She couldn't fathom his living in the place for weeks without at least getting himself a couch. Was it because he didn't have the money?

While he took off his jacket, rolled up his sleeves and set to work, Beth settled cross-legged on the rug. Dory was given the perch of honor in the wing chair, displacing the cat. She tried arranging the marmalade tabby in her lap and petting it. But, with an outraged yowl, the cat jumped to the floor and stalked away.

"Cleo seems to be a one-man feline," Jim apologized.

"Well, she certainly appears to like you." Dory watched as the animal rubbed up against his ankle.

Jim, who was laying out brass screws on the windowsill, shrugged and reached down to give the cat a casual scratch between the ears. "I don't know what I've done to deserve such affection. But I'll take whatever I can get."

The remark gave Dory something more to chew on. While she watched him attach the curtain rods to the wall and then helped with hooks and pleats, she mulled over his words. He seemed so alone, so unattached. Yet he'd been married before, or so Beth had reported. Dory wondered what sort of woman his wife had been and what had caused the breakup. Did he still miss her? Was that part of why his experience in Afghanistan had been so devastating for him? And when he said he'd take whatever affection he could get, did that mean he was willing and able to give it, as well? Or, like Neal, did he just want to soak it up without reciprocating?

Suddenly Dory found herself wondering what sort of children she might have had if Jim had been the sire instead of Neal. Black hair and brown eyes were dominant, weren't they? Might she have had a little boy with his father's dark intensity? There'd been a time when she'd dreamed of having a large family. But because of the circumstances of their marriage, Neal hadn't cared to have any more children after Beth was born. And, of course, it was too late now.

"They look great," Beth exclaimed when the first set of curtains was hung. "Now all you need is some furniture to go with them."

"Let's not get carried away here." Jim jumped lightly down from the kitchen chair he'd been standing on and stepped back to admire the effect. "I do like the color."

He glanced over at Dory, and once again she became conscious of her green cashmere sweater molding her breasts—all the more so because she'd taken off her jacket.

"Do you want us to help you hang them in your bedroom?" Beth queried.

"No, I think I can handle that on my own." He set the hammer on the chair and rolled down his sleeves. "How about my treating you ladies to hot fudge sundaes?"

"Hot fudge!" Beth's round face split into a wide grin and she jumped to her feet. "That sounds great! Lead the way!"

Dory cleared her throat. "Sounds kind of high calorie to me."

"C'mon, Mom, don't be a wet blanket."

Jim turned back to Dory. "I've been treating myself to ice cream desserts because I need to put on another five or ten pounds. But I can just make coffee if you prefer."

"Well, I definitely do not prefer," Beth declared.

"Ice cream sounds fine." This was not the time to try to restart Beth on her diet, Dory decided. The trouble was that there never seemed to be a good time.

Dory and Beth sat down at Jim's kitchen table and watched as he placed a jar of fudge sauce in a pan of water on the stove and then, while it warmed, dished out generous helpings of Dutch-chocolate ice cream.

"Just what I like, chocolate on chocolate," Beth commented.

Jim stood with his back to them, dribbling the heated fudge over the top of the glistening mounds. "Everybody likes chocolate."

Yes, Dory thought. Hadn't she read someplace that it had the same satisfying effect on you as good sex? An image of the brass bed with its white lace nightgown and black silk pajamas popped into her head. The thought made her choke slightly and drag her gaze away from Jim. For she'd suddenly become aware of just how closely she was studying his broad shoulders, and the lean span of his too-narrow waist and the compact masculine derriere below. It had been a long time since she'd had any sex at all, much less the good kind. When he turned and handed her a bowl swimming in chocolate, she decided to ignore the calories and dug in with gusto.

Beth took her ice cream out to the living room, where she'd tuned the television into one of her favorite soap operas. A moment after she was gone, Jim sat down across from Dory with his own ice cream.

"I really do want to apologize for that scene back there in the mall when I reacted like a character in a bad Hollywood thriller," he said. "I hope I didn't embarrass you too much."

"Of course not!" Suddenly it seemed like the most natural thing in the world to reach out and pat his arm. "Shopping trips are an ordeal for most men, you know."

Slowly he nodded. "Yes, but for me that goes double." He cleared his throat. "I suppose I should have warned you that I'm not at my peak performance in certain types of situations. But I'd been to the mall with my sister, and that time I did okay. I thought I'd be okay today, too."

"You couldn't know about the expo or be prepared for that crashing chandelier display."

"No, but things like that do happen. It's part of life's little parade of surprises. I can't go around reacting like a shell-shocked war dog every time I hear a loud noise. It tends to make people nervous."

"You didn't make anyone as nervous as you made yourself. Really, Jim, forget it. You were the only one who was bothered, not me, or Beth, or anyone else. Actually, I thought you handled yourself very well." She grinned. "In fact, I was impressed. You're a handy man to know if I ever get into a street fight."

As he gazed down at her, he broke into a slow, grateful smile. "You're a truly kind lady, aren't you?"

"I don't know what you mean."

"I mean you're that rare sort of person who'll always try to do the right thing or find the right word to ease tense situations and make other people more comfortable."

"Am I? Is that good?"

"How could it be bad?"

"Oh, I don't know." Restlessly she seesawed her spoon. Then suddenly she got up from the table and carried her dish over to the sink, next to the refrigerator. "Sometimes," she said with her back to him, "people who are always trying to accommodate others wind up being used as doormats."

"No one with an ounce of sense could ever use a person like you that way," Jim replied distractedly. He'd just realized that he'd left his sister's list taped up on the refrigerator and that Dory was standing within inches of it. Not wanting her to read the thing, Jim leaped to his feet, removed it and stuffed it into his pocket.

But when Dory heard the sheet of paper being yanked free of its tape, she swiveled around and collided with Jim.

"Oops!"

"Sorry." He rushed out to steady her. "Just getting something from the refrigerator."

She glanced down at his fingers, which were wrapped tightly around her upper arm, and inhaled sharply. "My fault," she whispered with a choked sound.

Instantly he released the pressure and withdrew his hand. Yet, standing only inches apart, a field of electricity seemed to still connect them. "If you have any faults, Dory Barker," Jim said gazing down at her soberly, "I haven't been able to detect a single one of them."

Beth's voice shattered the moment. "Hey, Mom," she said, poking her head around the corner, "it's getting late, and you said we could stop at the library before it closes."

"Oh, yes." Dory backed away from Jim and turned toward her daughter. "Oh, yes, I almost forgot."

A FEW MINUTES LATER, Jim closed the door and stood listening to Dory's and Beth's departing footsteps. When the sounds died away, he reached into his pocket and fished out the piece of paper he'd removed from the refrigerator. His expression grew rueful as he read his sister's bold scribble. Though Dory had been within inches of Maggie's "agenda," he didn't think she'd actually seen it—at least, he hoped she hadn't. After number nine, which read "meet eligible women," number ten went on to instruct playfully, "get the glands in gear and have sex with as many as you can lure between the sheets."

"Good old Maggie," Jim muttered as he reviewed how he and Dory had stood dumbstruck in front of that brass bed at the antique expo and then just now reacted to each other with such palpable chemistry when they'd accidentally collided at the sink. According to the agenda, he was still struggling with number three: "select and purchase items for apartment at area malls and shopping centers." Three was a long way from ten's mandate to seduce pretty ladies.

With one quick dismissive movement, Jim tore the list in two and walked back into his living room. It was getting dark outside. Before she'd left, Dory had drawn his new drapes against the approaching night. Now, except for the cat, they were the only color in the empty room. They enclosed it, giving it a new feeling of coziness even as they drew the eye.

He liked that new feeling, the new color that reminded him of spring grass and new leaves—and softer-than-silk cashmere sweaters. Decisively he picked up the hammer and the unopened packages on the floor and headed for his bedroom.

As he worked in there to set the curtain rod in place, impressions of the afternoon he'd just spent with Dory and Beth Barker flitted through his mind: the two of them standing in his doorway, looking so healthy and normal, so unlike the sick and brutally wounded who had been his daily diet of sights overseas; Dory's soft voice as she kindly guided him around the curtain department and then soothed him after the falling chandelier display incident; Beth's eager face as she accepted the bowl of ice cream he'd fixed for her. But the image he kept returning to was of Dory the way she'd looked standing next to the window and pulling the drapes.

It had been the simplest of acts, yet for some strange reason it had moved him. Somehow the picture of that slender woman with her girlish figure and soft blond curls gently shutting out the night burned in his mind like a lamp in the darkness.

CHAPTER FIVE

"IF YOU'LL TAKE A SEAT, Dr. Lucas will be with you shortly." Dory crossed off Mrs. Levine's name on the schedule and glanced over her shoulder at the closed door. Then she rechecked the clock on the wall. Almost noon. Any minute now Jim would walk out of Sam Lucas's office, where he'd been closeted for the past half hour. Dory swallowed nervously and then, irritated with herself, frowned down at the calendar before her.

It had been two weeks since she'd shopped with Jim. In that time, other than seeing him in ceramics class, where he was merely friendly, she hadn't heard from him. What had she expected, she asked herself. She wasn't at all sure that she cared to have him call her up and ask for a regular date. Even if she were ready for dating, she didn't really think he was yet. The man obviously had a lot of problems to work through. And anyway, she didn't see herself as his type.

Considering this, Dory gnawed her lower lip. He was an adventurous man, a man with a dramatic past. Doubtless, when he got around to wanting women in his life again, he'd be attracted to the glamorous sort who could match his past with colorful lives of their own. In fact, Dory told herself, she was relieved he hadn't shown any sign of pursuing the relationship. Yet she couldn't deny her pang of disappointment. Dory's frown deepened. Where Jim Gordon was concerned, her reactions didn't make much sense—and that worried her. In the past when her emotions had ruled her head, it had all turned out disastrously.

The door opened and Jim strode out, riveting her whole attention. His hair had just been freshly cut, and he'd put on another pound or two of what appeared to be solid muscle. In corduroy slacks and a dark brown leather bomber jacket he looked better than she'd ever seen him. When he stopped at her desk she found herself beaming up at him like a beguiled teenager. "Would you like to schedule an appointment for next week?"

"No, make it next month."

"Next month?"

"Sam says it's time to start cutting down."

"Well, I suppose that's good."

"Good for my bank account, anyhow." Brusquely he agreed on a time. As he took out his checkbook to pay for the session he'd just had, she realized that he was embarrassed. It embarrassed him to be seeing her under these circumstances—which surely indicated a more than casual interest in her. Or was she grasping at straws?

While he wrote out the check, Dory sent Mrs. Levine in for her appointment and then, suddenly charged with nervous energy, got up to tidy the office before she went out to run a few errands and pick up a yogurt for lunch.

"How've you been?" Jim asked as he put his pen away.

"Fine." Dory stacked magazines on one of the end tables, sorting out several of the older decorating and gardening issues. Then, carrying them with her, she walked across the room to accept his check.

"You're looking good. That blue dress becomes you."

"Oh, thank you." Dory wanted to say something more, something that would keep their conversation going. But she couldn't think of anything that wasn't boring or inane. She could tell Jim was experiencing the same difficulty. He stood gazing at her, his lips slightly parted as if unspoken words of great importance hovered between them. Yet neither of them said a thing and the silence stretched.

After putting the check away, she turned toward the coat rack and plucked her blazer off a hanger.

"Going somewhere?"

"Just to the Freemanis delicatessen down the street. I promised to give Mrs. Freemanis these magazines when we were ready to chuck them, and I left in too much of a rush this morning to pack my lunch."

"Want a lift?" Jim asked as he accompanied her out the door and through the exit to the small parking lot at the side of the building.

"Thanks, but there's no reason for me to bother you. I can drive myself." She stopped short. "At least, I thought I could." She'd just spotted the Plum. The car listed in its parking space, the right rear tire crumpled beneath it like a wad of squashed chewing gum. "Oh, no!"

Together they approached the disabled vehicle. "Your station wagon seems to be giving you a certain amount of grief," Jim commented.

"You might say that. I just got through paying a huge repair bill for a new solenoid," Dory groaned.

"This isn't anything so serious. Just a flat." He dropped onto one knee and peered at the misshapen rubber tread. "Looks like you picked up a nail."

"Oh, great. I'll have to get someone from a service station out here to change it."

"No, you won't." Jim walked around to the Plum's trunk. "I may not be the handiest guy in the world, but I do know how to change a tire."

"Really? You don't mind?"

He held out his hand. "No problem. Just give me the keys so I can get at your jack."

Gratefully Dory fished in her purse, and a moment later Jim was back on his knees, loosening the lug nuts on her mangled tire.

While he worked, she leaned against the sedan parked next to the Plum. "Are you sure you have the time to be a good Samaritan? I know you're back at work now."

"I don't have any appointments scheduled for another half hour," he told her as he deftly removed a lug nut from the wheel.

"How've things been going?"

"Fine." He hesitated and then, resting his weight on one knee, glanced back at her over his shoulder. "Today I was able to give Sam a good progress report. You'll be happy to hear I'm now buying necessities for myself and my apartment without the aid of a cheering section."

"Oh?" She cocked her head. "Not that Beth and I minded being your cheering section... What sorts of things?"

Wryly Jim began to tick off items. "New clothes that fit, a chest of drawers to put them in, a decent bed. And yesterday I even went out and bought a couch."

"You make that sound like quite an accomplishment."

"It was—a breakthrough, even." Jim rolled the ruined tire out from under the jacked-up car. "And you're the one who made me see that."

"Me? How do you mean?"

"It was after you and Beth left my place, after I'd hung the curtains you helped me buy and was wandering around admiring the effect, that I realized something."

Dory held the trunk so he could take out the spare and stow the ruined tire in its place.

"I realized why I hadn't bought them before, why I'd needed help to manage such a fairly simple task. It wasn't just my being uncomfortable in malls or my dislike of crowds and confusion that kept me from doing a little basic shopping."

"No?"

Jim shook his head. "That was more of an excuse than a real reason. For a month I'd been living in empty rooms, in conditions that amounted to camping out."

"Yes." Dory studied him, waiting with baited breath for what he was going to say. He rested one arm on the spare's rim, his gaze turned inward.

"It's no accident that I was camping out in my new apartment. Camping out is what I had to do for fourteen months in a field hospital. I lived in a tent. Half the time I ate food cold out of cans. My bed was a cot and a sleeping bag. My chair was a crate. And afterward, when I was taken prisoner, it was the same, only worse. What food I got was slop. For months I was isolated in a dark little cave that, except for the filth, was even more barren than my tent. Believe me, there were no pretty green drapes on the windows. There were no windows."

Dory frowned. "Are you saying that you think you were unconsciously trying to reproduce those privations in your apartment?"

Jim chuckled. "Not the filth, I hope. I do try to keep the place clean. But the emptiness, the isolation and discomfort—yes. Maybe that's one of the reasons I was so anxious to move out of my sister's place and into my own digs. All her thick carpets and overstuffed chairs were giving me claustrophobia. They live well, Maggie and Les."

Dory struggled to understand. "You're saying that when you first came back here, the luxury of your sister's surroundings made you ill at ease? But you're a doctor and doctors make good money. You lived comfortably before you volunteered for Afghanistan, didn't you?"

"Yes." Jim rolled the new tire around the corner of the car. "After we got out of medical school, my wife and I could afford to live well, and we did. We drove expensive automobiles, traveled, ate out all the time, dressed in clothes with impressive labels. Then, when our marriage fell apart, I felt the need to put all that behind me. In fact, today Sam suggested that my volunteering for Afghanistan was partly an act of penance, a way of shedding the outer layers of a life-style I had come to regard as superficial and self-indulgent."

"Do you agree with that?"

He nodded. "Yes, I may have felt some of that. But when I came back to the States it was something much stronger. Living with Maggie has always been a strain. Even when we were kids she was the original bossy little girl, and I never did like being pushed around. But after what I'd seen and experienced overseas, the luxury in her home seemed almost obscene. Crazy, huh?" As he finished bolting on the new tire, Jim shot Dory an ironic look.

Though he didn't tell Dory what was in his mind, he was remembering what his therapist had said earlier in their private session:

"Jim, there could be a network of reasons for a reaction like that."

"I know," Jim had replied, "that one of them had to be guilt. Deep down I didn't feel I deserved such luxury. Deep down I'm still punishing myself because of what happened to Tom. Only I'm finding new and more bizarre ways of doing it."

"I wouldn't put it like that at all," Sam Lucas had corrected. "I'd say you were recognizing your problems, facing and then tackling them. And that's a very mature and adult way in which to deal with life's difficulties."

Jim shook himself free of the recollection and smiled ruefully up at Dory. "Hey, I've just realized that I'm making you pay a heavy price for this tire change."

"What price is that?"

"You've been forced to stand there listening to me take my psychic temperature, which is a form of torture Sam Lucas won't tolerate for less than a small fortune."

Dory smiled. "I enjoy listening to you talk, Jim. And I'm very flattered that you feel you can talk to me."

Jim turned to lower the car off the jack. "It's hard to imagine a man alive who wouldn't want to talk to a woman like you."

Dory stared at his back. Neal hadn't ever wanted to talk to her—really talk. Because his formal education had been so superior to hers, he'd felt that she wouldn't understand anything but the commonplaces of adult exchange. They hadn't been able to share the thoughts and emotions closest to their hearts.

Feeling the need to lighten the mood between herself and Jim, Dory waited until he finished his task, thanked him for changing her tire and then said playfully, "I'm curious about this couch you've bought. Are you actually sitting on your new acquisition or just using it to prove a point?"

"I don't know. It hasn't been delivered yet." Jim started to laugh. "If I don't, I know someone who will."

"Who?" Dory gazed at him speculatively. Had he met another woman? Maybe that was the reason why he'd never called her, she thought jealously.

"Cleo, my cat," Jim said. He got to his feet and brushed off his hands. "She doesn't have a problem with luxury—not at all. She's going to love that nice squashy couch."

A wave of relief broke over Dory and she started to laugh. Jim joined her, his gaze fixed on her merry face. The wind had whipped her hair into delicious disarray and sharpened the color in her cheeks. He thought she looked prettier than he'd ever seen her. Automatically he moved toward her and reached out a hand. She extended her own to take it, but at the last instant he stepped back and dropped his arms to his side.

"I shouldn't touch you. I'm covered with grease."

"It doesn't matter."

"Yes, it does. You're so fresh and clean. I wouldn't want to get you dirty."

Dory was about to protest, but then the moment was broken by the sound of her name.

"Dory?"

Dory swiveled. "Neal?"

Her ex-husband stood a few feet away in the parking lot. His gaze went from Dory to Jim and back.

"What are you doing here?" Dory asked breathlessly. Flustered, she glanced back at Jim, who was staring at Neal with a frown.

Neal, too, looked distinctly unfriendly. "Since it's Friday, I'm knocking off a little early. But first I thought I'd stop in to have a word with you." Meaningfully he directed his gaze back to Jim, who still stood surveying him with faintly drawn eyebrows. "Got a minute?"

Taking the hint, Jim dropped the jack back in Dory's truck, locked it and handed her the key. "I'll be going now. See you later."

"Jim, thank you. Really, I appreciate what you did."

"It was nothing. Glad to be of service."

When Jim had left them, Neal strolled toward her. Trim and immaculately groomed in his hand-tailored gray wool suit, he was, as always, strikingly handsome. With his cream-colored overcoat slung casually over one arm, he could have posed for a man-about-town advertisement in a magazine like the *New Yorker*.

"What was that all about? Who was that guy?"

"Oh, just one of Sam's patients. He was helping me with a flat tire." Dory jingled the keys on her ring.

"Just one of Sam's nuts, you mean."

"He's not a nut," Dory exclaimed. She glared.

Neal's sapphire eyes narrowed. "Something going on between you two? Don't tell me you're finally taking an interest in the opposite sex. I thought you'd sworn off."

"I don't know what you're talking about."

"Oh, just the way you were looking at each other. I watched you talking to each other as if you were the only two people left in the world. I suppose you were offering tea and sympathy." He glanced at the publications in Dory's arms. "You always were a chump for a sob story. I'll bet you're still buying magazine subscriptions from kids who claim they're working their way through college."

Dory flushed. Only yesterday she'd written a check for a magazine she didn't want and couldn't afford. "Why are you here?" she questioned stiffly. "Is anything wrong? Saturday night is still on, isn't it?"

"What are you, a mind reader?" Sighing, Neal began pacing around the Plum, inspecting Jim's tire-changing job.

"You mean you're canceling Saturday? Oh, Neal, don't do it. Beth will be so disappointed."

"Look, I'm sorry. I know I promised her, but something has come up."

"Are you sure?" Since he was being so vague, Dory suspected that the "something" was a romantic weekend with his new girlfriend. Fine. But what about Beth?

"Of course I'm sure." Neal looked irritated. "I'll make it up to her, I promise. In fact, I'll take her up to Philadelphia next month, if you want."

"For the competition? But I'm going to want to be there, too."

"Good. We'll divide it up even-Steven. I'll take her up, and you can take her back." Neal spun on his heel and gave her the once-over. "You seem well enough. How've you been? Still messing around with that pottery stuff?"

"Yes," Dory answered distractedly. For some time now she'd been wanting to discuss her worries about the South Atlantic competition with her ex-husband. Yet they saw each other so infrequently that the right moment never seemed to arise. Right now in the parking lot wasn't a great time, either. But... As he gave the tire an experimental kick, she cleared her throat.

"Neal, now that you've brought the subject up, I wonder if I might have a word with you about this competition of Beth's."

He consulted his watch. "Okay, but make it short. I'm meeting someone for lunch."

As briefly as she could, Dory summarized her worries. "I'm just afraid that she's riding for a fall," she said. "Neal, you know how important this thing is to her, how much she's invested in it. What if she doesn't do well? What if she's humiliated?"

Neal's expression became impatient. "Dory, old girl, when are you going to stop living in a dream? In this world competition is the name of the game. You've heard the expression No pain, no gain, haven't you? Well, if Beth wants to win big, she has to go out there and put herself on the line for it."

"I know, but—"

"Oh, listen, stop being such a worrywart. She's my daughter, so she's got grit. She'll make us all proud of her." Neal flung his coat over his other arm. "Just try to get her to lose some of that blubber you've let her put on. Now I've got to get going if I'm to make that lunch date."

BETH GAZED at the beige meat loaf and gloppy mashed potatoes the lady behind the cafeteria counter had just dumped
on a plate. Revolting, she thought with a little shudder.

"Next," the attendant blared, and switched her bored
gaze to Beth. "You want meat loaf, hon?"

"Uh, no." Beth knew she should ask for the salad bar.
That's what she'd promised herself she'd do. But it was easy
to make promises like that after breakfast when your stomach was full and you'd had trouble zipping up your jeans.
Now she was tired and hungry. The thought of having
nothing to eat but tasteless lettuce was definitely unappealing. "Uh, I guess I'll have the pizza."

"Pizza," the attendant called down the line, and a moment later a cheesy slab of thick dough was slapped on a
plate and shoved in Beth's direction.

It smells really good, she thought with satisfaction. How
many calories could it have? After all, it was only one little
piece—well, maybe not so little. It covered the plate and
hung off the sides. She'd have diet Coke with it, she told
herself. After all, why did they call it diet Coke if it didn't
mean you were dieting when you drank it?

Actually, Beth's tray looked quite empty with nothing but
one slice of pizza and a plastic cupful of diet soda on it. As
she passed up the vegetables and soups, she felt downright
virtuous. But the dessert counter that day turned out to be
tougher to ignore than usual.

"Hey, butterscotch pie, allllriiight!" the tall boy ahead of
her declared. Grinning, he shot his arm out for a large piece
and then requested a chocolate sundae to go with it.

Butterscotch pie was Beth's favorite. Irritably she eyed the
contents of his already loaded tray—two slices of pizza, a
serving of mashed potatoes, a serving of baked apples, two
rolls with butter and two cartons of chocolate milk. And he

was beanpole skinny. It wasn't fair! So what if he was a basketball player. She was an athlete, too.

As if it had a will of its own, Beth's hand reached for the last piece of butterscotch pie on the counter. Then, guiltily, she paid for her selections and hurried into the crowded lunchroom.

Out among the large round Formica tables the sound level was at its usual ear-splitting intensity. Catcalls and whistles punctuated the roar. Rowdy boys anxious to show off their newly acquired booming baritone voices, shouted insults at one another. In one corner two girls giggled while they mixed together all the food on their plates, creating a mess they seemed to find indescribably funny and that no one in his or her right mind would care to eat. Nearby a tableful of ninth graders engaged in a game that involved tossing rolls and flipping kernels of corn off forks. Loud guffaws arose each time one of the freshmen got hit in the face.

Ignoring all this, teachers with bored expressions on their faces gossiped through lunch duty without even looking up.

Well, I'd be bored, too, if I had to do this every day of my life, Beth thought as she gazed around for a place to sit. Finding a suitable seat could be a problem. When Beth had first started at Centennial High, she'd been naive about her high school's political realities. Innocently she'd sat down next to a pretty, expensively dressed girl she'd admired at assembly.

Beth had soon been told very forcefully that she'd made a mistake. The girl had turned out to be Melissa Fairbanks, leader of the Golden Susans, and the Golden Susans only sat with one another in the lunchroom.

"What are the Golden Susans?" Beth had asked Sally, the bespectacled little redhead in her drama class. After Beth's expulsion, Sally had been kind enough to make room for her at a table on the other side of the cafeteria.

"They're the biggest social club in the school," Sally had explained. "Only the richest, prettiest, best-dressed girls are invited to join. I mean, if you're a Golden Susan, you know you're really somebody around this place."

"What if you've just been chased away from their table?" Beth had questioned. She'd glanced across the room where Melissa and her friends were looking her way and openly snickering.

Sally had shrugged her thin shoulders philosophically. "Then you're just like the rest of us peons—a big nothing."

Ignoring the way the Golden Susans were laughing at her and trying not to let her hurt feelings show, Beth had snorted and agreed. But inwardly she'd revolted against Sally's statement. She wasn't a big nothing at the rink, where she was one of the most advanced skaters in the club. And she wasn't a big nothing with her father. She was the apple of her father's eye. And she'd bet anything that her dad was handsomer even than Melissa's.

Nevertheless, from that moment Beth had been fascinated by Melissa Fairbanks, who, Beth was sure, had immediately forgotten her existence and didn't even know she was alive. Whenever Beth saw the slender, pretty cheerleader in the halls, she took careful note of what she wore and whom she was with. Beth even began to have a secret fantasy that someday Melissa and the other Golden Susans would regret the way they'd ignored and laughed at her. When she was the national figure skating champion and her name was in all the newspapers they'd be sorry, she told herself.

Now, as Beth sat nibbling on her pizza, she glanced over to where Melissa was holding court and wondered what it would be like to be part of her special circle. Beth had no direct experience of the charmed life that the popular kids in school appeared to lead. In fact, everything about high school seemed alien to her.

Back in her old neighborhood before her parents had divorced, she'd been happy and comfortable going to school with the kids she'd known since kindergarten. Now everything was different. All most girls seemed to think about was boys and getting dates and being popular. Beth had no idea what to say to boys, and she knew they weren't the least bit interested in her. The thought of being alone in the back seat of a car with one of them terrified her. Becoming a teenager wasn't at all the fun time it was cracked up to be, she thought. In a lot of ways she felt like a shipwreck victim who'd been stranded on an unfriendly shore.

"I'm going to get myself another Coke," Sally said, pushing back her chair and standing. "Want anything?"

Beth shook her head. She'd finished her pizza and pie and felt totally full. She glanced down at her straining jeans. "I feel like my zipper's going to pop."

Sally laughed. "Yeah, you know that old Laurel and Hardy movie we saw in drama class yesterday? Well, maybe we should work up a routine for our comedy presentation. I'll be Laurel and you can be Hardy."

Sally walked away before Beth had a chance to react. Maybe her friend, who hadn't matured yet and was still built like a skinny ten-year-old, could play the anemic-looking Laurel. But Beth definitely did not see herself as the roly-poly Hardy. Sally's remark had stung.

Ten minutes later, as Beth shifted her books and headed down the hall toward her algebra class, she was still brooding about it. Her jeans really did feel tight, and as usual, she wished she hadn't eaten quite so much. It would have been better to have salad instead of pizza, and the butterscotch pie was definitely a mistake. But it was too late now. Tomorrow she'd do better, she told herself fervently.

In her preoccupation Beth walked right past her classroom door. Since there were still five minutes left between bells, she turned down the hall to the right with the idea of checking out her hair in the bathroom. But as she approached the door, she slowed her steps slightly. Dina Van Allen, one of the Golden Susans, stood leaning against the painted cinder-block wall. There was a watchful expression on her sharp-featured face, as if she were standing guard.

Self-consciously Beth walked past, then turned and started to push open the door of the girl's lavatory. She was halfway through, when Dina shoved her roughly aside and stepped to block her path. "You can't go in there."

Beth stared. "Why not?"

"Because I said so, that's why."

"But . . ."

Dina leaned forward and gave Beth's breastbone a sharp jab. "Just find yourself another john, okay, geek? We don't want you in there."

It was obvious Dina wasn't joking. Her eyes were screwed up disdainfully. Beth felt her cheeks go hot with anger and humiliation. She wanted to scream at Dina that she wasn't a geek and that she had as much right to use the school's public lavatory as anybody.

Just then the bathroom door opened from the other side and Melissa along with three other Golden Susans came out. They had funny, embarrassed expressions on their faces and they were giggling as if they shared a big secret. At the sound of their laughter, Dina turned away from Beth just as if she'd never existed. "All taken care of?" she asked, her expression shifting to one of conspiratorial amusement.

"Right-o," Melissa answered with a wink. Then the four of them walked away.

Beth stared after them. When they disappeared around the corner, she pushed open the bathroom door and peered inside. It was empty, so the Golden Susans had had the place all to themselves. What had they been doing in here that was so funny and required so much privacy, she wondered.

CHAPTER SIX

DORY RAISED A HAND and squinted up into the cloudless blue sky. A crisp autumn breeze ruffled her fair curls and flattened her rose flannel shirt against her breasts. "Aren't we lucky with this weather!"

"Yes, it's beautiful!" agreed Ben, the engineer in her ceramics class.

He was seconded by several other class members. They had all car pooled to a little clearing in the wooded Patapsco State Park and were now unpacking their gear for the day—thermoses, bag lunches, spades, strainers and plastic bags. Once a semester Dory liked to spend a Saturday afternoon with her students on a nearby riverbank. "Because," as she'd explained the previous Thursday, "there's nothing like making a pot from clay you've dug out of the earth yourself. To understand pottery, you have to understand the whole process."

"All set," Ben declared as he shouldered his backpack. "Where to?"

With his sturdy build and short legs protruding out of a rather startling pair of embroidered gray lederhosen, Dory thought he looked like one of Snow White's dwarfs. She grinned and pointed. "The river is just down that path. But I'm not sure that everyone else is quite ready."

"We've just about got it all together," Linda informed her cheerfully. Clad in jeans and matching denim jackets, she and her daughter Janice marched up behind Ben.

Car doors slammed and then the rest of the group wandered over. Dory glanced toward the oak where Jim leaned with his arms folded across his chest. In faded jeans and a white sweatshirt, his rangy body made a bold contrast against the umbrella of brilliant autumn foliage, yet at the same time seemed to fit right in.

Noting the bemused expression on his face, Dory wondered what he was thinking. She hadn't been at all sure he would come along on this expedition, so she'd been surprised and pleased when he showed up at their meeting place in the community college's parking lot. But his presence also made her feel self-conscious. Now, as his dark eyes came to rest on her, she felt her stomach tighten.

He was affecting Janice similarly, Dory thought. Ever since their first class together, when he'd walked out after Janice's innocent remark about her brother, the girl had behaved like a frightened rabbit around him. Now she stayed close to her mother and seemed to look everywhere but in Jim's direction. The situation made Dory uncomfortable, but she didn't know what to do except ignore it and hope that in time things would smooth themselves out.

"Okay, if everybody's ready, let's roll 'em out," she called. She headed down the path, with Ben clomping along at her side. Janice and Linda followed and the others straggled behind.

The sun filtered through the yellow and scarlet leaves, casting a golden glow on the mossy ground beneath. "This is one of my favorite places," Dory said as she led her little band along the riverbank. She had spent so much time exploring the area on her own that she knew exactly where to find all the best spots for digging clay. But once they had arrived in the general vicinity she liked to let her students discover some of those mother lodes for themselves.

"At home, seems like I spend all my weekends complaining about the clay in my yard," Cloris, the grandmother who specialized in making wind chimes, commented ruefully. "Now I'm trying to find it."

"Well, around here you won't have to look far," Linda replied. She and Janice squatted on a hillock close to the water and poked the damp earth with their garden spades. Linda pried out a moist reddish hunk of mud and rolled it between her fingers. "This feels like the right stuff to me."

"Yuck," Janice commented after she'd tested her mother's find. Her hands were covered with mud.

Dory laughed. "One thing potters can't worry about is messy hands. Looks to me as if you've hit pay dirt, so start digging."

The other students scattered over the area and tested the ground with their spades or walked along the edge of the riverbank with their eyes glued to the ground. Ben had found a long stick. Like a small boy prospecting for hidden treasure, he used it to poke into holes around the tree roots at the water's edge.

After watching him a minute, Dory wandered among the other members of the group, offering encouragement or pointing out likely spots to explore. Every now and then her gaze strayed to Jim. Like Ben he was pacing the river's edge. Periodically he would drop to one knee and examine something he'd found, his expression totally absorbed.

"Having any luck?" Dory asked, coming up behind him.

From his kneeling position he turned to look back up at her, and the sun shining down through the golden leaves made his eyes sparkle and underlined the planes and angles of his attractive face.

"I've seen several spots where I can dig clay. But I thought that before I settled down to that, I'd just look around a bit. Where's Beth? I expected to see her on this outing."

"She's working at the ice rink, practicing for that competition she told you about."

"Hmm, too bad. She's missing a beautiful day." He pointed at a striated shelf of shale and rock above the river bed. "I'm no expert on geology, but you can really see some of the history of this area. I suspect that yellow band of sediment up there represents a drought. See how thin it is compared to the others?"

Dory glanced up at the layered stone and nodded. "I've never noticed that before. But I see something different each time I come here—new plants, new birds, lots of new insects."

Jim rocked back on his heels, his gaze sweeping the ribbon of clear dark water and the fiery sunlit foliage that bordered it. "Creeks and woods," he murmured.

"What?" Dory leaned closer, not sure she'd caught all of his last comment.

"I was just thinking that some of my happiest moments were spent in a place like this."

"Oh?"

"When I was a kid, my brother and I used to visit our grandfather's farm. It had a patch of woods with a shallow stream. Tom and I used to spend whole afternoons fooling around in the water, swimming, fishing, catching frogs and then letting them go—you name it." His voice died away and he sat very still, his face suddenly shadowed and stern.

Dory was almost afraid to speak. She hadn't expected he would ever mention his brother to her and suspected he hadn't intended to. Because of the setting and the unguarded moment the memory had just slipped out. "You and your brother were very fond of each other, weren't you?" she finally said.

He picked up a stick and used it to trace a random pattern in the mud. "I don't know that we were any different from any other pair of kids our age. We fought and sometimes were jealous of what the other one had or did."

"All families are like that. My sister and I used to drive our parents crazy with our constant bickering. But in our way we loved each other, and still do."

"You have a sister?" He turned toward her. "What's she like?"

"The opposite of me."

He cocked his head. "How do you mean?"

"Katie is a fashion buyer in New York City."

"Oh, that's a profession that involves a lot of travel, doesn't it? Is she married?"

"No, Katie never married or had children. But she's a couple of years younger than me, so she still has time. In high school she was a brilliant student, and when she graduated she was showered with scholarships. Now she leads a very glamorous life."

"Unlike you, you mean."

"Very unlike me."

They stared at each other assessingly, aware they'd revealed more of themselves than they'd intended. Then, almost brusquely, Jim dropped the stick, stood up and brushed at a mud stain on his jeans. "Maybe it's time for me to get started with my little shovel."

"Yes, maybe it is." Dory glanced at her watch. "We'll be stopping for lunch at noon."

"Sounds good." He started to turn away, then hesitated.

Dory followed the line of his gaze and spotted Janice and Linda hard at work on the other side of the river.

"I think it's time I made peace with that young lady," Jim said in a low voice. "Any suggestions on how to proceed?"

Dory didn't pretend not to know what he meant. "A smile and a kind word would do the trick."

"I hope you're right." He strolled off to retrieve his gear.

As he walked away, Dory fought the temptation to watch him. When Jim was around, her eyes too frequently strayed his way. Deliberately she turned and headed in the opposite direction to where Ben had started a major excavation. "You look as if you're digging your way to China," she said with a laugh as she hunkered down beside him.

But a few minutes after, when she glanced around at the rest of the group, she saw Janice laughing up at Jim, her young face pink with pleasure. So he'd done what he said he would and mended his fences with the girl. Well, good, she told herself, very good.

An hour later everyone was more than ready for lunch. Their appetites sharpened by exercise, fresh air and sunshine, they settled under a shady old willow and tore into their sandwiches and drained their soft drinks with gusto.

At first Jim sat with Linda and Janice, and the three chatted together like old friends. After about fifteen minutes, however, Jim got up and crossed over to Dory's spot.

"That looks good," he said, pointing at the chocolate chip cookie she was nibbling on.

"Thanks. Beth made a batch of these last night when I wasn't looking." She offered him a napkin filled with them.

"I wasn't hinting," he said as he accepted one.

"I know you weren't. Believe me, you're welcome to the whole bunch. I only brought them along because I didn't want Beth gobbling them. She's having trouble with her weight, so I'm encouraging her to cut down on the sweets."

"And she's not exactly enthusiastic about the idea," he guessed with a faint understanding smile.

"Not at all. She's always loved rich foods and desserts. When she was younger she was a skinny little thing and could eat anything she wanted. But now..."

"Now her hormones aren't cooperating and she's storing fat." He nodded. "In my pediatric practice I see it all the time. Adolescence can be a real trauma for some girls. Their bodies alter so abruptly. A lot of the crazy behavior teenagers exhibit during those years is due to the massive chemical changes going on in their systems. If they live through it, though, they outgrow it."

"You mean if their parents live through it."

Jim laughed, but then his expression grew more serious. "I guess I wasn't helping with that ice cream sundae I sprang on you back at my place."

"It was okay, but—" She had wanted to say "next time don't do it again." That, however, meant there would be a next time. Since Jim hadn't extended any follow-up invitations such a request seemed presumptuous. Dory changed the subject and asked him about his practice. "Do you treat many adolescents?"

"A fair number. It's amazing how many problems kids can be plagued with during those years." He shook his head.

"Well, you seem to have a good rapport with teenage girls. You certainly had Beth hanging on your every word, and now it looks as if you've made peace with Janice."

"Yes. You were right, it didn't take much. I should have apologized to her before." He finished his cookie and glanced across the clearing. "Did you know she goes to Beth's high school?"

"No," Dory admitted. "I didn't realize that."

"She says Beth's in her drama class."

"Oh?"

"She describes Beth as 'real quiet and shy.'"

"Really?" Dory frowned. "She's not quiet and shy at home, and I don't remember any of her teachers describing her that way in elementary school or junior high. In fact, she used to be quite a live wire, with scads of friends."

"Sometimes it takes a while for kids to find their feet in high school."

Yes, she thought. Because of the divorce poor Beth had had to leave her big comfortable house and move to an unfamiliar neighborhood, and she hadn't adjusted to the massive change in her life well at all. Figure skating was one of the few uninterrupted threads in her life. No wonder she clung to it so fiercely.

Jim slanted Dory an interested look. "You must remember what high school was like."

She picked up a small shiny stone at her feet and pretended to study it. Her memories of those years were not particularly pleasant. "Not really. That was a long time ago."

"Not so long ago, I bet. I was class of '74, but sometimes that seems like yesterday.

So he was thirty-three, Dory calculated—two years older than her. The natural reply would have been she was class of '76. But because, like so many other girls in her high school, she'd been gaga over Neal Barker, she hadn't graduated with her class. Neal Barker had been the best-looking, most popular boy in her high school, and she, like every other girl her age at school, had flung herself at his feet. Only, in her case that adolescent hero worship had had a result that changed both their lives.

After a confused and frightening tussle in the back seat of his car, Dory had become pregnant and then had stubbornly refused to have an abortion. Very much against his will and that of his family, Neal had grudgingly offered to marry her. And for the sake of her unborn child, Dory had felt she must swallow her pride and accept his proposal. Not the greatest of beginnings for a relationship all but doomed by differences in background and temperament.

Neal's wealthy parents had seen him through college and law school, while Dory had given up her education to care for her new baby daughter. And Jim, who was now looking at Dory expectantly, knew Beth's age. If Dory gave him the year she would have been a senior, simple arithmetic would tell him she'd disgraced herself in high school. "Yes," she said cautiously, "it does."

He studied her curiously. "You don't look old enough to have a teenage daughter."

"Thanks for the compliment."

"You must have married very young."

She stood and began to brush bits of leaf and dried grass from the seat of her jeans. "If you don't watch out I'll start boring you with my life story."

"I wouldn't mind. I've certainly chewed your ear off with parts of mine."

Dory looked down at her watch. "Well, it'll have to wait for another time. It's getting late. I think we'd better clear up here and finish our digging."

As Dory turned away to call to the others, Jim studied her. A shaft of sunlight caught the gold in her curls, turning them molten. Where she'd rolled up her sleeves, the downy fluff on her forearms seemed to glow. A bit of crumpled leaf still clung to the rounded rear of her denim pants. For a split second he had to control the urge to reach out and brush it away. He knew that if he were to do such a thing, it would only be an excuse to let his hand linger on the feminine curve of her bottom. His palm went warm at the thought, and he took a step backward.

Just like all the times before, he hadn't meant to get into such a prolonged discussion with her. In fact, since their curtain-buying expedition he'd been doing his damnedest to keep his distance—and not always succeeding. Yet, he could laugh at Maggie's list all he wanted, but in some ways it made a lot of sense. Nevertheless he was still putting his life back together, he told himself. His seesawing emotions weren't to be trusted, and where women were concerned, he was especially skeptical. Why risk hurting someone or being hurt himself?

But as sensible as he knew his decision to be, it hadn't kept him from thinking about Dory. In her class, when he could be sure she wouldn't notice, he allowed his gaze to linger on her. It was just that he liked looking at her, at her bright hair, her neat, graceful body, the rounded curve of her cheek—almost girlish in profile. He supposed, given Beth's age, that Dory was older than him. But she certainly didn't look it. There were times—like now, in her jeans and pink shirt—when she could pass for a teenager herself. Seeing her ex-husband in the parking lot that day had disturbed Jim. He'd kept picturing them together—on a couch in front of a television set, at the breakfast table, in bed— and they were not pictures he enjoyed. The guy must have been crazy to leave a woman like Dory, he thought.

Jim started to gather up his lunch papers, but his thoughts stayed pinned on her. He wasn't quite sure how it always happened, but somehow she kept surprising and intriguing him. Their conversations, for instance, so often took an unforeseen turn. He'd ask a polite question, expecting a rote reply. But she'd answer in a way that nonplussed him, made him stop and think. And then he'd find himself talking to her, really talking to her, revealing himself in ways he'd never counted on.

Dory Barker wasn't at all the pretty-but-conventional woman she seemed on the surface, he realized. Jim found himself wanting to delve deeper and know more. Why had she been so reticent when he'd brought up the subject of high school? Why had her marriage broken up? When she looked at her future, was she lonely or afraid? Just what was her life story?

A WEEK LATER Jim offered to stay after class and help Dory clean up.

"That's really not necessary," she protested.

"No problem," he told her. "I'm staying on to swim, anyway."

At that Dory gave in, and together they made short work of wiping down the tables and putting away the unused clay. "I'd forgotten about your swimming," she told him. "How often do you do it?"

"Three nights a week. It's good therapy—for mind and body."

"I've been told that swimming is just about the best, least stressful form of exercise," she concurred. "Actually, I've never seen the college's pool. What's it like?"

He stood eyeing her for a moment. "Why don't you come along and take a look? Maybe when you see the place, you'll like it and decide to take up lap swimming yourself."

"I doubt that, but I will come along and take a look." After she'd agreed, Dory wondered why she hadn't given herself time to consider. But now, of course, it was too late. She picked up her jacket, walked to the door and, when Jim had stepped past her, flicked off the light.

The pool was nicer than she'd imagined. Housed in a separate building, it was surrounded on three sides by a wooded area. While Jim changed in the men's locker room, Dory took a seat on a bleacher and glanced up at the pyramidal glass roof.

Lights in the pool area were so low she could see stars through the glass. Beneath the roof the pool lay like a huge rectangular aquamarine. It was almost empty. Only two swimmers disturbed the glowing water, while two others watched from the bleachers near where Dory sat.

Jim emerged from an entrance on the far left. He wore dark boxer-style bathing trunks with white stripes up the side, and as he padded barefoot across the damp tile, Dory studied him closely. His ribs still showed, and he could use another five or ten pounds, she thought. But other than that, there was little to criticize. He was a well built man, slim hipped and broad shouldered, and he carried himself well. He didn't walk or hold himself like someone who'd been beaten and starved.

When he spotted her on the bleacher he smiled and waved. She waved back and watched as he poised himself on the tile surround and then dived into the pool. When he surfaced he began to slice through the water with a graceful, rolling motion. His dark head swiveled from side to side as he took breaths, and the sound of his rhythmic stroking and breathing echoed in the moisture-laden air.

Dory had expected him to swim five or six laps. To her surprise, he did twenty. When he heaved himself out of the water near the diving board, she met him.

"I'm impressed. That was a lot of laps."

He shook his head, so that glistening droplets of water showered his neck and shoulders. "Not really. When I started I could only manage a couple. I've been trying to add one each time."

"You're a very good swimmer, very smooth," she said, noting the muscle in his upper arms. Then, as he bent to retrieve his towel, she noticed something else. There were scars on his back. Unthinkingly she reached out and touched a long, vivid weal. He flinched and she drew back.

"I'm sorry... I just... how did that happen?"

He tossed the towel around his shoulder so that the marks were hidden. "For talking back. One of my guards held me while the other used his belt buckle."

"Oh, Jim. I'm sorry. It must have been so awful!"

"It wasn't a day at the amusement park, but it's over, you know."

"Yes, I know."

They stood looking at each other. Water trickled slowly down his chest and into the waistband of his trunks. Moisture clumped his lashes into sharp black spikes. Behind them his eyes were reddened from chlorine.

"How about a cup of coffee before you go home?" he said.

"I think the cafeteria here must be closed by now."

"I know a place near your town house, a pub. You could follow me there."

As if agreeing to something much more momentous than a cup of coffee, Dory nodded soberly. "While you're changing I'll give Beth a call."

The pub was just closing when they got there. "Well, it used to stay open after ten," Jim apologized.

"There's a fast-food place across the street," Dory pointed out. "It's not much on atmosphere, but they do sell coffee and snacks."

"French Fry Heaven?" Jim shrugged. "Sure, why not?" He was familiar with the place. Since it was only a five-minute detour from the clinic, he occasionally used their drive-in window to pick up a take-home dinner. In fact, a couple of times he'd spotted Beth Barker inside, wolfing down fries and a shake.

As they stood in line to order, Jim decided against mentioning this tidbit of information to Dory. He knew she was concerned about her daughter's weight—overly concerned, it seemed to him. So the kid was carrying around a little baby fat. Chances were that in a couple of years she'd develop some self-control and shed it. People tended to associate food with love and reward. No wonder adolescents, with all their conflicts, so often turned to food for comfort.

Carrying a tray with cups of coffee for each of them and an apple turnover snack for himself, Jim followed while Dory picked out a table in an unoccupied area near the window.

"I really was impressed with your swimming," Dory said. "Have you always been so athletic?"

"I was on the swim team in college," he admitted, "and for several years now I've been interested in martial arts."

"Martial arts? You mean karate?" Dory wasn't surprised. She remembered how threatening he'd looked back in the mall. She suspected he'd been treated so roughly by his guards because they'd seen him in action and were afraid of him.

"At first I did karate. But then I got into t'ai chi. It's a much less aggressive, more contemplative Oriental discipline with a movement that looks almost balletic to western eyes. I think it was doing t'ai chi when I was alone in my cell all those months that kept me sane—or at least," he added with a mirthless chuckle, "kept me from going totally bonkers." He sat gazing at her for a moment. "Does it make you nervous being around me when you know I'm seeing a shrink?"

"Certainly not! I think I'm better informed than that."

"Not everyone is, and I debated before I signed up with Lucas—not sure I wanted therapy on my record. But I knew I needed someone to talk to, someone who could understand what I was going through, yet who wasn't a member of my family."

"Has it helped?"

"Yes." He paused as a teenage couple carrying loaded trays walked past. "I'm convinced I could have handled the situation on my own, but it would have taken longer. And since I was anxious to get back to work, that was time I didn't want to waste. I'm not sorry I sought help."

"Probably all people at some time in their lives would benefit from professional counseling. When I was in the middle of my divorce a couple of years back—" She paused, regretting that she'd brought the subject up. There couldn't be any point in telling Jim the details of her failed marriage.

"Is that how you started working for Lucas? Did you go to him for counseling?"

"No. But I probably should have. It was a crazy time. Looking back, there were things I could have handled better." And Beth's feelings about being uprooted were most of them, Dory thought.

"You seem to have survived the experience. That was your ex I saw in the parking lot that day, wasn't it?"

"Yes." She nodded tightly.

"Good-looking guy."

"Oh, yes. Beth worships him."

"Does that bother you?"

"No. Well, maybe a little." Dory toyed with her spoon. "She blames me for the divorce. Since her father can do no wrong, it must have been my fault."

"Obviously you don't think it was."

"Who knows? When a relationship starts off wrong and then keeps on without ever getting right, things become so tangled up. Who knows where the fault really lies?"

Jim nodded soberly, as if he understood exactly what she meant. "Listen, don't worry about Beth's attitude toward you. Girls that age are usually hung up on their fathers and resentful of their mothers. It's part of the maturation process."

Dory smiled. "That's right, I'd forgotten. You're an expert on young girls, aren't you?"

His eyebrows jerked up. "Hardly! And careful how you say that. My interest in them is purely professional, believe me. When it comes to my personal life, I like women who are fully grown."

Dory wasn't quite sure how to react to that. Just what kind of personal life did he have now? Did it have any more substance than hers, which was all but nonexistent? "You mentioned before that you're divorced, too."

"Yes. My wife and I split just before I signed up for Afghanistan, actually."

Dory hesitated to ask the obvious question, but he'd been quizzing her on some pretty personal topics. "When you were changing my tire you said something about your divorce and your going to Afghanistan being related."

"When you're in therapy you soon realize that everything's related. I think it's fair to say that if Lauren and I hadn't split, I wouldn't have thrown everything up the way I did."

They gazed across the table at each other. Then Dory looked down at her coffee cup. She tried to imagine what Jim's wife had been like, and failed. "Lauren is a pretty name."

"She was a pretty lady—is a pretty lady. Would you like to see her picture?"

Now Dory raised her eyebrows. He couldn't have surprised her more. "Sure."

Jim took out his wallet and flipped it open to a snapshot of a handsome couple dressed in white sportswear. The woman who was carrying a tennis racket, was a long-legged brunette with classic features. She had been caught laughing up at a young man whom Dory recognized from the picture she'd seen in the local newspaper.

"She's very attractive. That's your brother with her, isn't it?"

"Yes, that's Tom. When I got back home from overseas, I found this picture in one of my sister's albums and confiscated it. I'm not sure why." He ran a thumb along the exposed edge of the photograph.

"Maybe you miss your ex-wife and wish you could get back together with her."

Jim smiled wryly. "There's no chance of that. Lauren has remarried. And even if she hadn't, I know it wouldn't work. There was a time when we could have made it, but that time is past."

Dory was bemused. "You mean like launching a rocket ship to the moon? There's a window in time when two people can build something solid, and if they miss that slot it becomes impossible?"

"I see you read science fiction."

"A little."

"Well, I accept your analogy. No doubt about it, Lauren and I missed our rocket ship to the moon."

Might that imply a possibility of others taking off, Dory wondered. Suddenly she pictured Jim and herself clinging to a silvery missile speeding out toward the stars, and half choked on her coffee.

"Are you all right?"

"I'm fine." She cleared her throat. "Maybe you just wanted that particular picture of your brother."

"I have other, better ones. No, that wasn't it." He returned his gaze to the image in his wallet and frowned. "Looking at it now, I think maybe I do know why I wanted it. They were the people I cared about most in the world, and I lost both of them."

Dory hesitated, then threw caution aside. "I can guess how you must feel about your brother. Do you blame yourself for your divorce, as well?"

"Some. Lauren and I met in med school. We were both very ambitious. That worked fine when we were students together. But afterward, when we were each trying to establish our separate careers, it stopped working. I wanted a wife to come home to, not a frozen dinner and a note on the refrigerator. And after a while I started to want children." He paused, then added wryly, "In other words, I was a male chauvinist pig."

"Do you really believe that?"

"I don't disbelieve it. I know there were things I should have done differently and things I shouldn't have said."

"'Should have,' 'could have'—they're very sad words."

"Aren't they, though."

She hesitated, then laid her hand over his. "I'm sorry, Jim."

Her touch was feather light, and she withdrew her hand almost immediately. Yet Jim was galvanized by the contact—just as he'd been earlier at the pool when she'd touched his scars. Now he wanted to seize those soft fingers and savor their warmth. He wanted to explore a strand of her hair, which in the fluorescent light seemed to shimmer like soft, pale silk. Her blue eyes gazing at him were as clear as a child's, the whites a sharp contrast to the rich azure irises with their bordering narrow rings of black.

Once again he hadn't meant to talk about himself so frankly. And God knows why he'd showed her that picture. When he'd suggested this coffee stop, he'd only intended a brief diversion, the exchange of a pleasantry or two. He'd been curious to hear her story. Instead he'd found himself telling her more than he'd told anyone but Sam Lucas lately. And he was sorely tempted to confide even further. There were a million hopes, frustrations, disappointments, fears boiling inside him that he wanted to let spill out. The urge to unburden himself, to make an utter fool of himself to this gentle blue-eyed woman was so strong that he had to struggle against it. Because then what? If they really opened up to each other, where would they go from there?

The wooden legs on Jim's chair scraped harshly as he pushed it back and rose to his feet. "It's late. Maybe we'd better get going."

"Yes, maybe we'd better." She took a last sip of coffee and slid back her own chair.

Outside Jim crossed the street with her to the parking lot and saw her to her car. After she unlocked the door, she turned toward him. Moonlight bathed her face, but the expression in her eyes was shadowed. "Jim," she began hesitantly. "I hope I didn't embarrass you, asking so many personal questions."

"By now you must have realized how much I enjoy talking to you, being with you."

"Why, thank you."

"I'm not just saying that. You're a very nice person."

"Thank you again."

His hand lingered on the door handle of her station wagon. "There's an exhibit of Indian pottery opening at the Baltimore Museum of Art next weekend. I wonder if you'd like to take it in with me?"

"I'd love to, but I can't."

"Oh."

"I really can't, Jim. Next weekend is Beth's competition at the Philadelphia Skating Club and Humane Society. I couldn't possibly miss that."

"No, of course you couldn't. Sounds like an interesting place."

"It's just an ice rink."

"Well, with a name like that it must have an interesting history. Listen, maybe we could plan to do something together some other time."

"Yes."

His fingers, which had been itching for some kind of contact, seemed to take on a will of their own. He reached out and laid a hand on her arm. Under his palm it felt light and small and infinitely feminine. "Dory," he said again.

"Yes?"

Her face was lifted to his, her lips slightly parted. He wanted desperately to rest his mouth on hers, to put both his arms around her waist and close his eyes—to just stand there inhaling her fragrance. But that made no sense, he told himself, and stiffly resisted the impulse—no sense at all.

"Take care. Drive carefully." He opened the car door for her.

"Yes. Yes, I will," she said on a sigh, and then turned away. "I'm always very careful, you know. Sometimes I think I'm too careful."

CHAPTER SEVEN

"I THOUGHT YOU SAID she wasn't your type."

"She isn't."

Sam Lucas studied Jim over the top of his glasses. "Then what is it about Dory Barker that attracts you?"

"I don't know. I just like being around her."

"Most men do. I do myself. She's a pretty woman. But that's not what you mean, is it?"

"No," Jim admitted. "There's just something about her. I feel good when I'm with her. I feel comfortable."

"Hmm."

Jim gazed across the room at his therapist. This was to be one of their last sessions. Yet it hadn't been going very well. "Maybe I shouldn't have mentioned that I asked Dory out. You're obviously not pleased."

"She didn't accept, so it's a moot point."

"She wanted to accept. I think that if it hadn't been for this thing in Philadelphia, she would have said yes."

Sam rubbed a hand across his forehead. "Jim, in a relatively short period of time you've made a remarkable recovery from a potentially shattering ordeal. I know of patients with histories comparable to yours who've taken years to pick up the pieces. It's really a healthy sign that you're experiencing sexual attraction. Normally I'd be all for it."

"But in this case...?"

"In this case, I happen to be a friend of Dory Barker's. I know that she's been through a lot in the past few years and that right now she's very vulnerable. I'd hate to see her hurt."

"The last thing I want is to hurt somebody, especially Dory."

"I know that, Jim. Yet right now you're a very needy man. You're hungry for what a woman like Dory has to give—warmth, compassion, understanding. She'd be good for you. But if that's the basis of your attraction to her, would you be good for her?" Sam took off his glasses and began to polish them.

"You're thinking that when I stop needing those things I might hurt her."

"Not intentionally. It would just be part of your healing process to find that you didn't need her anymore."

Jim didn't answer. Sam wasn't saying anything that he hadn't already thought about himself. So why did hearing it make him angry?

When the session ended fifteen minutes later he still felt moody. Strolling into the reception area, he noticed it was empty. Since he knew that Dory was out running an errand, that was as he'd expected. But when he walked outside, a cream-colored Mercedes sports car pulled up and Dory's ex-husband got out. He started to rush past Jim, ignoring him and Jim knew he should just step out of the way. But something about Neal Barker's expensive pin-striped suit and pretty-boy looks exacerbated the bad mood he was in already.

"Need help?" Jim queried, planting himself directly in Neal's path.

"What? Oh, er, hardly." Neal looked him up and down coldly. "I'm on my way in to see Mrs. Barker."

"Dory's not in today," Jim retorted pleasantly. "I can give her a message, though, if you want. I'll probably be seeing her tonight." He didn't add "in ceramics class."

Neal stared, the expression in his light-colored eyes frigid. "That won't be necessary. I can convey my own messages."

"Suit yourself." Jim shrugged and walked on. *Now why did I do that,* he asked himself. Why had he bothered to needle a man he didn't even know?

"YOU'RE PERFECTLY WELCOME to drive up to Philly with us," Lydia Prentice offered. "There's plenty of room in the station wagon."

"No, thanks." Dory patted her friend's shoulder. "After the competition is over, Beth will be going back with me. And not having a car at the South Atlantics might be inconvenient. Emergencies could come up, errands might need to be run."

Lydia laughed. "Don't I know! I heard that last year Tina Martin flushed her contact lenses down the toilet. Without them she was blind as a bat and couldn't skate her freestyle program. Her father had to drive all the way back to Washington to get her another pair. Kids!"

The two women chuckled companionably. Once again they'd each gotten up at the crack of dawn to occupy folding chairs in front of the large Plexiglas window that overlooked the Columbia ice surface. Just below them Beth worked on her left back outside loops. At the far end Lydia's Gracie struggled through change double threes. Since Gracie had not yet passed her third test, she would be going to the South Atlantic sectional competition merely as a spectator.

"Still," Lydia added, "I hate to think of you driving all that way by yourself."

"I'm a big girl now, Liddy. I do lots of things by myself."

"That's just the trouble. You're alone too much of the time." The dark-haired woman shot her blond friend a searching look. "How do you feel about Beth wanting to go up with Neal and his new girlfriend? Won't that be kind of hard on you? I mean, I know how I'd feel if I had to watch my husband prancing around with his new woman."

"How?" Dory asked innocently.

"Like putting a bomb under the mattress in their motel room, that's how!"

"Hmm, it's a thought." She laughed at the picture that conjured up. "But I don't happen to have any gunpowder in my purse, so I guess I'll have to restrain myself. Anyhow, Neal is my *ex*-husband. There's a big difference."

"You know what I mean!"

Dory sighed. "Yes, I know. But Beth is thrilled about driving up in Neal's Mercedes, and she's in awe of his new girlfriend. It would be mean to make her go with me, instead. Besides, it's good that Neal is taking such an interest in her skating."

"You don't mind that she'll be spending the night with Gracie at the motel?"

"No, not at all."

"Bob and I are really looking forward to having a room to ourselves. We figured that the girls will be so excited they won't sleep, anyway. So they might as well be excited together where they won't keep us up all night."

"Sound thinking. I'm all for it."

"Still, that means you'll be all alone at night, too." Suddenly Lydia shot Dory a mischievous grin. "Too bad you can't rent some handsome man. Then you could parade him around in front of Neal. Wouldn't that be fun?"

"Oh, yeah. More fun than a barrel of monkeys!" Dory answered wryly. "Honestly, Liddy, I don't mind going to Philadelphia by myself, and I don't mind being alone in a motel room while I'm there."

"Well, if you say so," Lydia said doubtfully.

"I do say so."

BUT SOMETIMES WHAT YOU SAY to your friends isn't really what you mean, Dory mused the next afternoon. She had just, with a great deal of trepidation, passed a tractor-trailer hauling a shaky-looking load of cement blocks. Around her waves of northbound traffic on I-95 roared and thundered. Outsize trucks bore down on her little station wagon like monsters in flight, and sharklike sports cars zipped in and out of lanes with careless abandon. Nervously she glanced at her side mirror. A few miles back she'd come within inches of scraping off a fender on a speeding Porsche.

Dory hated driving these big roads and normally, because of her quiet life-style, managed to avoid them. Right now she was cruising at the speed limit and the wagon's engine sounded fine. But taking the Plum more than a few miles from home always worried her. She never knew when the car might let her down—as it had that night when she'd met Jim in the parking lot at the college.

The thought brought a smile to her lips, the first since she'd set off on this trip. The day before when Lydia had suggested hiring a handsome man to parade in front of Neal, she'd thought of Jim. How would it be if he were beside her now, sharing the driving? It would be quite an ego booster to appear in public with an attractive man like Jim. Liddy had thought that Dory might want to make Neal jealous, and Dory had been amused by the notion. But making Neal jealous really was beside the point. She just wasn't interested.

Oh, sure, during the divorce and just after, when her emotions had been flayed by her ex-husband's final rejection, she'd fantasized making him jealous. For so long she'd been so utterly dependent on him that she couldn't imagine what she'd do with her life now that she was on her own, and she'd pictured him crawling back to beg her forgiveness. But she'd found that just the daily struggle to maintain herself and her daughter had kept her plenty busy, and all that bitter feeling had died away, leaving an emptiness. Emptiness was better than pain and rejection, Dory had told herself.

Now that, too, was changing. During the past few weeks the emptiness had begun to shrink away. Like it or not, she was replacing it with a new interest—Jim Gordon.

Last week, when he'd finally asked her out, her heart had leaped. She'd had to say no, of course; she couldn't miss this competition of Beth's. But if he asked her out again, then what?

Dory's feelings warred. At the thought of starting a relationship with Jim, part of her tingled with excitement. Yet, another more cautious part of her shrank back. She was just getting over the pain of her divorce. She'd just shed a man who'd never really cared for her, who'd used her and then cast her aside. It was madness to let herself become fond of another man who might do exactly the same thing. Why risk it?

The sun was slipping away like a ghost when Dory finally threaded her way through Philadelphia traffic and arrived in the appealing neighborhood of old brick houses where the Skating and Humane Society was located. Neal had gotten there before her. She spotted his luxury car right away, even though it didn't stand out in the crowd. The parking lot at the historic rink was packed with Mercedeses, Cadillacs and other high-priced automobiles. Figure skating at this level was expensive. If it hadn't been for Neal's high-paying profession and his willingness to pick up the tab for lessons, there would have been no way Beth could have gone on with it.

Inside, this fact was even more evident. Though the rink itself was in a ramshackle old building, with nothing better than a wall lined with bleachers for seating, the crowd milling around the edge of the ice surface glittered. Teenage girls who'd been groomed within an inch of their lives flitted back and forth, their high-pitched chatter bouncing off the thirty-foot ceiling. If they didn't carry overflowing skate bags and wear rainbow-hued dresses covered with sequins, they had on Guess jeans and costly ski jackets.

The mothers, fathers and skating instructors in their retinues could have been attending opening night at the opera instead of a sporting event. Every third woman seemed to be draped in fur, and many appeared to have plucked the family diamonds out of the safe for the occasion. To Dory's left, one smiling matron in a floor-length black mink fairly blazed with jewelry.

Ruefully Dory glanced down at her modest storm coat and unadorned hands. If contestants were going to be judged on how expensively dressed their mothers were, Beth had lost already.

But maybe not—for the other half of Beth's family was doing a good job of compensating, Dory realized a few minutes later. She had spotted Beth, Neal and the woman who must be her ex-husband's friend, Deanna Ingram. The three of them were perched on the topmost bench of the bleachers. From them they could look down at the dozen or so skaters taking advantage of practice time on the Olympic-size ice surface.

It was cold inside the rink. With chilled hands jammed into her pockets, Dory stood gazing up at them. They hadn't seen her. Oblivious of her scrutiny, they laughed and pointed. Dory could see why Beth was so impressed by Deanna. She was a sleek, beautiful woman with shoulder-length brown hair and sharp, intelligent features. Her fashionably cut black leather coat with its strong shoulder line and flange detailing made the bulky furs worn by the women around her look slightly dowdy and ridiculous. Neal's blond handsomeness underlined her svelte appeal. His cashmere topcoat added just the right note of casual opulence. Between them Beth sat, her cheeks flushed by the cold and her eyes sparkling with excitement. Anyone seeing the three of them together like this would think that Beth was Deanna's daughter, Dory mused. They looked like such a happy and complete family unit, sitting up there joking and grinning.

Suddenly Dory felt like an intruder. It seemed gauche, even rude to butt in on them, and she had to fight the crazy impulse to turn and walk away.

"MORE CARROTS, dear?"

"No, thanks, Mom," Jim smiled across the table at his mother. He wished she'd relax. But all through this interminable get-together at his sister's place, she'd hovered over him like an anxious hen bent on protecting the last surviving member of her brood.

"These scalloped potatoes are delicious, Maggie. Have another serving, Jim. You look so thin."

"I'm full, Mom. Really."

"Maggie's good cooking will put some meat on your bones, Son," Ed Gordon rumbled from his seat next to his wife.

"Actually, I've gained back about as much weight as I need," Jim declared. He pushed his plate away and gazed frankly at his parents. The night before Ed and Barbara Gordon had driven up from their retirement home in Florida. They were staying with Maggie, but everyone knew it was really Jim they'd come to visit.

It was only the second time they'd seen him since his traumatic return from Afghanistan. The first time they'd been so shocked by his ravaged appearance and by their fresh grief over what had happened to their youngest, Tom, that they'd fled almost immediately, leaving Jim in his sister's capable hands.

Now, guilty and apologetic, they were back. Obviously they were hoping to make amends, hoping somehow to heal the ragged wound that had been inflicted on their family. Jim gazed at them knowing all that and feeling deeply sorry. They looked older, sadder. His mother's hair had grown a shade whiter, and there were new lines around his father's deep-set brown eyes. Tom had been their favorite child. While their children were growing up, they'd tried to hide the fact, but both Jim and Maggie had always realized it.

The older man cleared his throat. "Son, Maggie tells us you've gone back to work and that you're doing okay."

"Yes, I'm doing fine. How's it going down in Florida with you, Dad?"

"Oh, fine, fine."

"Doing any fishing?"

"A little."

"Catch any six-foot marlins?"

"Oh, I don't do any of that deep-sea stuff. But there's a little river not far from our place. I like to go out on it and hook a few catfish now and then."

Jim smiled. "Catfish always were a specialty in our family."

"That's right," his father answered with a chuckle. Abruptly the twinkle left his eyes. "Tom always used to love to fish."

"Yes, he did."

"You remember that time at your grandfather's when you and he came home with a load of crawfish and then left them on the back porch and forgot about them?"

"I haven't forgotten." It had been one of those golden summer days that linger in the memory. Two young boys barefoot in the muddy water, swatting at flies as they talked about everything and nothing. Jim could still recollect the feel of the sun on his back, the faintly briny odor of the crawfish as he'd helped Tom scoop them into a pail.

"Your mom was fit to be tied when she smelled those things."

"Now, Ed," Jim's mother murmured, and touched her husband's hand warningly.

"It's okay, Mom," Jim said. "I don't mind talking about Tom. I loved him, too."

"We all loved him," Maggie chimed in from the far end of the table. Silently her husband, Les, scooped up another substantial helping of potatoes. Obviously this was a discussion he intended to keep out of.

"We know you did, dear," Barbara put in quickly. "Everyone did. How could they help it? He was a wonderful, wonderful young man. And Jim, your father and I, we just wanted you to know—"

"Yes?"

"Well, it sounds funny to say it, but I think it needs to be said. We don't blame you for what happened. We know it wasn't your fault that Tom was killed. We know you did the best you could."

"Thanks, Mom" was all Jim could bring himself to say.

TWO HOURS LATER Jim pulled into the parking lot outside his apartment building. After he killed the engine and switched off the headlights, he sat in the dark for several minutes. It was a chilly night and the inside of the car soon turned uncomfortably cold. Still he sat, tapping one fore-finger against the steering wheel as he gazed out at the con-crete landscape. He was thinking about the dinner with his folks, thinking about how tough it had been.

Finally he sighed and eased out of the driver's seat. Mag-gie had called the night before with the news that their par-ents were in town for a visit. "Jim, they want to see you. You can't let them down."

"I know, but it isn't going to be easy."

And it hadn't been. Seeing them had brought everything back—bittersweet memories of Tom and their childhood together, painful memories of what had happened to both of them overseas.

Jim turned the key in his lock and let himself into his darkened apartment. After switching on the overhead light, he went to the refrigerator and took out a beer. When it was open, he settled into the brown wing chair. Immediately Cleo abandoned her spot on the new couch and leaped into his lap with a resounding *Brrrowww*.

Jim stroked the cat's short fur and smiled as he listened to her settle into a convincing imitation of a motorboat. Nevertheless a tissue of depression had begun to spin itself around him. During these past few weeks he'd been doing pretty well at fighting it off, he thought. But tonight it seemed to have the upper hand.

I'm alone too much, he thought restlessly. *What I need is someone to talk to—someone pretty and cheerful and un-derstanding—someone like Dory Barker.* He glanced at the phone, which sat on a table within reach. It wasn't really late, only nine o'clock. And he had Dory's number. She'd written it down for him when she'd invited him for dinner. What if he called and asked if he could come over—just to talk?

Given his recent conversation with Sam Lucas, that was probably not a good idea. Jim hadn't liked it when Sam had called him needy. But right now, he acknowledged, he felt needy—needy of a woman's smile, a gentle word or two. It couldn't hurt just to phone Dory and talk to her.

Refusing to give the matter further thought, Jim reached for the phone. But after he'd dialed the number no one answered. He sat frowning, listening to the hollow ring. Then he realized why no one was lifting the receiver. They weren't home, of course. They were in Philadelphia, at this Skating and Humane Society place Dory had talked about. Gently Jim removed Cleo from his lap and got up to check the road atlas he'd purchased recently. From here to Philadelphia wasn't all that long a drive.

"ALL THE KIDS look scared to death," Dory commented.

"Well, wouldn't you be if you were in their shoes—or I should say, in their skates?" Lydia answered. She had just come up beside Dory, who stood next to the ice, watching while the intermediate girls prepared to test their first figure.

"Yes," Dory admitted. In fact, as the tension built inside the arena, her own stomach tightened. The girls, even the ones who'd seem to brim with confidence earlier in the day, all looked a little nervous. It was one thing to work on variations of the figure eight by yourself or with your sympathetic coach. It was quite another to have to do it in front of a panel of stone-faced judges carrying rulers and clipboards.

"I'm almost glad that Gracie isn't competing," Lydia whispered. "She hates figures and will probably never get around to passing her third test. But Beth's figures are pretty good, aren't they?"

"Yes. At least, she's worked really hard this year. But I'm beginning to realize just how much of this type of competition is mental," Dory answered. She glanced over at her daughter. Yesterday Beth's cheeks had been flushed with excitement. Now she looked pale, and shadows darkened the area under her eyes. "Did the girls get any sleep last night?"

Lydia snorted. "They claim they did. But last night Bob and I heard a certain amount of giggling in the room next to ours. I don't think they got any shut-eye until the wee hours."

"Then maybe I should make Beth sleep with me tonight. How is she going to get through her freestyle tomorrow if she's walking around like a zombie?"

"Honestly, Dory, I don't think it will make any difference. From what I've heard, none of the girls sleep at these things, anyway. They're all too excited. I know that Beth and Gracie are getting a big kick out of having a room to themselves. I wish you'd let them go on staying together. Unless—" She shot Dory a searching look. "Unless you minded being in a room by yourself last night."

Dory contained a small spurt of irritation. "Of course I didn't mind! Why should I have?"

"Oh, it's just that since Beth has been spending most of her free time with Neal and Deanna Ingram, I thought you might be feeling left out."

While a panel of eagle-eyed judges lined up to watch the first girl trace her figures, Dory jammed her hands farther down into her pockets. "I'm fine, really."

"Bob and I thought we'd drive downtown and try dinner at a Chinese restaurant we heard about. Would you like to join us?"

Dory appreciated her friend's kindness, but suspected the Prentices were enjoying this chance to be together in a setting away from home and didn't want to intrude on them.

"Thanks, but I thought I'd take Beth out. If she does well she'll feel like celebrating, and if she doesn't she may need some consolation. Now tell me what you think of the kids she's up against."

Lydia ran an eye down the line of coltish teenagers waiting their turn for the judges. "I think that if I were Beth I'd be scared to death."

Worriedly Dory nodded.

The girl under the judges' eyes at the moment was a pretty little brunette from New York. While she glided around the ice in meticulous circles, Dory's gaze traveled to the spot where Beth stood waiting her turn.

Beth wore a plain blue skating dress with a warm-up jacket. The outfit was perfectly respectable, though not in a league with some of the dashing custom-made matching jacket and dress designs many of the other girls sported. A number of competitors had on eye-catching unitards decorated with stripes and stars. But Beth, Dory knew, would have looked chunky in anything so formfitting. In fact, it was best not to call attention to her figure.

Uneasily Dory allowed her glance to stray to her ex-husband. Last night and most of today she hadn't been able to do much but catch glimpses of him, Deanna and Beth together. A few minutes earlier, however, he'd come up behind Dory and snapped, "I thought you were going to do something about Beth's weight."

"What?" Dory had jumped a foot and then whirled around.

"You heard me. Just look at her over there. She's like a baby elephant in a herd of gazelles."

Dory had been shocked and angered by the comparison. "For God's sake, Neal, you haven't said anything like that to her, have you?"

"Of course I haven't. But I thought you were going to put her on a diet. Why haven't you?"

Dory gritted her teeth. "I've tried, and maybe if I'd had some real help from you instead of just constant criticism I would have succeeded."

Neal's expression had been scornful. "You've never been assertive enough. Not even with your own daughter." He'd walked away and left Dory standing there fuming. Now, as she watched Beth take the ice, she crossed her fingers inside her coat pockets and held her breath. *It's not how a person looks that should count,* she told herself. *It's what they can do!*

The thought was noble, but at first Dory feared she might just be kidding herself. Beth looked so pale and nervous as she stood on the ice. It almost seemed as if a breath of wind could knock her over. But the hours of determined practice paid off. Once she'd begun her tracing, she appeared able to banish her jitters. Her scores, when the entire round finished, might not be the highest, but they were more than respectable.

"Good going, honey! You were great!" Dory exclaimed as she rushed over to the other side of the rink to give Beth a hug.

"Thanks, Mom." Beth wriggled free of Dory's embrace. "But I wasn't *that* great. I mean, I'm only fifth. And tomorrow is the freestyle event. That's going to be a lot harder."

"Honey, I thought you were really wonderful," Dory insisted. "In fact, I think this deserves a celebration. Why don't we go out for something light and then take in a movie?"

Beth looked faintly embarrassed. "That sounds okay only—"

"Only what? I know there's a practice session at ten tonight. But we could be back in time."

"It's not that." Beth cast a flustered look over her shoulder.

Following the directions of her daughter's gaze, Dory spotted Neal and Deanna strolling toward them. Neal still wore his tan cashmere topcoat, but Deanna had changed into a sheepskin jacket with jeans and leather boots. It was a casual but put-together look that suited her modellike appearance. They were such an attractive couple that even in this stylish assemblage they stood out from the crowd.

"Dad made reservations for dinner tonight," Beth explained. "He and Deanna know this really neat French restaurant."

"Oh, I see."

"Maybe you could come along if you wanted."

"Oh, I don't think so, honey."

Beth shuffled her feet. "Yeah, well I guess not. Umm, well, I guess I'll see you tomorrow before the freestyle then."

"Not until tomorrow? You could stop into my room for a while after Daddy drops you off."

"Oh, but he has tickets for a play afterward. That big musical, you know—the one you were telling me about—is in town. So I won't be getting back until late."

Dory opened her mouth and then shut it. "You're going to miss practice?"

"Yeah, I know. But there's a practice in the morning. I'll be sure and make that."

"Listen, tomorrow's a big day. Don't stay up too late."

"I won't."

"Maybe we could have breakfast."

Beth nodded. "That sounds okay. I'll meet you down at the coffee shop."

"When?" Dory asked as her daughter turned to go.

"After practice, around eight." Suddenly all smiles, the teenager hurried toward her father and Deanna.

Dory stood watching the three of them for a moment. Then, beginning to feel conspicuous, she turned and walked away. But once she was back on the other side of the rink and lost in the milling crowd, she looked around uncertainly. If Lydia had been anywhere in sight she would have taken her up on her invitation. But it was close to dinner time. The couple must have already left for their Chinese restaurant.

Aimlessly Dory began to walk down the aisle next to the first row of bleachers. A general exodus from the building was well underway. All around her knots of friends and smiling family groups headed toward the doors that led to the parking lot.

To get out of the flow, Dory climbed up to a middle row of bleachers and sat down. As she listened to the voices and watched the faces of the people moving past, she hunched her shoulders. She'd never felt more alone. It would be nice if there were someone here she knew well enough to join for dinner. All of the restaurants nearby would be crowded, she suspected. Getting a table alone would be difficult, not to mention awkward. Maybe she should just pick up a snack at one of the carryouts and go back to her room, she thought.

As she contemplated this depressing prospect, Dory's spirits drooped further. *Maybe I should have included myself in Neal's fancy dinner plans,* she told herself wryly. *Then I could swap household hints with Deanna and keep him from letting Beth order all the richest dishes on the menu.*

"You're smiling about something, but I don't see it," a familiar masculine voice said.

Dory started and turned her head. Darkly handsome in jeans and a leather jacket with a sheepskin collar, Jim Gordon stood at the foot of the bleachers, gazing up at her quizzically.

"It's cold in here. Would you like to join me for a nice hot cup of coffee?"

CHAPTER EIGHT

"How... where...?" Dory closed her mouth, swallowed and then started over. "Jim, I'm...I'm surprised to see you."

"I know you are. I'm pretty surprised myself."

"How did you get here?"

"I drove up. I was thinking about you last night and most of today and—Philadelphia isn't so far—I just got in my car and drove up. Crazy impulse department, huh?"

Though he didn't allow his gaze to wander or show any other signs of nervousness, she could tell he was uneasy about her reaction. Dory tried to swallow her astonishment and let some of the genuine pleasure she was experiencing at the sight of him show through. "Well, hurray for the crazy impulse department! It's great to see you!"

"You really mean that? You don't mind?"

"Why should I mind?"

He rolled his shoulders. "Halfway here it dawned on me that this was a very important family thing for you and that you might not appreciate me sticking my nose in. I almost pulled over to the side and headed back."

"Well, I'm glad you didn't." She started to climb down off the bench. "As a matter of fact, I was just sitting up here feeling sorry for myself because I didn't have anyone to go to dinner with." Briefly she summarized the situation.

Jim took her hand and helped her jump from the last bleacher. It was the first time she'd felt his grip and the strength and steadiness of it surprised her. "That's rough," he sympathized.

"Oh, not really." A little self-consciously she withdrew her hand. "I understand why Beth would rather spend the evening with her father. And it's my own fault that I turned down the Prentices."

"Tough luck for them, but good luck for me. Will I do as a substitute?"

Dory stood looking up at him. This close to the ice it was cold enough that her breath puffed out in front of her, and she saw that his lean cheeks were faintly flushed from the chill. Somehow the vapor lights overhead shining through the frigid humidity put a sheen on his hair and lashes that made their darkness stand out sharp against his skin and the clear whites of his eyes. "Of course you will," she said softly.

"Where would you like to go?"

"I don't know. I really don't know Philadelphia all that well."

He glanced around the half-empty arena. "Well, I do. I did my undergraduate work at Haverford, which is right around the corner from here. There's a pub on Seventh called Bert's. They serve wonderful onion soup."

"That sounds great."

"Okay." He took her arm. "Then let's go."

Since Jim knew the area, they took his car. Much to his relief, the pub was still where he remembered it. However, it turned out he wasn't the only one who knew its reputation. When they arrived the place was jammed, and they had to stand in line. Waiting wasn't so bad, though. Almost all the expectant diners seemed to have come from the skating event, and they were in high spirits.

"They're even more gung ho than a football crowd," Jim murmured into Dory's ear over the rumble of good-natured voices.

"Well, this is a big event in the skating world," Dory tried to explain. "It's the play-offs of figure skating."

For about fifteen minutes they had been packed into the restaurant's small cramped lobby with what seemed like a million other hungry people. Yet those who weren't talking a mile a minute about the day's performances were smiling or laughing.

"Did you see that double lutz Ginny did?" one proud parent shouted to another. "I worked it out on my calculator. That cost me ten thousand dollars."

Dory chuckled at the bemused expression on Jim's face.

"That was a joke, I presume," he said.

"Yes, but not all that big a one. Figure skating *is* expensive."

He cocked his head. "I suppose this is much too personal a question, but if it's so expensive, how do you afford it?"

Dory didn't answer, because at that moment the hostess called their name and then signaled to a waitress, who led them to a booth. When they were seated, Dory glanced around at the dark wood surfaces and beamed ceiling. The atmosphere was smoky, laden with the fragrance of beer and good food and further enriched by the medley of exuberant conversations.

"This is a nice place. I'm glad we came."

"Good." Jim studied her. He wondered if he should ask her again about Beth's lessons. It was really none of his business. But that didn't stop him from being curious.

When he'd first met Dory he'd been too obsessed by his own troubles to spend much time worrying about anyone else's. But lately that was changing. Last night and all day today he'd kept thinking about her. When he'd finally gotten into his car and headed north toward Philadelphia, it had been against his own better judgment. But it was almost as if the power to decide had been taken out of his hands. Like the glow of a candle in the shadows, Dory's image had beckoned him.

When he'd pulled into the overcrowded parking lot at the Skating and Humane Society he'd felt foolish. She probably wouldn't even be in there, he'd told himself. And if she was, she'd probably be with half a dozen people he didn't know. He'd very nearly not gone in at all. But that would be stupid, he'd finally reasoned. At least he'd go in and take a look around.

It hadn't been more than a couple of minutes before he'd spotted her sitting alone on the half-empty bleachers. With her fair curls tight around her head from the humidity, her blue eyes luminous and her cheeks unnaturally pale, she'd looked like a lost angel and suddenly he'd been frustrated by the stream of people moving out the doors, making it difficult for him to get to her.

As he studied her now, sitting across from him so calm and ladylike, he still felt that surge of protectiveness. Yet there was an infinity of things he didn't know about her—and now, so many things he wanted to know.

After the waitress took their orders, he cleared his throat. "Please tell me to shut up if I'm being too nosy, but I really do wonder how much of a hardship Beth's skating is on you. Does her father take care of her bills?"

Dory slipped off her coat. Under it she wore wool slacks and a white cable-knit sweater. The rolled neck came up just high enough to emphasize the hollow of her throat. Jim kept finding his gaze drawn to the sensitive-looking spot. He kept wondering what it would feel like to the touch.

"Yes. Neal is extremely successful in his profession and he comes from a very well-to-do family. He's always encouraged Beth's skating. Sometimes—" Dory began to toy with a cut-glass salt shaker, slowly pushing it back and forth on the scarred wood in front of her. "Sometimes I wonder if she's skating more to please herself or to please her father."

The expression in Dory's downcast eyes was hidden by her light brown lashes. They looked incredibly long and silky, Jim noted. It was unsettling to start noticing details like this about a woman, things you really hadn't seen before. Faint freckles formed a starburst pattern on the bridge of her nose. One of them was shaped like a tiny crescent moon. And her mouth looked so soft, softer even than he'd remembered from that time in the parking lot when he'd almost kissed her.

"You're really worried about Beth's relationship with her father, aren't you?"

Firmly Dory pushed the salt shaker away. "Oh, I'm just worried about Beth period. And this competition—the whole thing makes me nervous. Sometimes I wish she'd never gotten started on all this."

Jim reached across and took Dory's hand. The move had obviously startled her. She quivered and then stared up into his eyes with a questioning look. "Relax," he said. "Beth's probably out having a whale of a time. We have an evening all to ourselves. Let's just save the worrying and enjoy ourselves."

ACROSS TOWN, Beth sat very stiff in her theater seat. Her eyes were glued to the elaborate production number underway on the stage. But she wasn't really thinking about the colorful costumes and energetic singing and dancing. At the moment most of her attention was focused on her stomach, which once again felt uncomfortably full.

Tentatively she rested a palm against her tightly stretched slacks. If only she hadn't eaten so much of that fudgy dessert. Deanna hadn't touched any, Beth reminded herself. But when her father had ordered the rich treat for himself and then encouraged her to join him, she hadn't been able to resist.

Beth glanced at her dad's boyish profile. He certainly didn't look as if his stomach were bothering him. And Deanna always looked so great. They were really enjoying themselves. Beth could tell from the way they kept looking at each other and smiling, as if they were sharing a bunch of private little jokes.

It had been that way at dinner, too. Beth had felt like a third wheel. That was part of the reason she'd eaten the big dessert, she acknowledged. She'd wanted to do something with her dad that Deanna wouldn't. But it hadn't been worth feeling sick and blimpy like this.

A wave of nausea swept over Beth. Abruptly she leaned back and squeezed her eyes shut. If only this were tomorrow night and she'd done okay in the freestyle event. Then she'd feel a lot more like celebrating. She might even be able to enjoy this stupid show, instead of wishing she'd stayed for the ten o'clock practice session.

Beth no longer had any fantasies about winning at South Atlantics—not after seeing her competition that afternoon. Those other girls were good, and they were so pretty and skinny—just like Melissa's crowd at school. Beth had felt like an elephantine klutz among them. Waiting for her turn at figures, she'd been *so* nervous! Even her toes had been trembling. She knew she was lucky to have come in fifth. And figures were her strong suit! What was going to happen tomorrow when she had to jump and spin in front of all those critical eyes?

"WHERE TO NEXT?" Jim queried as they made their way out of the restaurant. It wasn't nearly so crowded now. Most people had gone back to the arena for the junior pairs competition.

"Oh, I don't know. What time is it?"

Jim consulted his watch. "Almost ten-thirty. We lingered over our coffee a long time."

Dory nodded. "Too long. With all that caffeine in me, how am I ever going to get any sleep tonight?"

Good question, Jim thought. He knew he wouldn't be getting much shut-eye. But coffee wasn't the reason.

As Dory preceded him to the car, his gaze lingered on the back of her head, on the gentle slope of her shoulders and the way her belted coat suggested the neat span of her waist.

Once inside Jim's car, they sat in the darkness for several minutes, conferring about what to do next.

"We could go back to the arena and watch the pairs," Dory suggested.

"Is that what you'd like?"

"Not really," she admitted. "Pair skating has never appealed to me. During those overhead lifts I always worry about the girl falling and breaking her neck." She turned toward him. "It's just occurred to me to wonder if you have a place to stay."

"No," he conceded. "I drove directly to the Skating and Humane Society."

"Then maybe before we do anything else we'd better get you registered at the motel."

"Do you think there will be an empty room?"

"There should be. It's a huge place."

But when they talked to the desk clerk they were disappointed. "Sorry," the bald-headed man told them. "We're filled up. It's the South Atlantic competition down the road. All the out-of-towners are staying here so they can be close to the action."

Jim shrugged and then led Dory away from the desk. At the door she stopped to look up into his impassive features. "That's too bad."

"Nothing for you to apologize about. It was my idea to hotfoot it up here on the spur of the moment like this. You certainly hadn't invited me."

"I would have if I'd known you were interested."

A faint smile twisted his mouth. "It wasn't the skating I was interested in, Dory. And I don't regret coming. Dinner was fun. I enjoyed being with you. Come to think of it, I always enjoy being with you."

They gazed at each other. Dory looked away first. "What will you do?"

"Drive back home."

"But it's so late, and that's three hours away." She glanced up at the clock on the wall. It read eleven-fifteen.

Jim's eyes followed hers and then returned to her face. "What about you? Would you like me to take you back to the rink?"

"No. It's late and I just don't feel like it. I guess I'll go up to my room and try to put myself to sleep with a hot bath."

"May I see you to your door?"

"Of course."

They went outside and along the concrete walkway. "My room is on the second floor," Dory said, "up that staircase at the corner of the building."

He took her arm and then, when they reached the steps, followed closely behind as she began to climb. All the way up she was aware of him—his tread on the step below hers, his hand on the metal railing, the sound of his breathing.

Yet, despite the tight focus of her attention on him, she was also taking in other things with an unaccustomed intensity—the crisp clarity of the air, the dark inverted bowl of the sky with its pinpricks of stars, the rhythmic hum and swish of traffic from the street just beyond. For that brief time, all those details and sensations seemed strangely centered around her and Jim.

When she'd looked around to find Jim standing there at the rink, she'd been so very glad to see him. Now she didn't feel ready to have him leave, and crazy thoughts were ricocheting through her head. They hadn't even kissed, and she was wondering what it would be like if he spent the night.

"Are you comfortable in motel rooms?" he asked.

"No, I always have trouble sleeping in a strange place."

"Me, too, but take my word for it, it's possible to get used to anything."

Of course. She shuddered as she thought about the terrible place he must have stayed during his captivity. Had he been with a woman since then? There'd been no one for her since Neal had left. It wasn't healthy for a woman her age to be so completely without a man. For months now she'd been telling herself it was all right, but she knew it wasn't. Nor was it right for a man like Jim to go so long without physical solace. That might even account for some of the repressed emotions she knew he'd been keeping locked away inside himself.

Silently they walked down the narrow balcony where the outside entrance to her motel room was located.

"It's number 41," she told him, and began to search her purse for the key. He waited patiently, not saying a word. When she did find it, he took it from her, unlocked the door and handed the key back. "Thanks," she said as she fingered the oval shape of the number tag.

"I guess I should be going," he said, though he hadn't yet made a move to walk away.

"Jim." She took a step toward him, not knowing what would come out of her mouth and surprised by what did. "I don't really want you to."

"I don't want to leave, either."

He moved toward her, and suddenly she was in his arms. His head lowered, and her face lifted. In the chilly air their breaths mingled. They gazed at each other and then, as if seeking each other's warmth, their lips met.

When he kissed her, she had no further doubts. His kiss was firm, clean, knowing. If she let him make love to her, she wouldn't be doing him any big favor. This was a man who'd kissed other women and who knew how. Yet it felt right for him to be kissing her, far righter than she could have expected or even hoped.

"Dory," he murmured, "I . . ."

Suddenly she didn't want him to complete the sentence, afraid of what the next phrase might be. From down below a car door slammed and the sound of voices broke into the hush that had seemed to curtain them. The metal staircase clanged as several sets of feet began to mount it.

"Someone's coming up here," she said inanely.

"Yes."

They looked at each other for a few more seconds, and then all at once they were inside her room and Jim was shutting the door behind them.

"Do you mind?"

"No," she said.

The small crowd from the parking lot walked past and then on down the passageway and around the corner. As the intruders' voices died away, Jim and Dory stood in darkness. Lit only by the faint light from neon signs across the avenue, the room was a sea of shadows. A few feet away the bed loomed like a dark island.

"Dory," he began again, "you must know how I'm feeling."

"Yes, I'm feeling the same."

He reached out and laid his hands on her shoulders. She felt his fingers curl around them. Even through her coat, the contact was electrifying, alarming, thrilling. He was a strong man. If he wanted to stay, there was no way she could force him to leave. But the choice was hers.

"We don't know each other very well," he said.

"No."

"I'd like to change that. But if you tell me to go, I will. And we'll never speak of this again."

"I know. But I don't want you to leave."

A rough sound came from the back of his throat, and then he pulled her into his arms and they kissed again. This kiss was hungrier than the last, more urgent. It seemed to scorch Dory. But the heat that flamed up around them was as much hers as his. Even as her lips opened under Jim's and her hands clutched at his shoulders and the back of his neck, a part of her registered astonishment. Had this leaping fire been alive in her all along, buried under the ashes but still smoldering?

Time refused to stand still for such questions. Jim's mouth moved over hers and she felt the texture of his skin, the hard strength of his lean body. As she inhaled his masculine fragrance, so different from hers, she closed her eyes and abandoned herself to longings she'd begun to think no longer existed.

A few awkward, barely acknowledged steps and the bed came up against their knees. Then they were on it, their bodies tightly entwined as their feverish kisses went on, punctuated by soft, urgent little groans.

"My God, Dory," Jim murmured, burying his lips in her hair.

All the while his hands stroked her body, hers were doing the same to his. Restlessly her fingers roamed over his back, touching the ridge of his shoulder blades, feeling the hard knobs of his spine. But his jacket got in the way. Hardly aware of what she was doing yet quite determined, she began to push at the zippered opening.

Quickly he drew back, shrugged the leather jacket off and threw it on the floor. His shirt followed, and then he sat her up and helped her off with her coat. When it was gone, he touched the hem of her sweater and looked at her questioningly. Without a word, she reached down and pulled the knit garment up over her head. It, too, slithered off the polished cotton quilted spread.

Jim's dark gaze flickered over her. "You're so beautiful, so desirable..." His hand traced the curve of her breast above the line of her lacy bra, and then with his hand at her back he guided her toward him. His head came down and she felt his hungry kiss in the valley between her breasts.

Dory didn't even recognize the moan wrenched from her as she closed her eyes and let her head fall back. Reveling in the fiery sensations flooding through her was enough. Warmth swelled her breasts and their peaks went stiff and aching with excitement. She was glad when he slipped the bra straps from her shoulders and removed the unwanted undergarment.

At that moment, however, a sudden horrible realization dampened Dory's excitement. "Jim, please, Jim!"

"What is it?" As he kissed first one bared breast and then the other, his voice was thickened with ardor.

"Jim, I'm sorry." She pushed his head away and struggled to free herself. "I've just realized that I haven't got anything. I'm not protected."

There was a groan of frustration, then, "Is that all it is?" His breathing was ragged.

"Yes, but—"

"Dory, I'm a doctor. I know all about the birds and bees. Don't worry, I'll take care of it." Firmly he took her in his arms and silenced her with a kiss. At first she was stiff, worried. "I'll take care of it," he whispered again. "I promise. You can trust me."

She felt his mouth on her earlobe, then on her forehead. Her eyelids fluttered closed as his lips moved over them and then back to her mouth. His hands stroked her breasts and then moved down to the waistband of her slacks. Briefly she was glad that she'd worn her favorite underpants, the French-cut ones with the lace trim. Then it seemed that she stopped thinking altogether.

A moment later they were naked together, and it seemed so right—his lean strength and her yielding softness. His hands and mouth touched her in just the right ways at just the right times. He wouldn't let her touch him back.

"No, that would be too much for me, too much," he whispered, stilling her reaching hand as his own fingers sought out the most vulnerable and sensitive areas of her body.

It wasn't fair, she thought for an instant. She would be getting much more out of this than he. But as ripples of pleasure spread through her, it was impossible to retain that thought for long.

When the time came for him to enter her, she was eager. And when he withdrew before taking his release, she had experienced a culmination that left her limp and satisfied, if one could be satisfied in a situation like this.

"But what about you?" she whispered as they held each other and she felt him shudder and slowly relax against her.

"I'm okay."

"But—"

He kissed her temple and then raised himself up on his elbows so that he could look down at her. "Dory, you can't possibly realize what it means to be with a woman like you, to make love to a woman like you and to know that I've given her pleasure. That's more than enough."

She still felt apologetic and he could see that. He smoothed back a lock of her hair and kissed her again. After a moment he said, "It's chilly in this room. How about a hot shower?"

It *was* chilly, she suddenly realized. She hadn't felt it before, not with all that fiery excitement racing through her. But now, lying naked with the heat of his body warming only part of her, she realized she might be happier under a blanket.

"Yes."

They showered quickly. For Dory it was unnerving and exciting to stand under the hot spray, seeing Jim's nude body for the first time. In the room with the lights off, she'd had to use her imagination. But the reality was even better. With his dark chest hair and lean rangy build, he was so different from Neal. A couple of weeks earlier she'd liked what she'd seen of him in a bathing suit. He seemed more muscular now. And though there was no extra flesh on him, he didn't appear skinny. He looked sexy and extremely masculine.

She glanced down at herself and murmured through the gentle roar of the falling water, "It's strange to be standing naked like this with a man who isn't my husband."

He pushed a lock of wet hair out of his eyes, grinned and then cast an admiring glance over her body. "I don't see anything that should stay hidden. You're a very lovely woman. But you must know that."

Did she know that, Dory asked herself.

Afterward they toweled each other off and slipped back into bed. It was natural to want to lie close and cuddle. But after a moment, Jim drew back. "Touching you just makes me want to make love to you again, and it's too frustrating."

"I'm sorry."

"Why are you apologizing? This isn't something that either of us planned. There's no reason for you to take the pill if you don't need to."

She lay back with her head against his arm and looked up at the dark ceiling. "You know, it's been years since I've given birth control a thought. You're the first man I've been with since Neal left me."

"He left you?"

"Yes."

Jim curled his arm around her shoulders. "Why did he do a stupid thing like that?"

She hesitated and then said, "Because he never really loved me. We were forced into marriage when we were both too young to understand what it even meant." Haltingly she explained about her high school pregnancy.

"I thought you looked awfully young to be the mother of a teenager." Gently he stroked her hair. "It must have been tough, all those years married to someone you felt was only just tolerating you."

She'd been ashamed of the story and hadn't wanted Jim to know. Now that she'd told him, his sympathy had an unexpected effect on her. It had been many months since Dory had shed tears. But now a lump formed in her throat and she felt her eyes begin to burn.

"A moment ago you asked why I was apologizing when there was no reason to. I think it must have been just force of habit. For years I've been walking a tightrope, trying to be the perfect wife and mother, trying not to rock a boat I knew was full of holes and just barely afloat." She took a deep breath. "I was always apologizing to Neal for every little thing. No wonder he has no respect for me. I felt that what had happened was my fault, though it was both our faults. And I wanted so desperately for Beth to grow up in a real family."

"But that's over," Jim murmured soothingly. "And you don't have to appease anyone anymore."

"True," Dory replied. "In a lot of ways I think I'm just beginning to realize that fact."

After a moment he asked, "Are you still in love with your husband?"

"No. I don't know, maybe I never was in love with him. Maybe all along I was just in love with the notion that I had to put the mistake right and make it work."

"In that case, it's a good thing the two of you decided to go your separate ways."

"Even if it's making Beth unhappy?"

"Kids are resilient. Beth will be okay." He kissed her gently, but it wasn't long before the kiss started metamorphosing into passion. Again, chuckling ruefully, he pulled away. "Better not."

"No."

They lay murmuring in the darkness awhile longer, sharing thoughts that neither might have spoken aloud. Gradually, however, she felt Jim's body go slack and his breathing even out. When Dory was sure he was asleep, she disengaged herself from his arm and moved away. It must be quite late, she thought. *I should go to sleep, too.* But her eyes remained wide open, her mind churning like a thresh-ing machine.

Just then footsteps echoing on the staircase and then the sound of high-pitched female voices outside her door made her stiffen. Oh, Lord, she thought, Beth! What if for some reason Beth had decided to stop by her room, after all? But the voices faded down the passageway.

Gradually some of her panic eased and she relaxed. She was sure Beth wouldn't come to her room now. It was far too late. But, she reproached herself, when she'd invited Jim to spend the night with her, she hadn't even given her daughter a thought. Carried away by the feelings he'd aroused, the need, she hadn't done any logical thinking at all. She hadn't even remembered about birth control until they were practically making love.

Dory flushed at that thought. Carefully she turned her head on the pillow and studied the man beside her. In the shadows she could make out only small bits of his profile, the straight line of his nose, the thrust of his chin, the curve of his shoulder. Was she sorry about what they'd done? No. There was nothing to be sorry for. It was high time for both of them. It couldn't have been as good for him as it had been for her. But he was right. That wasn't her fault, and next time she would make it up to him.

On that possibility, Dory's train of thought lurched slightly. Would there be a next time? Should there be? She began to gnaw her lower lip. *I could fall in love with this man,* she realized with a disquieting jolt. It wouldn't be hard at all. But what about Jim? He hadn't said a word about love tonight. Neither had she, of course—because they'd both known that love wasn't the issue. What they'd shared was sex and sympathy. They could both walk away from that unscathed, even strengthened. But would that continue to be true if it happened again?

Maybe for him, she thought. But for her—maybe not.

CHAPTER NINE

JIM WOKE UP the next morning totally disoriented. For a full minute he lay in the unfamiliar bed, looking around and wondering, with that sense of panic that still started off so many of his days, where he was. But he could see that he wasn't walled up in a filthy cave. Thin gray light filtering through drawn curtains revealed the characterless furnishings and rough-textured walls he recognized as modern American motel. Then the sound of running water near his head began to register.

Someone was in the bathroom taking a shower. And that someone, he realized with an eye-opening jolt, had to be Dory Barker.

A tantalizing, disquieting mosaic flooded his mind: Dory Barker lying beneath him transfixed with pleasure, her lips opening beneath his, her arms wound tight around his neck, her fingers exploring the sensation-taut muscles of his back. Had it really happened? He glanced at the slight depression in the pillow next to his and saw a blond hair clinging to the case. Obviously her head had rested there only a few minutes earlier. As Jim acknowledged the fact, he reached for the hair, let it curl around his finger and felt his body responding anew.

He glanced toward the closed door and then started to throw back the sheet. Maybe he would join Dory in the shower; maybe he would let his hands explore the seductive wonders of her neat, infinitely female body again. Last night they'd been too tired to enjoy a shower together properly. Last night just standing under the hot water had been enough. Now he'd like to devote a lot more energy to the activity and feast his eyes on her in the daylight.

Abruptly a pipe in the wall thudded as the water was turned off. He heard the plastic rings of a shower curtain being pushed back along a metallic rod. Too late for a romantic romp in the tub. Of course, he could still tap on the door and offer to help Dory towel-dry. It was a service he'd certainly enjoy performing.

Nevertheless Jim hesitated. Reconsidering, he leaned back against the pillows. The fact was that despite their night of passion, he and Dory really didn't know each other that well, and he didn't feel right about leaping out of bed in his birthday suit and barging in on her in the bathroom. Wryly he shook his head. It didn't make a lot of sense, but, then, neither did last night.

He wasn't even sure how last night's flare of passion had come about. It wasn't what he'd intended when he'd driven up. Or had he? Admit it, maybe that was what had been in the back of his mind all along. Guiltily Jim groaned. As his mind replayed Sam Lucas's warning to stay away from Dory, his renewed desire began to fade.

Sam had known he just wasn't ready to walk into something serious. Oh, sure, last night no one had mentioned any commitments. But Dory was no casual romp in the hay. She was a vulnerable, sensitive woman who'd had a rough deal from her husband and deserved something better. How did she feel about what had happened last night? What was going through her mind now? And what the hell was he going to say to her? Jim pushed back the blanket and reached for his pants.

On the other side of the bathroom door Dory stared at herself in the mirror. Slowly she buttoned her blouse up to the top and then tucked it into the waistband of her slacks. She couldn't stay in there any longer, not if she was going to meet Beth for breakfast on time. But she couldn't leave without talking to Jim. Was he awake, she wondered. And if he was, what would she say to him?

Dory took a deep breath, turned the doorknob and stepped out.

"Good morning."

"Good morning yourself." She was surprised to see him already dressed, sitting on the edge of the bed with his hands on his knees. As her eyes met his she recalled how he'd looked earlier that morning. He'd been so appealing with his dark head against the white pillow and his chest bare above the sheet. Dory's first instinct had been to move closer, to reach out and touch one of his smooth naked shoulders and then slip into the circle of his arms. But instead of doing that, she'd drawn back to consider.

This was her first sexual encounter as an unmarried woman. What were the rules, she'd wondered. Last night there hadn't seemed to be any. They'd come together like starved and lonely people, each of them too badly in need to worry about conventions or consequences. But this morning was a different matter.

Could a man and woman kiss and cuddle in the light of day without it meaning anything? Maybe some could, but Dory knew she wasn't one of them. As she'd studied Jim's profile a knot of feeling had tugged at her vitals. It wouldn't be hard to care deeply about this man, not hard at all. But how was he feeling? Until she knew, she'd better play it safe. Quietly Dory had gotten out of bed, collected her clothes and gone into the bathroom to shower.

Now, as she gazed across the room and took in the wary expression on his unshaven features, she congratulated herself on her caution.

"You didn't need to get dressed for me," she told him. "I imagine you want to shower."

"Yes, but I don't have a bathrobe or anything. Somehow I didn't feel right about wishing you the top of the mornin' in my Jockey shorts."

Dory smiled. "It would have been okay. I wouldn't have been shocked. As I recall, you look very nice in your Jockey shorts." To mask her unease, she walked over to the desk and began checking her purse.

"You're an early riser," he said. "It's only seven-thirty."

"I'm meeting Beth for breakfast."

"Oh. I guess that means you don't want to have breakfast with me."

Her hands stilled and she glanced back at him over her shoulder. "Did you want to?"

They looked at each other and then both said at the same time:

"Dory, about last night."

"Jim, about last night."

It was so ludicrous that after the first startled instant they began to laugh, which cleared the air somewhat. Jim got to his feet, walked over to where she stood by the desk and touched her arm. "Dory, I don't know what to say about last night. I didn't expect it to happen."

"It came as a surprise to me, too." She searched his face. "Are you sorry?"

"No. Are you?"

"Not a bit," she said with what she realized was perfect sincerity. "I enjoyed myself. It was good, and I have no regrets. It's just that I'm such a novice at this that I don't know what to do now. I don't know what, if anything, happens next."

"Neither do I." He tightened his fingers on her shoulder. "I wish we'd woken up at the same time. I'd like to have breakfast with you and talk things over."

"I'd like that, too. But I promised Beth. This day is too important to her."

He let his hand drop and he nodded. "Of course it is."

"Jim, do you understand?"

"Yes, of course I understand. This competition is a big deal for the both of you. I had no right barging in the way I did."

"You didn't barge in. Last night I was very glad to see you. I think you must know that."

"But today is different, isn't it?"

Dory had the sensation they were talking at cross-purposes. Did he want her to tell him to leave? Was he feeling his way toward a comfortable escape route? Well, she'd give it to him. "It's just that I'm going to be at the rink, and I don't know how interested you are in watching a bunch of adolescent girls spin and jump for hours on end. You could stay and spend the day here if you wanted."

He shook his head. "No, this is between you and your daughter. I don't want to make things awkward for you. Besides, I came up here on impulse. There are a million jobs I should be attending to back home."

"Yes, well, I understand."

"May I call you tonight to ask how it went?"

"Of course you can. Please do."

They left it at that, and after a stilted goodbye, Dory slipped on her coat and went downstairs to the coffee shop. Part of her mind still on the unsatisfactory conversation with Jim, she paused in the doorway to look around the crowded eatery. She spotted Beth waiting in a small booth.

"Hi, honey. How was your evening out with your father?"

"It was okay."

"Was the show good?" As Dory slid onto an orange plastic bench she turned away from her own problems in order to concentrate on her daughter. After giving Beth a quick once-over, she decided she didn't like what she saw. Beth looked glum and pale.

"The show was okay. I already ordered my breakfast."

"Oh?" Dory opened the menu.

At that moment a waitress came and set a small glass of juice down in front of Beth.

"That isn't all you're having, is it?"

"They were giving away free doughnuts in the lobby, and I had a couple."

"I see." Thinking about all those sugary empty calories, Dory pursed her lips and then ordered bran cereal, juice and coffee for herself. After the waitress was gone, she said, "I hope you didn't stay out too late. You have a big day coming up."

"Mom, I *know* what kind of day I have."

"Of course you do. That was a stupid thing for me to say." Dory smiled encouragingly. "Nervous?"

Beth sipped her juice and then stared around the room. Shadows smudged her eyes and her shoulders were hunched and tense. "Why should I be nervous? It's not as if I have a chance to win anything."

"Of course you do. You did well in figures."

"Fifth, that's not so good. Besides, figures are what I'm best at. I haven't been doing so well in freestyle lately. Last time I tried my triple salchow I fell all over the place, and my double axel has always been shaky."

Dory remembered something Beth's teacher had said recently about Beth's extra pounds affecting the double and triple jumps girls were expected to compete with these days.

"I've never cared so much for the jumps, anyway. To my mind they're not what's pretty about skating."

"Yeah, well, the judges care. If you want to win in competition, you have to land all your jumps."

"Is winning so important? Why don't you just tell yourself you're going to do the best you can and leave it at that?"

"Of course winning is important," Beth retorted. She shot her mother an anguished look. "I'm sorry, Mom. I know I'm not being very nice, but I'm really nervous." She pushed her juice glass around on the table. "Everybody is here to win. That's the whole point. Besides, what's Dad going to say if I mess up this afternoon?"

"Beth, your father's not going to say a thing. He loves you. We both love you. It doesn't matter to us whether you win or lose. Listen, the only one making a big deal out of this competition is you. As far as I'm concerned, if it's making you that unhappy, we can go home right now."

"Oh, Mom . . ."

"Beth, I'm serious."

Instead of replying Beth jerked her head at a table across the noisy restaurant. "See that girl in the ski jacket? That's Jennifer Reid."

Dory recognized the attractive little brunette, slim and sprightly with her wedge-cut hair and expensive, new-looking skiwear. "She's the one who came in second in figures in your class."

"Yeah, and she's the one who's going to win."

"How can you possibly know that?"

"She trains at Wilmington with Williamson, and I've heard people talk about her. They say she never misses a jump."

Dory sighed. Beth's attitude this morning was really beginning to worry her. "Honey, these girls are all human, just the same as you."

"Then why do I feel like such a klutzy slob next to them?"

"You're just overreacting because you're nervous. That's natural enough, but really, honey..."

Beth tuned her mother out. Why do any more than pretend to listen? She knew all the reassuring things Dory was going to say, and she didn't believe a single one of them. Oh, her mother meant well. It was just that she couldn't possibly understand how it was at school—and now here.

The minute Beth had seen the girls she was up against in this competition, she'd known she didn't have a chance. Jennifer Reid and the others were just like the Golden Susans. They were pretty and slim and had that special look—as if someone had lovingly polished them until they glowed. They wore all the right clothes and did all the right things and made other people appear gray and dull by comparison.

Up until today Beth had consoled herself that she had something Melissa and her crowd didn't have. On the ice she was better than any of them and would someday be a champion. When that day came she had pictured them all being impressed and sorry they had excluded her. But now, she knew in her heart that her fantasy was going to be taken away, and she was going to be left with nothing.

JIM TOOK one last look around the motel room. For a moment his gaze lingered on the unmade bed and he considered leaving a note behind. But what would he say? Besides, Beth might find it and that would only embarrass Dory. Reluctantly he walked out and let the door lock itself behind him. As he descended the metal staircase he considered stopping in the motel's café for a cup of coffee. But Dory was there with Beth. They would all see each other and it would be sticky. He and Dory had already had enough awkwardness. He turned into the parking lot and got into his car.

On the way out of town he stopped at the drive-in window of a fast food place. Then, juggling a cup of hot coffee, he headed toward the interstate. But as he threaded his way through Philadelphia traffic he kept asking himself if he was doing the right thing, if maybe he shouldn't go back.

Impressions of Dory collected in his mind, her face, the soft curls that framed it, the way her body had felt against his, the way her voice had sounded as she'd gasped with pleasure. When he'd taken her into his arms her response had given him more of what he needed than a dozen sessions with the likes of Sam Lucas.

On the other hand, Jim knew that if he turned around and went back he would be telling her that he wanted it all to happen again and that he wanted her to let him into her life. How would she feel about that? From her behavior that morning he wasn't sure. Worse, he wasn't sure how he felt about it himself.

"She could do a lot better," he muttered. "She's a beautiful woman who deserves a lot better man than I am." Sam Lucas had spelled that out for him. Dory had been hurt. She was vulnerable and needed a man she could lean on, a man who could offer her the kind of rock-steady security on which a woman could rebuild her self-esteem.

Jim wished he could be that man, but he knew he wasn't. Oh, sure, things were a lot better with him than they'd been a couple of months back. He'd done a lot of rebuilding in his life, and he intended to do a lot more. But, like a man walking through a bog, he still had to test every step he took.

What if he was just reaching out to her because he needed her warmth as part of his healing process? How could he be certain that what he felt for Dory would last and that he wouldn't wind up hurting her? He couldn't, and that wasn't fair to her. A wave of guilt assailed Jim. Because, despite his qualms, he knew that he still wanted her and that tonight he would call her in the hope that she still wanted him.

ANXIOUSLY DORY PACED back and forth at the end of the ice surface. What she wouldn't give for a decent chair! Her back ached from sitting on hard, cold bleachers all morning.

"Oh, Dory, there you are!" Rosy-cheeked from the brisk weather, the Prentices with their daughter Gracie waved as they pushed through the swinging doors and then hurried toward her. "There was such a crowd at the motel, it took us longer to check out than we expected. I'll shoot myself if we're too late to see Beth skate!" Lydia exclaimed.

"Plenty of time. Everything's getting underway ten or fifteen minutes late." Dory gestured at the ice, where five brightly clad girls zoomed around at blinding speeds. "The first flight just went out for their five-minute warmup."

"Oh, good," Lydia said cheerfully. "Then we can all watch together. There are seats up there at the top. Why don't we nab those?" Even as she spoke, Lydia, the inveterate manager, seized Dory's arm and started guiding her toward the vacant row.

At first Dory dragged her feet. She felt far too jittery to sit down again. She was pretty sure she didn't feel like socializing, either. On the other hand, the Prentices were the best and oldest friends she and Beth had and she didn't want to offend them.

"Goodness, those girls down there all look so young and cute," Lydia said after they'd found seats. She turned to Gracie. "That could be you out there next year if you pass your fourth test."

Gracie shook her pert ponytail emphatically. "Not me. I'd be too nervous."

Unable to stop herself from playing the prying mother, Dory leaned toward Gracie and asked, "How late did Beth get in last night?"

"I don't know. Around midnight, I guess."

"Did she get any sleep?"

Gracie shrugged. "I was sort of groggy when she came in, and the lights were off. I did hear her moving around in her bed a lot, though. I mean, I know if it were me I couldn't have slept at all."

Dory nodded. Judging from Beth's haggard appearance and uptight behavior all morning, she'd probably spent the night tossing and turning. Dory gnawed at her lower lip. She'd been perfectly serious when she'd told Beth that it would be all right with her if they left. She knew, however, that Beth couldn't consider doing anything so chicken-hearted. She had to go through with the whole competition or lose face. Nevertheless, right now Dory wished they were both safely back in their town house.

Of course, if they hadn't come to Philadelphia for this ordeal, she wouldn't have spent last night in Jim Gordon's arms. Dory's gaze flicked sideways to the bleachers several yards away where Neal and Deanna Ingram had seated themselves. The night with Jim had changed things some-how. Dory felt as if she were looking at her ex-husband and his lover through the wrong end of a telescope. They seemed so distant and unreal, whereas her lovemaking with Jim dominated her mental landscape like a mountain range at the edge of a desert.

Somehow, for the time being, she had to forget Jim. All her attention had to be focused on Beth.

"Beth will be skating in the last flight?" Lydia asked.

"Yes." Since the girls would be freestyling roughly in the order of their placement in the figures section of the competition, Beth would be coming out with the third group of five girls in a field of fifteen.

As the practice ended and the first skater took the ice, an air of expectancy rippled through the arena and everyone clapped. Dory told herself to relax and enjoy the performance. It was hard to do that, though. She couldn't keep herself from sympathizing with each misstep, holding her breath at the takeoff of each jump and groaning with every fall or two-footed landing. If she was going through this much angst when girls who were total strangers skated, what was it going to be like when Beth finally came out, Dory asked herself. Was she going to be one of those mothers she'd heard about who had to leave the arena when her own child performed?

"I gather you and Beth didn't have dinner together last night, after all," Lydia whispered after the third contestant had finished her less-than-perfect program.

"No. She went out with her father."

Lydia clucked. "And left you all alone? I wish you'd gone with us. Did you have to have dinner by yourself?"

"No, I ran into an acquaintance."

"Oh? Who?"

"Nobody you know. Listen, I want your opinion on the dress I made for Beth," Dory said, changing the subject. "Do you think it stands up to the outfits these other girls are wearing?"

"If you mean the royal blue with the handkerchief hemline that you showed me last week, I think it's beautiful— maybe not as flashy as some of the glitzy numbers I'm seeing out there loaded with all those sequins and rhinestones, but a lot more flattering and tasteful. I'm sure it will give Beth all kinds of confidence."

But confidence was not something Beth had a firm hold on. Dory could tell that the minute she saw her daughter step out on the ice for her flight's five minute practice. Above her brilliantly colored dress her face was ashen. And when she started skating around for her warm-up, she moved in a jerky, stiff-kneed way that made her look wooden.

Oh, God, Dory thought with an inward groan. *She's so nervous she can hardly see straight. This is going to be a disaster.*

CHAPTER TEN

THE ONLY SOUND in the car was the hum of the engine and the occasional swish of another automobile roaring past in the fast lane. Dory took her attention off traffic on the interstate long enough to shoot a worried glance at Beth. She slumped in the passenger seat, her eyes fixed on the windshield and her face expressionless.

Dory flicked a brief look at the gas gauge. "We're getting close to Baltimore. Would you like to try to find a radio station?"

"No."

Dory cleared her throat. She couldn't stand the thick silence anymore. Somehow she had to cut through the wall Beth seemed to have built around herself the past few hours. "Honey, I know you're feeling bad. But I wish you wouldn't take it so hard. Just because you didn't skate your best at a competition, the world hasn't stopped spinning."

"My world has."

"Now what can you possibly mean by that? Sweetheart, you're barely fourteen years old. You have time. There will be other competitions."

Beth's voice was brittle. "Not for me there won't, not after the way I made a fool of myself in front of a thousand people."

"You did not make a fool of yourself. Taking a bad fall on a triple jump is not making a fool of yourself. In skating it happens all the time."

"Mom, I know what I did out there. I skated like a clown. I ruined my jumps. I even chickened out on my double axel and turned it into a single. Everyone was laughing at me."

"They were not laughing at you," Dory insisted. It was certainly true. The audience had been sympathetic with Beth's plight. For it had been obvious the moment that she stepped on the ice that she was in trouble. Her nervousness had been so palpable that everyone in the arena had felt it. They had all groaned when she'd fallen or misstepped. But it had been Dory who'd watched with her heart in her mouth and her hands clenched into white-knuckled balls. If there'd been any way that she could have scooped her daughter off the ice right then and there and carried her home, she would have.

"I'm not going to skate again, ever!" Beth said fiercely.

For a second Dory felt a swell of relief. Life would be so much easier if Beth gave up her passion for this demanding sport. No more getting up at the crack of dawn, no more reminding Neal about Beth's bills for lessons and ice time. But then Dory brought herself up short. Skating was her daughter's life. If she decided to quit, it shouldn't be like this. "You don't mean that," she said quietly.

"Yes, I do. What's the point of going on? Besides, I can't ask Dad to waste his good money on me anymore, not after the way I humiliated him this afternoon."

Dory overreacted by taking her foot off the gas pedal so sharply the driver behind her honked angrily as he swerved out and whooshed past. Quickly she took control of the car again. "Beth, you did not humiliate your father."

"Oh, yes, I did. When he and Deanna came around to say goodbye after it was all over, they were trying to be nice. But I could see the way Dad was looking at me. He was embarrassed that I was his daughter, and he was even more ashamed that Deanna was there to see how I messed up."

Dory wanted to deny that. But she had seen the expression in Neal's eyes, too and knew that Beth's observation wasn't completely without foundation. Casting another anxious glance at her, she saw a tear trickle out of the corner of the distraught teenager's eye and her heart squeezed with pain. She wanted to reach over and take Beth into her arms the way she had years earlier. But she couldn't very well do that and drive, and her daughter was too old to be treated like a toddler with a scraped knee. All Dory could do was reach over and pat Beth's knee.

"Honey, we're almost home. Until we get there, just relax and think about something else. What we both need is a good night's sleep. You'll see, tomorrow things will look different."

Beth didn't reply, and a moment later when Dory glanced over at her again, she'd closed her eyes. But Dory knew that her daughter was just playing possum. Behind that blank face a whirlpool of misery churned away. And Dory didn't know what to do about it.

Two hours later, alone downstairs and feeling restless, Dory's unhappy state of mind hadn't improved one bit. Carefully she opened a bottle of white wine she'd been saving for a special occasion and poured herself a glass. Drinking alone was an indulgence she allowed herself only rarely. But tonight seemed like the right time to break a few rules.

Sighing, she carried the glass into the living room, kicked off her shoes and sank down into her favorite easy chair. Claiming schoolwork and exhaustion, Beth had gone up to her room soon after they'd gotten in. Dory had tried talking to her, but reassuring clichés were all she'd been able to come up with. She couldn't really blame her daughter for not wanting to listen to those.

Now the house was quiet, too quiet, really. As Dory sipped her wine, she could hear the clock on the mantel. Against the rhythmic ticking, her thought clamored chaotically.

Except for offering as much sympathy and stability as she could muster, there really wasn't much she could do about Beth's unhappiness, she told herself. Dealing with failure was part of growing up. Beth was big enough now to make some of her own decisions. Nevertheless Dory's heart ached for her daughter. This afternoon she'd suffered right along with her. When Beth had stumbled and fallen, so had she.

After a few more minutes of pained reflection, Dory turned her thoughts to the other big problem in her life— Jim Gordon. He'd said he was going to call her tonight. If he did, what should she say to him?

Of course, he might not call at all, she warned herself. It was a bruising thought. All her married life Dory had lived with rejection. Right now she didn't need another dose of it. She curled her knees up under her and took a fortifying sip of wine.

On the other hand, Jim didn't strike her as a man who said things without meaning them. So, if he wanted to see her again, what should she do?

Dory gazed down into what was left of her wine and acknowledged that she was frightened. It would be the height of stupidity to allow herself to fall in love with Jim. Certainly he hadn't exactly behaved like a besotted lover that morning.

For crying out loud, the man had likely been without a woman for months. He'd probably leaped at her out of simple, basic lust. There'd been a certain amount of that in her own response, after all. Emotionally he was going through a healing process and for all she knew might not even be capable of love right now—certainly not the kind of love she wanted and—yes—needed.

The phone jangled, snapping the thread of Dory's disturbing analysis. She'd tucked her legs under her so tightly that they were half-asleep. Limping into the kitchen was a big effort. By the time she got there the phone had rung six times.

"Dory?"

"Yes?" She recognized the deep masculine voice.

"It's Jim. I was just about to give up. I thought you hadn't gotten back yet."

Dory steadied herself against the counter. "We've been back home for a couple of hours."

"You sound kind of strained. How'd it go with Beth's skating?"

"Not too well, I'm afraid. She was awfully nervous and dropped several places after her freestyle." Dory gave him a brief account of Beth's unfortunate afternoon.

Jim was properly sympathetic, but after saying all the right sorts of things, his voice took on a slightly deeper timbre. "How are *you* doing?"

"I'm okay. I was just in the living room relaxing with a glass of wine."

"Oh? Sounds inviting. Would you like some company?"

Despite the thoughts she'd just been having Dory was tempted to say yes. Today had been such a terrible strain, and she felt so down. At times like this, a woman needed someone. It would be such a luxury if she could put her head against his shoulder and close her eyes while he murmured a few soothing words.

"Thanks for the offer, but I don't think so. It's late and I'm tired. I was just about to go up to bed."

The word "bed" was out of her mouth before she could censor it. It hung there between them, conjuring up sensual memories that seemed out of place in the sterile environment of her kitchen.

Jim cleared his throat. "I've been thinking of venturing forth on another shopping expedition."

"Goodness."

He chuckled. "Yes, I think it must be a sign that I'm on the road to recovery, don't you? Anyway, even after all these weeks my apartment still looks like I just moved in. There are a dozen things I need to buy for it."

"Oh? What kinds of things?"

"Lamps, a coffee table, bedspread. I know I told you that I no longer needed a cheering section, but I was wondering if you might be willing to lend me your expertise again. Or are you still too traumatized by our last mall adventure?"

Dory frowned. Now that she had decided not to let things go any farther between them, she was almost afraid to see him again. But she couldn't bring herself to tell him that on the phone. When she explained the reasons for her decision, she needed to be with him so that she could be sure he understood.

"When?"

"Anytime this coming week will be fine with me."

"Okay," she said softly. "How about Friday after work?"

"Great. I'll pick you up."

"YUCK!" Upstairs in her room, Beth stood in her bra and panties, staring at her nearly naked reflection in the full-length mirror on her door. She hated what she saw. What she saw was disgusting.

To the left of the mirror the wall had been covered with corkboard. A patchwork of souvenirs were pinned to the dark expanse—snapshots, tickets, programs from ice shows and the like. One of the snapshots had been taken two years earlier, before her parents' divorce, and showed a laughing Beth in a skating dress. Now Beth peered at the photo comparing it to the fat person with cottage cheese thighs and bulging hips and breasts whom she saw in the mirror.

That skinny little girl was me, she thought. *I was pretty then, and I could really skate. What happened? Why did I turn into someone else?* In a way she felt as if the real Beth was the one in the picture. That was the person she identified with, not the fleshy Beth who'd bumbled around on the ice in Philadelphia like a sick elephant. That one had humiliated and betrayed her.

Beth heard her mother's footsteps on the staircase. Quickly she grabbed her nightgown off the hook and pulled it over her head. She was just yanking it down around her knees when Dory stopped outside her door.

"Honey, are you all right?"

"I'm fine," Beth mumbled through the flannel folds.

"Can I come in and talk to you?"

Beth rolled her eyes, then opened the door a crack and peered out. "I'm just about to go to bed, Mom."

"You sure you're okay?"

"Yes. I heard the phone ring a little while ago. Was that Dad?"

Dory shook her head. "No, honey, it was Mr. Gordon. He wanted me to help him shop for his apartment again."

"Oh." Beth withdrew her head. "Well, good night. I think I'll go to bed now."

Dory had put her hand on the door. "Would you like me to come in and talk to you a little bit?"

"No. I'm tired, and I want to got to bed." Beth pushed the door shut and then, to convince her mother, switched off the light and plopped heavily down onto her mattress. A minute later she heard Dory proceed down the hall to her own room.

When the muffled sound of her footsteps on the carpet died away, Beth sighed and stared up into the darkness. So Dad hadn't called. Well, maybe he and Deanna weren't back by now. But she was sure they were. They'd left the arena in Philadelphia even before Beth and Dory had. After the way she fell all over the place and embarrassed them, they couldn't wait to get out of that place, Beth thought. As she remembered the expression of distaste on her father's face, the way his eyes hadn't quite met hers when he'd come over to say goodbye, her own eyes began to burn.

She'd been hoping he would call and say something to make her feel better, such as "Hi honey! Listen, don't let the turkeys get you down! Next year you'll go back to Philadelphia and wow 'em!"

But he won't say anything like that because I made him ashamed of me, she thought. *He probably doesn't want to have anything more to do with me. He probably wishes I weren't even his daughter.*

She'd always known that her father wanted everyone and everything around him to be perfect. Wasn't that why he'd left her mother in the first place? Beth remembered how he'd always criticized her mother—even though, to Beth's mind, her mom was about as pretty and nice as you could expect of a person that old. But she hadn't been good enough, and now he'd replaced her with Deanna, who was so gorgeous she could be a model or even a movie star.

And Beth knew exactly what kind of teenager Deanna had been. She'd been slim and popular and perfect like Melissa's crowd at school and like the girls who'd won at Philadelphia. Beth knew that was the kind of daughter her father really wanted, not a big fat nothing who couldn't even land a double axel. She clenched her fists and felt the hot little ball of misery that had been in her chest ever since South Atlantics grow larger.

As tears dripped down her cheeks, the ball suddenly became a huge empty space right in the center of her. She hadn't eaten much of anything all day, she remembered. For dinner her mother had just fixed another one of those stupid salads and Beth had been feeling so low that she'd only picked at it. Now she was ravenous.

Carefully she got out of bed, opened the door and then tiptoed out into the hall. Her ears picked up the sound of a running tap, which meant that her mother was taking a bath and wouldn't be able to hear any suspicious noises. Relaxing, Beth hurried down to the kitchen and flicked on the light.

A half-carton of vanilla ice cream was tucked in the back of the freezer. She took it out and ate a spoonful, but it wasn't sweet enough. In the pantry she found some maple syrup and brown sugar, with which she filled up the carton. Then she squooshed the syrup, sugar and ice cream all together and ate the whole thing. But it still wasn't enough.

Her mother kept an unopened tin of assorted nuts around for guests. Beth ran it through the electric can opener and grabbed handfuls to cram into her mouth. She ate so fast she hardly took the time to savor the salty richness of the nuts before they were gone. Glancing over her shoulder, she hid the empty tin at the bottom of the garbage and then went back to the cupboard.

It was stocked mostly with unappealing boxes of bran cereal and cans of vegetable and bean soup, but desperation was the mother of invention. Beth slathered an inch of peanut butter onto a graham cracker, sprinkled as much coca on it as would stick to the peanut butter and topped it with another graham cracker.

When that had disappeared she felt slightly sick. Yet she still hankered after something more. But there really wasn't anything else. Her mother had stopped keeping sweets in the house, and sweets were what Beth really craved. Frustrated, she hunted through the refrigerator. But all she found was cottage cheese, milk, vegetables and the like.

Feeling cheated, Beth slammed the refrigerator door. Then she cleared away the evidence of her binge and snuck upstairs. But after she'd crept back into bed, she lay like a lump of woe, her hands protectively covering her distressed stomach and more tears flowing down her cheeks. She hated what she'd just done, and she hated herself.

She felt so lonely and unhappy. If only someone would come to comfort her and tell her things were going to be all right. In the old days when she was little her mother used to do that. Always she would stop in at night and sing a lullaby or read a bedtime story. Suddenly Beth felt angry at her mother. Why didn't she come now? In the old days she'd always known when Beth did something wrong and she'd made her stop and do it right. Why, Beth thought with irrational resentment, hadn't she known what was going on downstairs and put a stop to it?

Then Beth thought about her father again. If he could have seen her stuffing her face like a pig he would have been revolted. With a pang, she pictured the disgusted expression on his handsome features. He wouldn't want to have anything more to do with her.

More tears began to gush out of Beth's eyes. *I have to change back to what I used to be when Daddy loved me,* she thought. *I have to be skinny again like the girls who won in Philadelphia and like the Golden Susans.* But how? It was easy to say she would stop eating when she was stuffed to the gills the way she was now. But Beth knew that tomorrow she would get hungry again. How would she make herself not eat then?

IT WAS FUNNY how the answer came the very next day, almost as if someone had been listening in on her troubled thoughts and decided to take pity on her.

That morning, under her mother's solicitous eye, Beth had only bran cereal and juice for breakfast. "Do you intend to start patching again next week?" Dory asked.

"I don't know," Beth told her. "I have to think about it."

Dory didn't press and sent Beth off to school with a kiss and a hug that Beth barely tolerated. She had so much on her mind, like how tight her jeans had been this morning—she could barely zip them up—and how she was going to make up for last night's excesses by not eating anything at all for lunch.

But by noontime in the cafeteria it was the same old story. She was hungry and the pizza smelled so good. As she pushed her tray along the metal rails in the line of boisterous students, telling herself to take the salad instead of pizza, she noticed Melissa Fairbanks two places ahead of her.

Melissa, so slim and sprightly in her lambswool sweater, with her pert bottom encased in denim baggies that ended in a pair of super expensive pink leather Italian flats, wasn't going for the salad. She'd loaded her tray with not one but two slices of gooey pizza and was reaching for a thick wedge of lemon meringue pie, as well.

It wasn't fair, Beth had thought with a resentful scowl. Why should she have to starve herself when Melissa could pig out without gaining an ounce? Defiantly she'd passed up the salads and requested pizza for herself.

But after she ate it, she felt so upset she could hardly sit still in her chair.

"What's wrong with you?" Sally asked. "You've been acting really funny all morning. Didn't your competition go well?"

Beth regretted ever having told her lunch companion about Philadelphia and was glad she hadn't made as big a deal out of it as it really was. "No," she answered gruffly. "I bombed."

Sally shrugged. "Too bad, but I think it's fantastic you can do that kind of stuff on the ice at all. I mean, whenever I go to the rink all I can do is wobble around, hanging on to the boards."

Easy enough for Sally to say, Beth thought. She hadn't devoted her entire life to skating and pinned all her hopes on becoming a champion. She hadn't made a big fool of herself in front of all the people who really mattered to her. A wave of unbearable heat flooded through Beth and suddenly she couldn't sit on the hard little cafeteria chair another minute. "I have to go to the bathroom," she told Sally. "If I'm not back before lunch period is over, I'll see you in drama class."

"Sure."

Beth emptied her tray, requested a hall pass and walked out. Instead of stopping at the nearest bathroom, however, she decided to walk down to the one in the middle of the building. It was most likely to be empty at this time, and she felt like being alone. She'd only said she had to go because she wanted to get out of the cafeteria. But as she hurried along the corridor she realized she really did have to empty her bladder.

To her surprise and chagrin, when she rounded the corner she saw that Dina Van Allen was standing in front of the door marked Girls just the way she had the last time Beth had tried to use this particular lavatory.

"What are you doing here?" she said when she spotted Beth.

"Going to the john, what else?"

Dina lifted her eyebrows in that superior way all the Golden Susans had, as if no one else in this world counted for anything but them. "This one's taken. Go somewhere else."

Beth stood staring at her. When they'd turned her away before, she'd let herself be buffaloed. A cauldron of angry emotions seethed and bubbled inside of her. She felt like a volcano about to spew lava. Her whole body went rigid with fury. Like a warrior robot made of steel, she pushed her hand out flat on the bathroom door.

"Oh, no, you don't!" Dina stuck an arm out to block her.

With a strength she hadn't known she possessed, Beth flung it aside and shoved past. However, once beyond the barrier, she stopped short. Jessica Palmer and Christa McLeod, two other Golden Susans, who stood planted between her and the stalls, stared at her, and something about their expressions, half frightened, half defiant, hit her like a blow to the solar plexus.

"Get out!" Christa snapped.

Beth wanted to, but then she heard the sounds coming from a closed stall. Her gaze dropped to the floor and her eyes widened as she recognized the distinctive pink shoes. That was Melissa Fairbanks in there. "What's wrong with her?" she demanded. "Is she sick? Shall I get a teacher?"

For a minute Christa looked really scared. "Don't you dare get a teacher, you little sneak!"

"But—"

"There's nothing wrong with her. If you know what's good for you, you'll just go away and forget you ever saw this."

Beth took a step backward, but now her curiosity was really aroused. "I don't understand. If she's not sick, then why is she throwing up?"

"She just ate too much, dummy!"

"Ate too much!" Beth remembered the tray loaded with pizza and pie. She remembered wondering how Melissa could eat like that, yet stay model thin. Then she remembered trying to get into this bathroom weeks ago and being stopped by this same group of girls. "You mean," she asked incredulously, "that she does this all the time?"

"Only when she eats too much," Jessica snapped. "We all do it."

"You do! But how? I mean, I thought it only happened when you were sick."

"That shows how ignorant you are. We can make it happen, and it's easy."

"It is?"

"Yes, lard face! And it's a whole lot better than being a fatso like you."

Beth didn't react to the insult. Her mind was too busy. No wonder they were all so thin! It had never even occurred to her that what went into your stomach didn't have to stay there. It was kind of icky when you first thought about it, but Melissa Fairbanks did it, and she was the most popular girl in school. If Melissa did it with such good results, it must be okay.

The noises in the bathroom stopped and the toilet flushed. Then Melissa came out. Her face was red and she glared at Beth. After she'd rinsed her mouth out at the sink, she said, "What's *she* doing in here?"

"We couldn't stop her, Missy," Christa explained apologetically. "She just barged right in."

"Typical!" Melissa snorted. She put her hands on her hips and planted her feet wide. "Well, now that you know, what are you going to do about it?"

"I don't know," Beth mumbled. What *was* she going to do?

"Well, Miss Sneak, let me just give you a warning. If you say a word about this to anyone, we'll fix it so that no one in this school ever speaks to you again. Got it?"

Beth got it all right, and she knew that Melissa and the other Golden Susans could do exactly what she'd said. Beth didn't know what a pariah was, but she understood the concept. She wasn't exactly Miss Popularity now, but it would be awful to be laughed at and mocked everywhere she went.

"I don't want to tell anybody," she said. She gazed at Melissa, thinking how pretty she looked and how slim—just like the girls in Philadelphia.

Suspiciously Melissa cocked her head.

"But there is something I'd like to know," Beth added.

"What?"

"I'd like to know how you do it."

CHAPTER ELEVEN

WHEN DORY SAW Jim's car pull up and stop in front of the house, she smoothed her skirt nervously. After the doorbell rang, she made herself count to ten before answering. She didn't want him to think she'd been at the window watching for him—even though she had. All week it seemed that when she wasn't worrying about Beth, she was fretting about Jim Gordon.

"Hi," he said.

"Hi," she replied, allowing her eyes to feast on him. Since the weather had turned quite nippy, he was wearing a dark green parka of the ruggedly appealing type she'd seen in L. L. Bean catalogs.

"I like your coat."

"My sister ordered it for me. She's the motherly type. Worries that I don't keep myself warm enough."

"She has good taste. That color suits you." In fact, it was getting to be almost eerie how every time she saw him he looked better than the time before—stronger, healthier, more vital, more relaxed. It would be flattering to think that their night together had had such a tonic effect. Certainly, on a physical level, it hadn't given her anything to complain about.

The thought made Dory feel slightly warm. "I'm all ready," she said quickly. "Just let me throw on my coat, and we can get going." She didn't want to invite Jim in for a drink. With Beth doing homework upstairs until her father came to collect her for the weekend, what could they talk about that wouldn't make them both feel ridiculous?

"I hope I'm not taking you away from anything important," he said as they descended the steps.

"Nothing but housework and the evening news on television. That's usually depressing, and if I want I can always catch it later on tonight."

He nodded and helped her into the car. When she was seated and he'd gotten into the other side and pulled away from the curb, he asked about Beth.

"Actually she seems okay," Dory replied.

"You sound surprised."

"Well, I guess I am a little. Beth had so much invested in this competition. When it didn't turn out well for her, I really expected more of a reaction. Oh, she was very upset right afterward, and it worried me. But lately she's been..." Dory hesitated, not sure how to explain her uneasiness. It wasn't as if anything seemed actually wrong. The only bad moment she'd had with Beth was when Neal had been late in calling to invite her for their usual weekend. But after Dory phoned him and insisted he treat Beth as if nothing had happened, things had been okay.

"Were you going to say that Beth seems back to normal?" Jim questioned.

"Not exactly. She's seems—oh, I don't know—distracted."

"Well, maybe she's just rethinking some things, readjusting her priorities."

"I hope that's it. She hasn't gone back to skating yet, though I know she misses it."

Ruefully Jim shook his head. "Teenage girls can be a mystery."

"Oh, yes, I forgot. You're an expert on the subject."

"Hardly. Most of the kids I deal with are younger. It's just that I do hear about the patients my colleagues have. Some of the stories are unbelievable, and some would break your heart. I think it's tougher to be a teenager now than it ever has been before."

"Why do you think that?" Fascinated, Dory turned in her seat so that she could watch the play of emotions on his expressive face.

"Because our world is so much more complicated," he replied seriously. "Take the media, for instance. These kids were raised on television. Since infancy they've been bombarded with images of what they should be, how they should look, what they should feel. And some of those standards are pretty discouraging to measure yourself against." He flicked on the turn signal to change lanes and checked the rearview mirror. "Not every kid can be popular, good-looking, fun loving and always wear exactly the right kind of blue jeans. Some of us are lucky if we can ever learn how to be any one of those things during the entire course of a lifetime."

"So you're saying our kids are under more pressure to excel than we were."

"I know they are. And what makes it worse is that they don't have any clearly understandable rules to play by. They're given so much freedom, and in a lot of cases, it's freedom they don't really want and definitely can't handle."

Thinking of her own high school days, Dory nodded. "I was terribly confused when I was a teenager. And I made a royal mess of my life."

"Oh, I don't know." He shot her a glinting smile. "You don't look messed up to me. In fact, right now you look very pretty."

"Why, thank you."

His expression sobered, and he directed his gaze back to the windshield. "Dory, I've been thinking a lot about you this week."

"I've been thinking a lot about you, too." Should she explain to him now that she'd decided it would be best for her to back off from their relationship, Dory wondered. She'd planned on having this discussion when they'd finished their shopping. But he'd given her the perfect opening.

She was just steeling herself to begin the speech she'd rehearsed, when he said, "I know you have a lot of doubts about getting involved with me, but let's not talk about that now, shall we? Let's just relax and have fun. We can talk about the serious stuff later, okay?"

"Okay," Dory agreed. She was relieved. Why ruin the afternoon before it even got started?

They went to the same sprawling shopping mall where they'd purchased his curtains, and spent a pleasant half hour idling along the concourse, admiring window displays. Jim seemed like a different person, relaxed, ready to be amused.

"You don't seem so bothered by the crowds," Dory remarked.

"It's not so bad today. I'm finding, as the weeks pass, that it's easier to handle this sort of thing."

"Good, I'm glad."

"So am I!"

Finally they ventured into a discount linen outlet, where, with Dory's approval, Jim selected a handsome gray-and-white plaid comforter and matching sheets. Emboldened, they went next to a lamp store. There, after much debate, Dory persuaded Jim to buy a gray ceramic lamp to match his new bedclothes.

"But I already have a lamp in the bedroom."

"Is it as nice as this one?"

"No, it's just one of my sister's castoffs." He cocked his head, studying the graceful shape of the lighting fixture. "But you're right. This would definitely give my boudoir a little class."

After stowing these purchases in the trunk of his car, they went back to check out a small but well-stocked print gallery.

"My sister, Maggie, has been complaining about my bare walls for weeks. She says it's not natural," Jim commented as they looked around the store.

Dory stopped to peer at a beach scene in glowing shades of blue and yellow. "Well, I suppose she's right. But I wouldn't buy a picture just to have something on the wall. If you're going to hang a painting or photograph where you'll see it every day, it should do something for you, mean something to you."

"I agree, and that's why I've gone without. For a long time, nothing seemed to mean anything. I didn't even see my walls. But that's beginning to change, and there is a picture here that I've been thinking about buying."

He led her to a framed reproduction of a river scene. The artist must have painted the original very early in the morning. Its colors were the muted gray-greens of dawn, with lacy willows on the grassy riverbank blending into mist rising off the dark unruffled water. In the distance a rowboat floated on the river's tranquil surface. Inside it two small figures, one with a hat and one without, had dropped their fishing lines into the water.

"It's beautiful." Dory glanced up in time to catch the expression on Jim's face as he gazed at the painting. "This means something to you, doesn't it?" she asked softly.

"Yes."

Dory recalled the conversation she'd had with Jim at the state park that Saturday when her class had met to dig clay. He'd surprised her by talking about his brother. He'd recollected how as children they'd played together in the water. She returned her attention to the painting. The figures in the boat could easily be two young boys.

"Does it remind you of a day you spent with your brother?"

He nodded. "When I first came across the picture, I thought it would be the last thing I'd want to have on my wall where I could see it every day. I was sure it would be too painful. But I haven't been able to get it out of my mind. And now my feelings seem to have changed, and I find that I really do want it."

"Then you should have it," Dory said.

He looked at her. "Think so?"

"Yes, but you don't really need my opinion. You've already made up your mind about this, haven't you?"

"Yes," he admitted. "I guess I have."

A few minutes later, as he wrote out a check for the painting, Dory stood watching and feeling strangely happy and proud. She knew buying that picture was a significant step for Jim, that somehow it meant he was beginning to come to terms with his brother's tragic death and his own feelings of guilt and loss. She also sensed, though she could think of no logical reason for it, that she'd played some positive role in that change.

Jim tucked the painting under his arm, and they proceeded along the concourse. Near the exit to the parking lot he surprised Dory by stopping in front of the half-moon-shaped entry to a Chinese restaurant. "It's almost dinnertime. How about picking up some carryout to eat at my place? After I hang the picture we can celebrate with it and a bottle of bubbly I happen to have stashed away."

"Oh, I don't know." Going with Jim to his apartment had not been part of her plans. She'd expected to tell him her decision in the car just before he dropped her off back home. Now, however, that did seem rather churlish. Perhaps it would be more civilized to wait until after dinner to explain her reasons for wanting to nip their relationship in the bud.

"All right, but I can't stay long."

"Why? Didn't you mention that Beth was spending the weekend with her father?"

"Yes, but I'm expecting an important call," Dory fibbed.

"Well, you shouldn't take important calls on an empty stomach."

A few minutes later she and Jim returned to his car toting a bagful of delicious-smelling little white cartons. Back at his place they made a picnic of their carryout meal. Then, after Jim carried his new picture around the living room, considering all the options for its placement, they hung it over his attractive new tweed couch. When it was up and they'd both agreed that it looked beautiful, he opened a bottle of champagne and proposed a toast. "This isn't exactly original, but I'd like to drink to new beginnings."

"To new beginnings," Dory said, and clinked glasses with him.

Yet all the while she wondered how to tell him that she didn't intend their new beginning as lovers to go any farther. All afternoon she'd been intensely aware of him physically, hungrily taking note of all the most minute details of his appearance. New things about him bombarded her. She hadn't remembered how his dark hair grew in an endearing little whorl at the back of his neck or that there was the slightest of bumps at the narrow bridge of his nose. And one of his eyebrows was slightly more arched than the other, giving that side of his face a faintly saturnine cast. Her fingers itched to trace the errant eyebrow's shape, smooth it into something less ruffled.

This concentrated sensitivity was perfectly natural, she defended herself. After all, Jim was the only other man besides Neal who'd ever made love to her. Of course she couldn't help noticing things about him. It would be strange if she didn't.

But now that they were alone in his apartment, the physical awareness had become much more overwhelming. To hang the picture, he'd taken off his jacket and rolled up his shirt sleeves. While he'd stood on the couch, hammering in a nail, she'd kept noticing the fine dark hair on his forearms, the graceful strength of his hands, even the shape of his fingernails. Earlier, as they'd shared the cartons of Chinese food, their hands had brushed. Each contact had sent ripples of warmth surging through her.

After they each drank to the new painting, he said, "Thank you for coming with me to shop. It was fun."

"Yes, it was. Thank you for inviting me."

Taking another sip of champagne, Dory reflected on just how true this really was. Jim was different—no longer the strained, intense person she'd first met, but a man who could smile and laugh—a man who could be lighthearted.

"You really are doing a lot better these days, aren't you," she blurted. "It's not just that you've regained your health. You're happier."

"Yes," he answered after a moment. "I think the worst is behind me. In fact, I'm about to discontinue my sessions with Dr. Lucas. Even he says I don't really need a therapist anymore. And you know, Dory, I owe a lot of that to you."

"To me?"

Jim gazed at her warmly. "Knowing you, having your friendship has meant a lot to me."

Dory felt her heartbeat accelerate. "I'm glad to have you for a friend, too."

It was on the tip of her tongue to add "and to protect that friendship, I think we should make an effort to keep things strictly platonic," when he said, "You know, we're not through in here yet."

"What?"

He pointed at the pile of packages still lying in one corner of the room. "You're the one who talked me into buying that lamp. Don't you want to see how it looks in the bedroom with my new comforter?"

Dory set down her glass. "Oh, I don't think you need me for that."

"Of course I need you." He gathered up the plastic bags and took her hand. "Come on."

It was silly for a grown woman to be nervous about going into a man's bedroom, especially when she'd already slept with that man, Dory told herself. Nevertheless, as he led her into the small, rather barren little chamber, she felt distinctly uneasy.

Inside the doorway she stopped short. "My God!"

Jim stood to one side and grinned, watching her reaction. "What do you think?"

"It's the bed, the brass bed we saw at the antique expo."

"One and the same."

"You actually bought it!"

"I actually did. As a matter of fact, I was so taken with it that I went back and put down a deposit the next evening. They needed it for their display, so it wasn't delivered until a week ago."

"But why on earth..." Dory was still having a little trouble assimilating the fact of the huge, ornate brass bed, which totally dominated Jim's tiny cubicle of a bedroom.

"I thought this room needed a bit of dressing up," he informed her with a perfectly straight face. "Before I got the bed it was about as homey in here as the inside of an abandoned refrigerator." As he spoke, Jim walked past her, shook out his new comforter and then spread it out on top of the mattress. He stood back to take in the effect. "Looks quite inviting, doesn't it?"

Dory started to laugh. "Yes, but I don't know that 'homey' is exactly the word I'd use to describe that bed."

"What word would you usc?" One of his eyebrows lifted and his dark eyes held a wicked gleam. "Sexy?"

"Well, 'spectacular' was more what I had in mind."

"Spectacularly sexy is how it strikes me. And you know what? I'll always associate it with you. Whenever I walk into this room, I think of you. And now that you're actually here..."

"Yes?" Dory's lips parted.

"All I can say is that it's pretty overwhelming." Jokingly he ran a finger around the inside of his collar. "Whew, all of a sudden it feels awfully warm in here."

"I hadn't noticed."

"I'm sure you will in a minute. What do you think about this idea? Maybe we should take our clothes off and lie down on my new comforter so that we'll be prepared for the heat wave I sense is coming our way?"

Dory put her hands behind her back and clasped one wrist as if it were an anchor. "It's an interesting suggestion, but I can't stay much longer. In fact, it's time I went home now."

"Don't go, Dory." He took a step toward her.

"Oh, but I must."

"You're just saying that." He drew her into his arms and kissed her until she was breathless, until her heart was pounding so loudly in her ears that she could hardly hear the words he whispered when he finally lifted his mouth.

"I've missed you this week."

"Oh, Jim, I . . ."

"Did you miss me, too?"

"Yes." She sighed.

"I knew it." He began to drop kisses on her cheeks and then arched her back so that he could bury his lips in the warm hollow of her throat. "Don't go. Stay."

"Oh, Jim, please..." Again his lips discovered hers, and she couldn't find the strength to utter another protest. Had his kisses been this drugging before? She supposed they must have been. But they seemed even more masterful now, even harder to resist.

"I want to make love to you properly," he whispered. "I couldn't before, but this time it will be different."

She knew he meant he had protection, and her last reasonable objection was swept away. Dory's legs felt weak, and she was having trouble remembering why she had wanted to resist him. It was because he was dangerous to her, of course. But at the moment he seemed more desirable than dangerous.

Seeing in her flushed face the answer he sought, he kissed her again, and Dory's will to resist evaporated utterly. "Let's make proper use of my new quilt and ridiculous bed," he said. Easily he lifted her into his arms, carried her to the bed and laid her gently on the plump new comforter.

"How can I prepare for a heat wave when all my clothes are still on?" she asked as she gazed up at him.

"You can always count on your friendly amateur meteorologist to help out with such problems." With a tender smile, he sat down at her side and began to slip open the tiny pearl buttons on her blouse. "Your eyes are so blue," he said, pausing to drop a kiss on each of her temples. "When I look into them I think of lakes reflecting back cloudless skies."

"And right now your eyes are very dark," she told him.

"Dark with desire for you," he teased. But then as he pushed aside her blouse and looked down at her breasts, cupped in the lacy bra she'd elected to wear that day, his smile slipped. "So feminine, so lovely," he murmured, and pressed his lips against the soft flesh.

At his touch, insistent and possessive, Dory's insides seemed to dissolve. Her hands went up to cradle his head and draw him closer to her. And then suddenly they were kissing with a passionate intensity that squeezed every other emotion dry. His body came down on hers and they strained together, their legs entwining. Eagerly she opened her mouth to him, welcoming his tongue with hers.

"Oh, Dory, I need this," he whispered hoarsely as he drew away to yank off his shirt and then undo his belt buckle.

"I do, too," she answered. At that instant she knew with her whole being that it was true. She needed to be held and loved. She was a woman, and she needed a man. Ignoring everything but the compulsion of the moment, she reached down to unzip her skirt.

This time, fully protected and knowing each other better, they made love with satisfying abandon. Once again, Jim was a knowledgeable lover. His hands and lips stroked and petted, kissed and caressed, arousing her body until it clamored for his. When he penetrated her, she found that he was a demanding lover as well as an educated one. He took a driving control and didn't leave her until he had achieved his goal. Only when he heard her indrawn gasp of pleasure did he take his own.

Finally, weak with satisfaction, they slipped under the new comforter and fell into each other's arms.

"My God, Dory, that was wonderful!"

"Yes," she agreed, snuggling her cheek against the relaxed muscle of his shoulder.

He began to stroke her hair. "I hope I didn't hurt you. I wanted you so badly that I'm afraid my self-control wasn't the greatest."

"I thought your self-control was just fine."

"I only hope you felt one tenth of what I did."

"Is it so important?"

"Of course it's important. As far as I'm concerned sexual pleasure means giving as well as receiving."

As Dory reflected on that, she found herself thinking about her ex-husband. At best Neal had been, she now realized, a perfunctory lover. Yet he must be quite another man in bed with Deanna. A beautiful, independent and experienced woman like Deanna wouldn't tolerate a bedmate who left her unsatisfied. But, of course, Neal's attitude toward Deanna would be very different. He hadn't been stuck with her the way he had his wife. No, he'd chosen her.

Suddenly filled with hope, Dory glanced up at Jim. The way a man felt toward a woman was reflected in their intimacy. Jim had been so considerate, so tender. Surely he shared some of the budding feelings she was beginning to cherish for him.

Snuggling closer, she murmured, "You're a wonderful lover, Jim."

"Thank you." He squeezed her and laughed, but she could tell he was pleased.

"Am I the first woman you've been with since..."

"Since Afghanistan?"

His body stiffened slightly, and she regretted the question. But it was too late now.

"Yes," he said. "Except for a couple of days with a French nurse I met in Peshawar, just across the southern border from Afghanistan. That was where the International Medical Corps had its base and where Tom and I actually spent most of our time.''

''Oh, I see.'' Dory tried to picture the type of woman who would take the kind of risks Jim and his brother had taken. ''That nurse must have been an unusual person.''

''She was. In Europe she'd raised money for the Afghans. Then she flew to Pakistan, walked deep into Afghanistan and brought food and medicine to war widows and orphans. I remember she wore a heart around her neck with two little words engraved on it.''

''What were they?''

Jim grinned. ''Break it.''

''And did you?''

''Not me. That lady wasn't about to get her heart broken by the likes of me.''

Dory stared at him. The nurse sounded like a heroine to her, a woman you'd never forget as long as you lived. Yet he'd mentioned her so casually. Obviously he didn't attach any importance to their liaison. This punctured the little balloon of happiness Dory had begun to blow up for herself and reminded her of how different men were from women in their attitude toward sex.

Unaware of the turmoil his description of the nurse had produced in Dory, Jim began to describe some of the conditions he'd lived with overseas, the shattered villages and cities he'd seen and the terrible injuries he'd treated.

''By the time you're finished with med school, you're used to wading through blood and pain. You feel as if you've seen it all. But in Peshawar my days were filled with bullet wounds, amputations, the medical problems of thousands of refugees. I saw things that will probably haunt my nightmares as long as I live. The worst of it was the children. I'll never forget a little boy, a really cute little kid, who came in one day. He had a complex congenital heart problem. Here in the States I could have sent him to a pediatric cardiovascular surgeon who could probably have corrected it with open heart surgery. But all I could do there was offer antibiotics. I knew he wouldn't live to be more than twenty.''

Dory lay her hand on Jim's chest. "Did you decide to become a pediatrician because of a special feeling for kids?''

"Yes, I suppose I did. Most adults think of them as either being cute or a lot of trouble. But it's hard to be a kid trying to figure out how to fit into a world you didn't make and probably don't like. I think I empathize with that more than most people.''

"Then it must have been really terrible to see what they were going through in that war.'' Though she was perfectly warm under the comforter with him, Dory shivered. It was a shame Jim didn't have children. He would make a wonderful father. As she considered that, Dory moved away from him slightly. "We talked about your wife before. You said the marriage didn't work because of the pressure of your two careers.''

"Yes,'' he admitted. "At least, I think that's what drove us apart, though part of me still can't make sense of what happened. I mean, it should have worked for us. We were young and in love, and we had so much in common. We'd both chosen medicine for a career, which meant that we understood what the other was interested in and what the other was going through. We had everything and so, according to the popular wisdom, it should have been perfect. Instead it turned sour.''

"She must have been an unusual woman, beautiful, intelligent and ambitious.''

"Lauren was all those things.''

In fact, Dory meditated, she sounded a lot like Deanna Ingram. The notion made her restless. She tried to imagine herself doing the remarkable things the nurse he'd described had done. Acknowledging that it was impossible, she turned and propped herself up on her elbow. "Have you always been attracted to women who are so overwhelming?"

Jim looked surprised by the question. Then he laughed.

"I'm not sure what you mean. I'm attracted to women who are bright and capable, naturally!"

Dory gazed down at him. "Then what do you see in me?"

As the even more surprising question sank in, his jaw dropped. "I don't know what you mean," he finally managed. "Are you saying that you're not bright and capable?"

Dory took a deep, ragged breath, then let it out slowly. Her heart had started to thud and every muscle in her body seemed to tighten. "Jim, those are just words. The fact is that I'm nothing like the kind of woman your wife was—or, from the sound of it, the other women in your life have been. I was pregnant and then married before I finished high school. I spent most of my adult life being a housewife and mother, and if my marriage hadn't been so unsatisfactory, I would have been content.

"Now I'm trying to put a new life together. I have interests I want to pursue. I'm working on my pottery and going back to school. I have visions of someday owning and operating my own craft shop. But truthfully, I'm not an ambitious person in the way very successful women have to be when they compete in a world dominated by men. And I'm not a heroine, either. Basically all I've ever wanted is to be happy and useful and comfortable and to make the people around me feel the same."

"That sounds extremely ambitious to me."

Solemnly Dory gazed at him. Though she hadn't put it into words, she acknowledged that what she really wanted was to love the people closest to her and to have them love her back, and in particular she wanted this from the special man in her life. Maybe it was time she stood up for herself and refused to take anything less. "I'm not the sort of woman you're usually attracted to, am I?"

"No," he admitted reluctantly. "Most of the girls I dated before I married Lauren were like me, students with big plans for a career. After Lauren and I split, there was just the occasional brief affair, usually with someone I'd met professionally."

Like the incredibly heroic nurse, Dory thought. "Then tell me something. What do you see in me?"

"Do you realize how funny it is for you to be asking me a question like that in a situation like this?" With a wry smile he indicated the bed where they lay naked, no longer in each other's arms, but with their bodies still close enough to touch.

Dory was well aware of their situation. "I know it's slightly ridiculous, but humor me."

"Okay." His eyes wandered over her, lingering on the creamy curve of her breasts. "You're a lovely person. You're warm and kind and very feminine. It felt wonderful to make love to you just now." He reached out and stroked her shoulder. "But it feels good just to be around you."

"You mean like being in a kitchen where homemade cookies are being baked?"

He was nonplussed, and he let his hand fall away. "That's not the image that springs instantly to mind."

"Then try this—you're attracted to me because I'm motherly and uncritical, and that's what you need right now."

Abruptly he sat up and frowned down at her. "Now that really is a strange thing to say. What are you getting at?"

Clutching the sheet over her breasts, Dory pushed herself up into a sitting position, as well. "I guess what I'm really asking is where do we go from here?" Though her insides trembled, she met his eyes squarely. "Jim, be honest with me. Where do you think our relationship is headed?"

"Isn't it a little early to be asking me something like that?"

"For you, maybe. Not for me. For me it may even be too late."

"You're speaking in riddles."

Starting to shiver all over again, Dory cast around for her discarded clothing. When she spotted her bra and blouse at the corner of the bed she pulled them to her. Half-turned away from Jim, but hotly conscious of his troubled gaze on her back, she struggled until she got her bra on and then awkwardly poked her arm through one sleeve of her blouse. Vainly her free arm searched for the other sleeve, which was crumpled and half inside out.

"Dory, stop please. Talk to me. Why are you acting this way? What did I do wrong?" He stilled her frantically questing hand. Then he straightened the sleeve of her blouse and gently guided her arm through it.

As she fumbled with the buttons, Dory had never felt more idiotic and unhappy in her life. Scalding tears stung her eyes. But they were partly tears of anger, anger at herself.

"Look, I know this is very uncool. I know a sophisticated woman doesn't ask these questions of a man with whom she's just beginning an affair. But as you've probably figured out by now, I'm not a sophisticated woman. And you're not just any man. I can't be casual about going to bed with you. With me 'making love' isn't just a pretty euphemism for sex. Being with you like this means something to me."

His voice took on a rougher edge. "You make it sound as if I'm some sort of two bit Casanova. Casual sex has never been my forte. Being with you like this means something to me, too."

"Yes, but what?" Her blouse buttoned at last, she swiveled to face him. "Before he left me, Neal told me I was the sort of woman strong men like him are attracted to only when they feel in need of comfort."

"He said that? My God, what a bastard that man is!"

"Maybe he's not exactly Mr. Sweetheart, but I really think he was just being honest. That's how he saw me, as a kind of motherly cushion he was content to come home to when things hadn't gone well at the office, but that otherwise he could ignore."

"Are you comparing me with your ex-husband? If you are, I have to tell you that I don't appreciate it."

Dory shook her head. "No, you're not at all like Neal. You're a much nicer, more complicated person than he is. But you are a strong man, Jim, and you've just gone through a lot of trauma in your life. It wouldn't be surprising if what you needed right now was a brief but temporary affair with a transitional woman."

His eyebrows shot up. "'A transitional woman'?"

Dory took a deep breath. Now that she'd started this, she couldn't turn back. And, for a change, she wanted to say exactly what was on her mind.

"I think you know the sort of woman I'm talking about. She's in all the movies. Sometimes she's the shady lady with a heart of gold. Sometimes she's a barmaid or good-natured waitress. She's the motherly, nurturing sort of woman a hurting hero can go to for solace while he's patching himself back up. She's a woman who, when he feels whole again, will give him a smile and a joke and then send him on his way to the kind of female who is more his match, the kind of female he can really fall in love with." *The kind of female you were formerly married to,* Dory thought, *not me, but a woman like Lauren or Deanna.*

Jim sat very stiffly, his arms folded across his naked chest. "Instead of throwing up this smoke screen about movie heroes who have nothing to do with me or you, why don't you just say what you really mean? Tell me the truth. Do you regret what we've just done here together?"

"No, I don't, and I'm not throwing up a smoke screen, either. What's on my mind is that I don't want to play the doormat role I've just described. In a lot of ways I played it for my husband. I was young and inexperienced and felt I had to. But I'm older now, and I'm not up for it again. I'm sick of it."

A long, taut moment of silence stretched between them. Then Jim glanced around the room, where their clothes were still strewn like crumpled storm victims. "Dory, I don't think we can finish this conversation here. I'm going to leave so that you can get dressed in privacy. Why don't you meet me out in the kitchen for a cup of coffee?"

"All right."

He pushed back the covers, and she averted her eyes while he got out of bed to pick up his shirt and pants. But just before he walked out of the room, she risked a quick glance. Though she'd seen him naked during their lovemaking, that had been different. Because of the passion he'd aroused in her, all she'd been able to take in was hard masculine flesh, dark eyes that seemed to burn into her soul and lips and hands that made her ache with urgency.

Now, as he walked through the door, her gaze raked his long lean back, which tapered to narrow hips and tightly rounded buttocks. Only a few minutes earlier his legs, lightly furred with hair, had twined with hers. Dory flinched at the memory, because now she was quite sure it would never happen again. Her words just now had been a way of ensuring that it would never happen again. Instead of playing the game men and women play she had opted to protect herself by breaking the rules. She had flung down all her cards, and now the game was over.

Cold, her nerves jumping, Dory finished dressing, then visited the bathroom. There she allowed herself to touch Jim's towel and run her thumb along the handle of his hairbrush. Then, squaring her shoulders, she walked out.

He'd been very quick. As she made her way through the living room she could smell the aroma of freshly brewed coffee and hear him moving around the kitchen.

"Smells delicious," she said, hovering in the doorway.

He glanced up from the mug he'd just filled. His clean-cut features had taken on a distinctly wary cast. He probably thought she needed a therapist herself, and maybe she did.

"Sit down, Dory. We need to talk."

Dory crossed to the small Formica table, where cream and sugar had already been set out, and pulled back a chair. When she'd seated herself, he placed a steaming mug in front of her and took the chair opposite. Facing each other, both of them fully dressed and as guarded and on edge as duelists preparing to engage, they sat in taut silence.

"Dory," Jim began. "I was so happy when you came back here with me. Believe me, you're the first woman I've felt that way about since—"

"I know," she put in quickly. "I do believe you."

"But you're right," he continued heavily. "There are a lot of things I'm not sure about, a lot of emotions I don't yet have a handle on. I'm getting there, but it takes time."

"I understand that." She fingered the thick brown handle on her mug. "Maybe that's the trouble. I understand it too well."

"I would never just use you and then discard you. I hate people who do that to others. But I can't make any sort of promises to you, either. It's much too early for that."

"Of course it is." She took a quick, scalding sip and pushed her mug away.

"Can't we play this casually? Go on seeing each other, see how things develop?"

She shook her head. "No, I don't think so."

He gazed at her in bafflement. "Why not?"

"Because I'm going to fall in love with you, Jim." In her lap she laced her fingers and clenched them. "And that's not going to be good for either of us—not good for you because you aren't in any shape to take on the responsibility or the guilt and not good for me because I'm not in any shape to take the pain and uncertainty." She pushed her chair back and got to her feet. "And now I think it's time for me to go home."

CHAPTER TWELVE

SEVERAL DAYS LATER Sam Lucas looked up from the file he'd been studying and said, "I'm impressed." He closed Jim's folder and laid it on his desk. "For a man who was practically at death's door a few months back, you've made remarkable progress."

"Thanks." Uncomfortably Jim shifted in his chair.

Sam eyed him with admiration. "On a physical level, what you've done is amazing. Looking at you now, I'd never guess what you've been through. Why, when you were first examined you'd been beaten and starved so severely that some of your doctors thought any kind of recovery was questionable. In fact, I'd be thrilled to look as healthy as you do now."

"A case of before and after. And I did it all without steroids," Jim joked, flexing the not inconsiderable muscle of his forearm.

"I know you did it with hard work and determination, Jim, and you're to be congratulated. You should be very proud of yourself." Sam cocked his grizzled head. "How's work?"

"Fine. Exciting, actually. There are a lot of innovative things going on at the health plan these days. I've been asked to head a task force looking into ways of controlling the outbreak of Lyme disease. It's kids, you know, who are at greatest risk."

"I don't doubt you'll do a great job. I noticed a big improvement in your state of mind after you started back to work."

Jim nodded. "What can I say? It's nice to be needed and to be doing something you feel is useful. In fact, I find that my commitment to my work is even greater than it used to be."

"Any depression?"

Jim shrugged. "I get to feeling low every now and then. But it's nothing I can't handle."

"That's the key," Sam said. "Let's face it, life is stressful. Bad things happen and we get depressed. It's just a question of surviving our low moments and going on to enjoy some of the good things. You seem to be a survivor."

"I hope so."

"I know so." Sam steepled his hands over his knee. "I'm convinced you're ready to deal effectively with whatever comes your way. Now before we end our last session, maybe you'd like to ask me a question."

"As a matter of fact, I would." Jim got up and paced to the window, where he stood looking out with his hands in his pockets. "It's interesting you should say I'm ready to deal with anything, because right now I'm in a situation I'm not sure how to handle at all. This may seem sort of off the subject, but I expected to see Dory at her desk when I came in. Thursday isn't normally her day off, is it?"

"No, it isn't," Sam said. "She rearranged her schedule with Lorraine this week."

"Did she say why?"

"No, she didn't offer any explanations. Just asked if she could do it."

Jim swiveled to face his therapist. "I think I know why. I think she must have spotted my name on the appointment schedule and decided she didn't want to run into me today."

Sam's eyebrows began to creep upward. "Now why would you think a thing like that?"

Jim's lips twisted wryly. "Not because I'm paranoid. It's because last week she told me she didn't want an involvement with me."

"I see. Obviously you ignored my warnings about Dory." Sam looked perturbed.

"I tried. Honestly I tried. But I couldn't leave her alone. I'm too attracted to her." Jim rubbed a hand across his forehead. "However, if it's her vulnerability you're worried about, let me assure you that the woman is perfectly capable of protecting herself from the likes of me. She's decided that I'm only interested in her because I'm lonely and in need of comfort."

"Oh?"

"She called herself 'a transitional woman.'"

"Interesting," Sam commented after a moment's reflection. "Do you know what she meant by that?"

"Yes, I think I do. A transitional woman, as I understand it, is a sort of human hot water bottle a man uses to make himself feel better and then tosses aside when he doesn't need her anymore."

"Hmm, and what do you think about that?"

Jim turned back to the window. "At first I was furious about her saying those things." Jim didn't describe the circumstances under which Dory had made her accusation. But they were very present in his mind. He'd just made love to her—sweet and glorious love. He had been filled with tender feelings.

Her attack, coming at a time when he'd felt so vulnerable to her, had cut him deeply, all the more so because he'd feared there might be a smidgeon of truth in it. He couldn't help but remember that when he'd first met Dory he hadn't seen her as his type at all. But that had changed. He had changed.

"Now I don't know what I think," he told Sam. "All I know is that I've been very disturbed about our last conversation. I came here hoping she'd changed her mind. I expected to see her out in the office, and I'd planned on persuading her to meet me for a cup of coffee. I still think that if we could just talk this thing out—"

"Dory isn't stupid," Sam interrupted. "Doubtless that's why she changed her schedule. She doesn't want to talk to you."

"No. That's quite clear. When I called the community college I was even told she hadn't signed up to teach another eight-week ceramics course. They sounded more surprised than I was." A hard light came into Jim's eyes. "But I don't have to meet her here or in class. I know where she lives. I'll go there and make her talk to me." He started for the door.

Hastily Sam got to his feet. "Jim, wait. Listen to me."

"Why? You've just given me a clean bill of health and assured me I can handle anything that comes my way. Our time is up, isn't it?"

"Not quite. Sit down and let me give you some advice."

"As my doctor?"

"As a friend of both yours and Dory's."

Jim hesitated, clearly unwilling. But then, with a sigh of resignation, he dropped back down into the chair opposite Sam. "Okay, let 'er fly."

"I'm not a firing squad."

"Then why do I have the feeling you're about to shoot me down?"

"Jim, think about this," Sam said earnestly. "Consider what you've been through and how troubled you were in body and spirit when you first started seeing me. It hasn't been that long, has it?"

"No," Jim admitted. "Just a couple of months. But a lot has happened in that time. You said it yourself, I've come a long way."

"But you still have a ways to go. Dory Barker is the first woman you've felt any physical attraction for. Isn't that so?"

"Yes, but it isn't as if I haven't known other women. I'm as experienced with the opposite sex as most men."

"All that was before your incarceration overseas. This is after. You have to think of that experience as a chasm in your life, a dividing line. Successfully crossing it has made you stronger, but it has also made you different than you were before. You're just not really sure in what ways."

The analogy unsettled Jim. He sat up very straight. "All right. I'll buy that. I *am* different. A lot of the attitudes and opinions I used to cherish have changed."

"Of course. When you put iron into a white hot flame you forge steel. You have to give this new person a chance to find out who he is and what he really wants."

"What are you suggesting?"

"Be fair to yourself and to Dory," Sam urged. "Don't bully her back into a relationship with you until you can be sure it really is what you want. Jim, it's time to grow a little bit, expand your horizons socially, test yourself. You're a good-looking man, the kind the opposite sex is drawn to. Start seeing other women."

"WELL, LONG TIME no see." As Gracie hurried to put on her skates, Lydia Prentice strolled over to the spot where Dory had positioned her folding chair in front of the big Plexiglas window at the ice rink.

"You're late. I was beginning to wonder if you were going to make it this morning," Dory said with a welcoming smile.

"You were wondering about me? Well, I like that!" Lydia pulled a chair up next to Dory's and plopped down into it. "We were beginning to think Beth had retired from skating. This is the first time since South Atlantics that you two have shown up for patch, and it's been three weeks, hasn't it?"

"Yes, three weeks," Dory conceded. "All this time she's been threatening to quit skating. But last night she suddenly announced she wanted to get back to work on her fifth test."

"Were you glad?"

"Very."

"Even though it meant getting up at the crack of dawn again to drive her here?"

"Yes, even despite that. Liddy, I was worried about her."

Lydia nodded. "I can imagine. After what happened at South Atlantics I was concerned for the poor kid myself. When you didn't come to patch I called a couple of times to ask how she was doing. But I never seemed to catch you at home." She gestured out the window. "I must say, from here she seems perfectly fine."

They both looked out at the Olympic-size sheet of ice, where a dozen youngsters were engrossed in tracing various versions of the figure eight. Beth, clad in warm-up pants, ski jacket, heavy mittens and a knit hat pulled down low over her shoulder-length hair, was working in concentrated silence at the far end.

"Yes," Dory agreed, "she seems to be doing all right."

"Well, hurray! I was afraid a big disappointment like that one in Philadelphia might throw Beth into a real tailspin."

"I was afraid of the same thing. But it doesn't seem to have happened. In fact, if anything, Beth has been unusually chipper of late."

"Really?" Lydia narrowed her eyes. "Well, she's looking good."

"Yes."

"In fact..." Lydia squinted. "She looks thinner."

"She is thinner. I believe she's taken off something like five pounds."

"She has? Well, good for her! If I were in her shoes, I'd probably have added a few pounds. I can just picture it. I'd have been consoling myself with milk shakes and chocolate chip cookies."

Dory shook her head. "No, she hasn't done that at all. For the past couple of weeks she's been eating what I feed her without complaining or asking for more. And obviously she's not cheating at school or filling up with fries and shakes at the fast food place up the street when nobody's looking. I'm very proud of her."

"You should be. Denying yourself like that when you're down takes a lot of willpower." Lydia patted her own rounded stomach. "I should have such willpower."

Dory laughed and then said with a faintly puzzled expression in her blue eyes, "Maybe I was wrong to worry. Maybe the debacle at South Atlantics wasn't all negative. I don't want Beth to compete again, but if that bad experience has somehow given her the willpower to improve her eating habits, then something positive will have come out of it."

"Maybe." Lydia's eyes brightened. "But you know what? Sometimes I think we spend too much time worrying about our kids. If you're not telling me about Beth's problems, I'm yakking to you about Gracie's. Let's change the subject."

"To what?"

"To you."

"Me?"

"Yes, indeedy. You're seeing someone, aren't you?"

"What?" Dory shot her friend a startled glance. "What are you talking about?"

"Don't give me that innocent look. A couple of weekends ago I was at the mall shopping with Gracie. We spotted you coming out of that Chinese restaurant with the most gorgeous hunk of man. We did our best to catch up with you to say hello and check him out, but the two of you disappeared out the door, looking as thick as thieves. Now don't pretend you don't know what I'm talking about. I demand to know who he is."

Buying time, Dory took a sip of her coffee. She might have guessed that Lydia would catch on to her secret. Where gossip was concerned, the good-natured brunette had been born with a sixth sense.

"Liddy, he's just a friend."

"Friend, my eye! Where did you meet him?"

"No big mystery. He was enrolled in my ceramics class this fall."

"Hmm." Lydia batted her lashes. "Now I know why you're so devoted to clay. I didn't manage to zero in for a close-up, but what I did see of this guy looked absolutely scrumptious—tall, dark, great body with broad shoulders and a teeny tiny bottom. Now come clean. I know you weren't teaching him how to wedge clay in that Chinese restaurant."

Dory sighed. "What is it with you, special radar? It was perfectly innocent. He's just moved into a new apartment. I was in the mall helping him pick up a few things he needed for it."

Lydia nudged Dory's shoulder. "Oh, and what were you helping him pick out? Sheets?"

Dory felt herself turn bright pink. That was exactly what she'd helped Jim select, among other things.

As she caught her friend's chagrined expression, Lydia crowed. "Oho, so I hit the nail on the head. Well, I hope that after you advised Mr. Gorgeous to buy those sheets and pillowcases, you went back to his place and helped him try them out for wear and tear."

Dory's embarrassment turned to something much more painful. Her hand began to tremble so violently she spilled coffee all over her pants. Mortified, she jumped up and averted her face. Blindly she began to dab at the hot liquid soaking into her jeans.

"Oh, my God! Did I make you do that? Honey, I'm sorry!"

"No, it's nothing. Really it's nothing at all." Frantically Dory brushed at the stained denim.

"You're just rubbing it in. Let me get some napkins."

"Really it's okay."

But Lydia rushed away to the snack bar and returned seconds later with a huge wad of paper napkins. "Here, let me," she insisted, dropping down on one knee in front of Dory.

"No, honestly..." Dory tried to turn her tear-streaked face away.

"Hey, what is it? What's wrong?" Lydia peered up. "You're crying!"

"No, I'm just..."

"You're crying!" Lydia leaped to her feet and put an arm around Dory's shoulders. "Oh, honey, is it something stupid that I said?"

"Oh, no..."

"Is it that guy?"

When Dory didn't answer, Lydia guided her back to the metal folding chair and sat her down. "Here, use this." She proffered an unused napkin.

Shamefacedly Dory accepted it and blew her nose. "I'm sorry. I'm behaving like an idiot."

"I'm the one who's behaved like an idiot, teasing you that way. Me and my big mouth. Honey, what's going on? Have you let that guy get under your skin?"

Dory gave a watery chuckle. "You might say that."

Frowning, Lydia dropped back down on the chair next to Dory's. "Well, that's progress, sort of. For a while there I wondered if you were ever going to get over Neal's walking out on you."

"Oh, I've been over that for a long time. I just hadn't met anyone who interested me."

"And now you have, but he's a rat? Honestly. Men!"

"Jim's not a rat. Lydia, you've got it all wrong."

"Well, at least you've told me his name. Now let's see what else I can get out of you. C'mon, if he's a nice guy, what's the problem?"

"It's—" Dory pushed a strand of blond hair off her forehead. "It's complicated." Hesitantly she gave her friend an edited version of the way her relationship with James Gordon had developed.

When she finished, Lydia regarded her thoughtfully. "He sounds like a fascinating man."

"He is. Maybe he's too fascinating and that's the problem."

Impatience flickered across Lydia's blunt features. "You know, Dory, you've always sold yourself short. It's because you got pregnant in high school and had to live with Neal, who always put you down after he condescended to marry you, I suppose. But it's time you woke up to the fact that you're a beautiful, intelligent, warm and extremely appealing woman. There's no reason this Jim guy couldn't honestly fall in love with you. It doesn't have to be just some fling before he moves on to one of the Deanna Ingrams of the world. Why can't you just relax and give it a chance?''

Dory sat up very straight and stared out at the ice. ''That's what he said, too. And maybe in a couple of years I could. But right now, to quote an old song, 'I'm just not ready to take a chance on love.' There are other things I have, to do with my life first.''

''Like what?''

''Like finish my education and start achieving some of the goals I've set for myself. For some time now I've been thinking about opening my own pottery shop.''

''I think that's a great idea. I've seen your work. You have a lot of talent.''

''I'm enrolled in a small business program at Howard Community. And there are all kinds of other courses I want to take—literature, history, fine arts.''

''And that's great. I'm all for education. But it's no substitute for certain other things.'' Lydia eyed her friend. ''You know what I think?''

''No, but I have a feeling I'm about to find out.''

''I think you're already in love with this Gordon character. That's what's got you so scared.''

Dory's blue eyes flicked to Lydia's brown ones and then darted away. Her friend was too good at reading expressions. She didn't want her to guess at the pain she'd suffered ever since breaking off with Jim. The doubts, the sleepless nights, the struggles not to lift the telephone and dial his number—those were going to stay her own personal secret.

''I think I'm old enough,'' she said carefully, ''to know the difference between love and a strong attraction. Love is something that grows and develops over a period of time. Jim and I don't know each other well enough for that."

"Maybe not," Lydia agreed dubiously. "But it's obvious you're pretty hung up on this guy." She reached out to give Dory's wrist a quick, companionable squeeze. "I know it's none of my business, but will you listen to some advice from an old friend?"

"Of course," Dory replied, mustering a smile.

"You need to get out more."

"Now where have I heard that before?" Dory rolled her eyes.

"I know you've heard it all from me before, but this time you should listen. In my opinion, one good reason this Jim Gordon has knocked you for a loop is that you've been alone too long. You need to get out and meet more men."

"Liddy..."

"Honey, going out with a man doesn't mean you have to marry him, or even let him kiss you good-night. All it means is that you're socializing a bit with the opposite sex and not letting life pass you by."

Dory gazed at her friend. "All right," she finally said.

Lydia looked startled. "All right what?"

"All right, maybe you have a point."

"JESSICA'S JUST TAKEN on a very exciting challenge," Maggie confided. She beamed at the young woman seated on the couch next to Jim. "She's going to be coordinating government research programs in Antarctica."

Jim managed to avoid choking on the sherry he was sipping. "Oh," he commented after clearing his throat. "That is impressive."

"Tell my brother about it," Maggie insisted.

Jessica, an extremely attractive brunette with long straight hair, a svelte figure and intelligent green eyes, smiled deprecatingly. "There's really not that much to tell. Right now I'm just going through a preliminary orientation. The government won't actually send me to Antarctica until next month."

As she described the clothes she had been issued to withstand the subzero conditions at the U.S. government base at McMurdo and the special UV filtering sunglasses she'd just had made up to ensure against snow blindness in that unfriendly climate, Jim gazed at her thoughtfully. Jessica Burch was the third young woman his sister had invited him to dinner to meet, and it seemed as if each one was prettier and more accomplished than the last. This time Maggie had really outdone herself, he mused.

"Excuse me if I sound gauche, but how are you qualified to direct research in Antarctica?" he asked curiously.

Jessica adjusted the designer scarf draped around her slender shoulders. "Well, my formal education includes a doctor's in electrical engineering, and since entering government service I've been in charge of several high level research projects. Working in Antarctica will be breaking some new ground for me, though—or perhaps I should say ice." She chuckled and Jim noted that she had a pleasant, throaty laugh. "Actually, I don't think of myself as a cold weather person. I don't even ski." Her large green eyes swept over Jim. "Do you?"

"A little."

"Then maybe I should get you to teach me."

"The county is sponsoring a cross-country ski trip the weekend after Christmas," Maggie chimed in. "You two should sign up."

"That's an idea," Jessica said. Then she glanced down at her watch. "But I'm afraid I have to get up very early in the morning tomorrow." She looked expectantly at Jim. "Do you mind?"

"Not at all."

Everyone stood and Jessica extended her hand to Maggie. "This has been a very pleasant evening. Dinner was delicious. Thank you for inviting me." She turned to Les and said with a grin, "Thanks for the ride here. See you in the office tomorrow."

Jim's brother-in-law groaned. "Right."

Jim helped Jessica into her stylish cashmere coat and then walked her out to his sister's BMW. As he opened the door on the passenger side he was almost glad his own car was in the shop being repaired and Maggie had lent him the use of hers. Somehow he couldn't picture a sleek female like Jessica in anything less than a BMW. Doubtless she drove something exotic, sporty and foreign.

Before selling or giving away his worldly possessions to volunteer overseas, status cars had been very important to Jim, too. In addition to having his clothes tailor-made and eating at all the best restaurants, he'd owned a Jaguar. If and when he recovered fully from the kidnapping, would he go back to being like that, he wondered. No, he thought not. Sam Lucas was right. Afghanistan had changed him. He was a different person now, with different values.

"Does your sister do this sort of thing to you often?"

Jim finished backing the car out of the driveway, then turned toward Jessica. "What?"

In the light filtering in from the streetlamp, she looked amused. "I think, you poor unsuspecting man, that you know what I mean and are just too polite to admit it. How frequently does Maggie lure you to her house for dinner and then shove strange women at you?"

Jim chuckled. "Actually, you're the third one she's introduced me to in as many weeks."

"You don't say? Well, I admire her fighting spirit. I suppose I shouldn't ask, but I'm weak and can't help myself. How do I stack up against the others?"

"Very well. Neither of them had a doctor's degree."

Jessica slapped at his knee and pretended to pout. "Leave my education out of it. I think you know what I meant, and it wasn't that."

"Okay, you're even better looking than they were—and that's saying something."

In the darkness her lips curved upward. "Why, thank you, kind sir. And now, would you like to hear my reaction to you?"

He shot her a wary glance. "I don't know. You appear to be the honest type."

"Believe me, I am the honest type. When Lester asked me home to dinner, I had my suspicions. But until I move over to Antarctic research and development on a permanent basis, he's my boss. So I figured, what the hell, his wife's a good cook, and it's a free meal."

"You can't beat Maggie's cooking."

"I have to admit that when Les locked me into his Mercedes after work and on the drive out to his house started telling me about the brother-in-law I was going to be meeting, I got just a wee bit nervous."

"I can imagine." Jim guided his car through a green light and then shot her a questioning glance. "What did he say about the peculiar fellow?"

"Not much, just that you were a medical doctor and had been through a divorce fairly recently and needed to get back into the social swim."

So good old Les hadn't told his co-worker about the Afghanistan business. Jim was glad. It wasn't something he wanted to talk about with virtual strangers. Or with anybody really—except maybe Dory. But talking to her about it had been a mistake. "I sound like a real loser, don't I?" he commented.

"I concede that I didn't have my hopes up. I tell you this only so you'll understand why my jaw dropped to the carpet when you first walked in the door."

He hadn't noticed her jaw doing anything unusual, but he decided to play along. "Why? Did I have my jacket buttoned backward?"

"If you had I wouldn't have noticed," she shot back. "I was far too busy admiring your dazzling white teeth, big brown eyes and curly black locks. You can't have been divorced long. You know what the single man to single woman ratio is in these parts? Around the Washington, D.C., area a bachelor with your kind of looks is like raw meat in a pool of piranhas."

"Thanks for the warning."

"It's not a warning. In case you hadn't guessed, it's an opening salvo in what I hope is going to be a mutually enjoyable campaign."

Jim had to laugh. He also had to admire her audacity. He'd encountered aggressive women before, but not too many had Jessica Burch's style and sense of humor. And, being human, he was flattered. Dory had never come on to him like this, and never would, he realized. She was far too diffident.

Jessica lived in the Bethesda area in a classy high rise off Connecticut Avenue. "You can just leave your car in visitor parking," she told him after they pulled past the entrance to the unguarded parking lot. When she saw Jim lift his eyebrows, she added, "Well, you were planning on coming up for a drink, weren't you?"

"I thought you had to get up first thing in the morning."

"I do, but I never let that interfere with more important things. Now come on, don't be shy. I know you've been wondering all evening about my window treatments."

Jim could only guess what a window treatment might be. Nevertheless he was both amused and intrigued. "Honest, Miss Burch, I can't wait to see how you've done your windows," he murmured.

Not surprisingly, Jessica's apartment was every bit as elegant as Jessica herself. Pale pink carpet cushioned the floor and was set off by contemporary furnishings in shades of black, rose and pearl gray. Shiny, egg-shaped vases holding sprays of artfully arranged silk flowers, bits of etched crystal and a fireplace outlined in black marble drew the eye. The shiny surface of a black lacquer dining table reflected back pale pink candles in crystal holders.

Before going into the kitchen to mix drinks, Jessica lit the candles and opened the vertical blinds on a bank of floor-to-ceiling windows so that Jim could admire the city lights. When she returned with a scotch and water for him and a Campari for herself, she nudged him into the black tweed modular sofa facing the window, kicked off her shoes and curled up on it herself.

"Now tell me about your sister's first two candidates. What were they like, and why didn't they make it?"

Jim grinned and shook his head. "You don't mince words, do you?"

"No, why should I? Are you turned off by outspoken women?"

"I don't think so. I don't remember my wife ever holding back when she had something to say."

"Yes, but you divorced her, didn't you?"

"It was the other way around."

"Hmm, the woman must have been mad. But I'll ask you about her later. For the present, I'm more interested in my recent rivals. Who was number one, and why didn't it work?''

Jim took a sip of scotch. "She was a very nice high school teacher my sister had met through her PTA affiliation. Since we both work with kids, Maggie figured we'd have a lot in common. But maybe that was the problem. We bored each other."

Jessica nodded. "I, too, am all for leaving my work at the office, where it belongs. Now on to the second candidate. Why didn't you click with her? Fat ankles? Big nose? Buck teeth?''

"None of the above. On the contrary. She was extremely pretty."

"Drat! Then why no sale?"

Jim shrugged. "Got me. Chemistry, I suppose."

"Ah, yes, chemistry." Jessica set her half-finished Campari down on the kidney-shaped glass coffee table and moved closer. "It's the one vital ingredient, isn't it? With it, nothing else really matters. Without it, what's the point?" She reached out and slowly ran a manicured finger down the length of Jim's red silk tie. "Well, Mr. Gordon, when you walked in that door a few hours ago my test tubes started to smoke. And they've been bubbling away ever since. How about yours?"

Appreciatively Jim chuckled. And after a moment's deliberation, he set down his own glass. Why not, he asked himself. She was beautiful, intelligent, interesting and willing. He liked her sense of humor and the challenge in her slanted green eyes. Since Dory had walked out on him, he'd been lonely. The night before he'd dreamed of warm lips, soft skin and scented hair, then woken up in his empty bed feeling frustrated and lonelier than a castaway. For what Jessica was tempting him to, he even had his ex-therapist's approval. So, why not?

"I don't know about smoking test tubes, but I'm more than willing to try a few experiments."

Jessica closed her eyes and leaned toward him. "Ready for ignition, Dr. Science."

Jessica's lips were as soft and delicious as they looked. The fabric of her silk blouse slithered sensuously against his fingertips, and her hair smelled of something erotic and sinfully expensive.

"Mmm," she murmured as he let his mouth investigate hers. Quickly, a little too quickly, her lips parted, inviting a more intimate exploration. But instead of taking her up on it, Jim drew back.

Sensing the abrupt change in his mood, Jessica flicked open her eyes. "Why have you stopped? What's wrong?"

"Nothing's wrong."

"Oh, yes, there is. You're sitting there frowning. Has the breath mint I snuck on the ride back failed me?"

"It's nothing like that. It has nothing to do with you. You're a very beautiful and desirable woman." He got off the couch and walked over to the chair where he'd draped his overcoat.

"Then why do I have the feeling I'm about to join your sister's other two unlucky ladies?" Jessica demanded. She leaped to her feet and followed him. "You're not going to tell me you've decided you don't like the opposite sex, are you?"

Firmly Jim shook his head. "No, I'm not going to tell you that. I definitely like women, and I definitely like you. But I'm afraid the timing just isn't right."

Her eyes narrowed. "Which probably translates to mean there's another woman someplace whom you happen to like even better than you do me and who has first dibs. Are you still hung up on your ex-wife?"

"No, I'm not. It's not her. But you're right. There is someone." Jim held out his hand. "Look, thanks for the drink and the conversation. But it really is getting late, and we both have to be up early."

"Are you sure about this?" Jessica asked, gazing at him with frank disappointment.

"Yes, I'm sure." Before heading out the door, Jim saluted. "Good luck in Antarctica."

CHAPTER THIRTEEN

THE ELEVATOR RIDE back down to the lobby of Jessica's apartment building seemed to take forever. *Or maybe it's just that I'm in a state of shock,* Jim thought as the doors finally slid open and he made his way through the marble-tiled reception area and outside into the chilly darkness.

A beautiful, intelligent, exciting woman had just thrown herself at him. "And I rejected her," Jim muttered. "Either I really am crazy, or I'm in love."

He was pretty sure he knew which it was. As Jessica's willing lips had opened under his, Dory's image had planted itself firmly in his mind. Those gorgeous big blue eyes had seemed to be staring accusingly at him and suddenly the whole enterprise had been quite futile. "I'm not mad. I'm just in love," Jim said under his breath.

Stunned by this revelation, he walked into the parking lot without really paying much attention to his surroundings. It wasn't until he was within twenty yards of his sister's BMW that he noticed someone had broken into it and was rifling the glove compartment.

"Hey!" Jim shouted. "Stop that!"

But the thief had already heard Jim's footsteps and turned to flee. Cursing under his breath, Jim took off after the man. It didn't even cross his mind to hesitate—that it might be safer and wiser at that time of night and in this deserted spot just to let the culprit go. At that instant all he knew was his gut reaction of anger. Someone, some unknown and unprovoked stranger, had been trying to do him an injury, and he wasn't going to let him get away with it—never again!

The thief was lean and wiry, and very fast as he dodged between the rows of silent cars. Even a couple of weeks ago Jim wouldn't have had a chance of catching up with him. But lately he'd been devoting all his spare time and energy to building his strength and stamina. His weight lifting was beginning to pay off and he'd stepped up his jogging regimen.

When the robber jumped the metal guard rail at the edge of the parking lot, Jim, despite the encumbrance of his overcoat, followed him over it with ease. Suddenly his target whirled and pulled a wicked-looking knife from the sleeve of his sweatshirt.

"Stay where you are, mister! Don't get any closer!"

Though his face was indistinct in the darkness, Jim could tell from his voice that he was young. Jim's captors had been young men. That hadn't kept them from being brutal. At the back of Jim's mind the thought was only the vaguest of whispers. As he confronted the knife on which moonlight glittered with cold menace, he was functioning purely on instinct. All he knew was his anger and his intention to get the weapon away from his opponent, teach him a lesson.

It was over in an instant. When the kid rushed in, Jim deflected his bow with an elbow block, knocked the knife from his hand and, as the weapon clattered to the pavement, picked its former wielder up by the shoulders.

"Hey, stop! I didn't mean anything! Put me down!"

For the first time Jim stared directly into his assailant's face. For an instant his fury, which had built to a crescendo, seemed to cloud his vision. But then the terrified young face registered and he realized it was just a kid—a scared eighteen-year-old who looked as if he might have a drug habit.

Slowly all Jim's ferocity drained away. While still keeping a firm hold on his captive, he set him down. The young man wriggled and struggled in Jim's grip, but soon realized escape was futile. When he quit cursing, he spit out, "Okay man, whatcha goin' ta do?"

"What do you think I should do?"

"I don't know, man. For a minute there you had me worried. You looked like you wanted to kill me."

"Did I?" Jim chuckled. "Well, don't worry. I'm not going to kill you. I'm going to try to make a life of crime a little less appealing to you by turning you over to the nearest policeman. I think we ought to find one a couple of blocks from here."

BY THE TIME Jim got back to Columbia it was almost midnight. He went out of his way to drive past Dory's town house anyhow.

During the weeks since their parting he'd done that several times. After work, using the excuse that he didn't feel like cooking, he'd picked up a take-home meal from the drive-in window at French Fry Heaven. And then, as long as he was in the neighborhood anyway, he'd cruised past Dory's to see which lights were on so he could try to imagine what she might be doing. This late, of course, there were no lights on at all. Obviously she and Beth had gone to bed.

In a thoughtful mood Jim guided his automobile back to his apartment complex. This had certainly been an instructive evening, he reflected.

As he mulled over his experience with the young thug in the parking lot, whose name had turned out to be Denny, a sense of satisfaction spread through Jim. Having to go down to the police station with Denny and answer a lot of questions had been a time-consuming pain, but it had been worth it.

"You took an awful chance going after this guy," the sergeant at the night desk had chided. "You'd have been smarter to just let him get away. A drugged-out kid like this could stick a knife in you and leave you to bleed to death."

"I realize that now," Jim had replied. "I won't do anything so foolish again."

But even as he'd answered Jim had known that he'd had to run after and then confront and overcome young Denny the thief. His self-respect had been at stake.

Smiling faintly, Jim got out of his car. As he walked to his door, his thoughts turned back to Jessica and the other earth-shattering revelation of the evening. As he recalled the dinner at Maggie's, Jim's smile widened. Maybe the first two young women his sister had introduced him to had just been unlucky picks, but Jessica Burch was another story. If he couldn't get excited about a zinger like her, he was a lost cause. It confirmed what he'd already known in his heart. Dory was the one he wanted. He was in love with her. Somehow he had to talk to her and convince her of that.

Jim chose the next evening to make his first move. All day he'd toyed with the idea of calling Dory, but finally decided against it. On the phone it would be too easy for her to turn him down. He needed to see her in person.

He waited until eight o'clock, when he judged she'd be through with dinner. But his careful timing didn't do him any good.

"Mom's out," Beth said when she answered the door to his nervous knock.

His face must have fallen a yard, because Beth looked concerned. "Hey, long time no see. I'm the only one here, but why don't you come in to get out of the cold and talk or something? I'm just watching television and doing homework."

Jim thought he probably shouldn't take her up on it. But he'd been so anxious to see Dory and now felt so disappointed. At least, just being inside her house, he could feel a little closer to her.

After he strolled into the cheery little room he asked casually, "Is your mom out because she's decided to go back to teaching?"

Beth shook her head. "Nah. She's got a date."

"Oh?" Jim sank down into the nearest chair. He felt like leaving, but now that he'd accepted Beth's invitation to come in, he couldn't just walk out again. He gazed at the teenager, noting that she looked different but too taken up with the problem of Dory to focus on how and why. "Do you know how late she'll be out?"

"No, but it'll probably be late. They went to dinner at the Watergate and then a music thing at the Kennedy Center."

"Oh." Dinner and a show at the Kennedy Center, he thought—glamour, bright lights, romance. Why hadn't he ever taken Dory out for an evening like that? No wonder she thought he didn't really care for her and was just using her. Oh, sure, he had to budget carefully because he was paying back his sister and brother-in-law for the ransom they'd put up. But he made a good salary. The money situation was beginning to loosen up now. He could afford to treat a woman like Dory the way she deserved. And he would, he promised himself—just as soon as he could persuade her to give him the chance.

He wanted to question Beth about the man Dory had gone out with, but when he looked up and saw the teenager staring at him quizzically he changed his mind. In search of some topic that would do for five minutes of conversation before he excused himself, he glanced around the living room.

"I see you've already got your Christmas tree up."

"Christmas is only a week away."

"That close?" Jim shook his head. "I haven't been paying proper attention." He got up and went over to examine some of the objects dangling on the small but fragrant pine in front of the window. "These are cute. They look like petrified cookies," he said, pointing at an ornament shaped like a fanciful mermaid and then another in the shape of a unicorn.

"That's exactly what they are," Beth told him. "My mom and I made them when I was little. She used to love to do stuff like that. She's a real Christmas freak."

"How about you? Are you a Christmas freak, too?"

"Nah." Beth shook her head. "Too fattening—all those gloppy sweets that everyone stuffs themselves on during the holidays! That's not for me!"

It was then that Jim realised why Beth seemed so different. "Have you been on a diet?" he asked.

"You might say that."

She preened—ever so slightly, but enough so that he could tell she was very proud of herself and had been miffed he hadn't said anything about her weight loss before.

"Well, it seems to have been a very effective one. You must have taken off at least ten pounds since I saw you last."

"Thirteen, to be exact." To demonstrate, Beth got up and pulled the waistband of her jeans out from her stomach. There was a considerable gap. "These used to be really tight."

"You're going to have to get yourself a new wardrobe."

"That's what my mom says, but I want to wait until I've taken off another five."

"Another five pounds?" He cocked his head. "You look almost too skinny now. If I were you, I wouldn't worry about taking off any more weight. Girls need a little fat, you know."

"Oh, no!" Vehemently Beth shook her head. "Fat is disgusting. I hate the way it makes me feel and look. Yuck! I never want to be fat again and look the way I used to!"

"You weren't fat before, just pleasingly plump," Jim told her mildly. He was a bit taken aback by the emphatic way she'd expressed herself. But teenagers were like that, always going overboard on something or other. Then he remembered another curious thing. A couple of times when he'd picked up food at French Fry Heaven lately, hadn't he seen her inside feasting on the kind of gloppy food she'd just decried? But, no, he must have been mistaken. She couldn't have lost all that weight if she'd been snitching shakes and fries.

He studied her more closely. She seemed all right, a little pale perhaps. And her skin appeared a bit dry, which was unusual in a person her age and might indicate some sort of vitamin deficiency—or might just be due to chapping from the cold dry weather they'd been having lately.

"Why are you staring at me like that?"

"No reason. You're feeling okay, aren't you?"

"I'm feeling fine," she retorted belligerently.

He decided to drop the subject. It was time he got going, anyway. "Tell your mother I stopped by, will you?"

"Sure." Beth walked him to the door. "I'll leave a note on the refrigerator. It was nice seeing you."

OUTSIDE THE RESTAURANT the lights of Washington, D.C., twinkled like a thousand winter fireflies. Inside it was cozy and warm. In one corner a pianist at a grand piano played sophisticated arrangements of popular ballads. Their romantic strains mixed with the gentle tinkle of wineglasses and pleasant conversation.

"Dinner was so good. I'm not sure I can get up from this table. But if we don't want to miss the show we'd better pay the check and get going," Lydia said.

Grant Felson reached inside his pin-striped jacket for his wallet. "Let me get this."

"Oh, no," Lydia and Tom protested.

But Grant shook his head and raised a hand. "I insist." He smiled at Dory, who sat next to him. "It's been my pleasure."

This was the second time she'd double-dated with Grant and the Prentices. On the first occasion, before they'd introduced him to her, she'd been filled with doubts. She'd expected it to be just another awkward evening with someone who didn't really interest her. But Lydia had been so insistent, and she knew her friend was right. She couldn't go on sitting home alone the rest of her life.

To her surprise, she'd liked Grant right away. He wasn't what anyone would call handsome, but physically he wasn't unattractive, either. He had intelligent, humorous blue eyes, a confident bearing and an authoritative way of dealing with the world. It was he who had driven them all to the Watergate, guiding his maroon Volvo sedan through merciless six o'clock Washington, D.C., traffic with ease—always, to Dory, an impressive feat.

"He's a widower," Lydia had told her. "His wife died last year after a long illness. It was terrible for him, and he's just now beginning to get out and socialize."

That had made Dory sympathetic. She had been even more touched by his gallant manner toward her. All during their first evening together he'd held doors, pulled out her chair and listened closely to her every word as if pearls and not mere pleasantries were falling from her lips. And when he'd dropped her at her door, he'd held her hand as if it were made of glass, then shaken it gently.

When Lydia had suggested this dinner and concert date together, it had seemed ridiculous to refuse. Besides, they were going to hear the *Messiah*, which Dory loved, and especially loved hearing at Christmastime.

An hour after they left their table at the Watergate, she sat in one of the Kennedy Center's red velvet seats while Handel's magnificent music washed over her. It made her think of the Christmases past when Beth had been little and when she and Neal had been struggling to make their marriage work. What would Christmases be like in the future, she wondered. And for that matter, what about this holiday that was almost upon them?

As the soprano began the haunting strains of her aria, Dory's thoughts turned to Beth. Usually by now Dory had finished all her Christmas shopping. But there were still some clothing items she was waiting to buy for Beth because she couldn't be certain of her size. It kept going down.

A little frown began to pucker Dory's brow. At first she'd been delighted by her daughter's weight loss. She was proud of Beth's newfound self-control, the way she had started uncomplainingly eating only the healthful, low-calorie foods Dory provided. And there was no denying that when she'd shed some of her baby fat, her real prettiness had begun to shine through.

But lately Dory had begun to worry all over again. Wasn't Beth losing weight awfully fast? Wasn't she getting a little too thin? Dory had started increasing her daughter's portions and offering her healthful fruit and yogurt desserts and big deliciously sweetened oat bran muffins to go with the low calorie salads and soups they'd both been consuming. She'd watched carefully to make sure Beth ate these things, and she had—every bite. So Dory *knew* Beth was getting enough to eat. Yet her weight continued to drop.

Oh, well, Dory told herself, surely over the holidays she'd put some back. No one could resist all the goodies spread around so freely at this time of year.

After the concert, Grant piloted them all back to Columbia and dropped Tom and Lydia off at their front door. Then, alone with Dory in the front seat next to him, he drove his Volvo back to her town house. As they cruised through the darkened streets, Dory wondered if she should invite him in for a drink or a cup of coffee. It was late and she didn't really want to. But maybe she should.... She was still debating the question when they pulled up in front of her house.

"I really enjoyed the concert," she said sincerely. "Thanks so much for taking me."

"The pleasure was very mutual, Dory, very mutual, indeed."

He wore a navy-blue overcoat with a white silk scarf. In the automobile's darkened interior, the scarf and the streaks of white in his neatly brushed hair gleamed palely. Dory began to feel a bit nervous. Saying good-night to Grant wasn't going to be quite the simple matter it had been last time. He wasn't making any move to get out of the car and open the door for her.

"Dory," he said, turning toward her, "you're a very nice person and a lovely woman."

"Why, thank you, Grant." Why were men always telling her that she was a nice person? It was beginning to irritate her. She was tired of being so darn nice.

"I'm grateful to the Prentices for introducing us."

"What a lovely thing to say. I'm glad to have met you, too."

"Do you really mean that?"

"Why, of course I mean it." Dory began to feel even more uncomfortable, and in the enforced intimacy of Grant's car, also somewhat trapped. But she didn't want to let that show. If she was a "nice" lady, this was a "nice" man, she told herself, and he *had* shown her a couple of truly pleasant evenings. The least she could do before she said good-night was exchange a few private words with him.

He turned toward her more completely and rested his arm along the back of her seat. "I suppose Lydia has told you about my wife?"

"Yes, she mentioned that you were a widower and that your wife died after a long illness."

Through the gloom he gazed at her earnestly. "That was a year ago, which may not sound like such a long time. But believe me, when you're alone and lonely, it can certainly seem that way."

"You haven't gone out much with other women?" Dory queried hesitantly.

He shook his head. "Oh, now and then. But there hasn't been anyone I've felt particularly drawn to. I was beginning to think there wasn't going to be—until now."

"Until now?" Dory's stomach began to jump. *Oh, dear,* she thought.

"I want to see you again—soon. Only this time I'd like it to be just the two of us, so we can really get to know each other. What do you say?"

"I don't know. The holidays always take so much time, and besides working I'm taking college courses." Suddenly Dory knew the answer she wanted to give was no. But she didn't know how to turn him down without hurting his feelings. The poor man had suffered a great loss and had been lonely for months.

"You could spend a weekend with me at my place in Virginia."

"I thought you lived in D.C."

"I have an apartment there. But my real home is the farm in Virginia. It's a nice place with trees and fields and horses. The house is old but spacious and Vivian, my wife, did a lot of work on it before she died. She had beautiful taste in furnishings. I know you'd like it."

"I'm sure it's very nice, but . . ."

"Say yes, Dory. I know you want to. I know this is going to be perfect for both of us." Without warning, he drew her toward him and kissed her soundly.

At first she was so startled by his unexpected move that she did nothing at all. Then, as she began to take in the feel of his skin against hers, the scent of his hair and clothing, she stiffened.

His mouth had settled on hers so firmly that she couldn't breathe. She felt as if he were drawing all the breath out of her, choking her. Panicking, she began to push at his shoulders. But he was a large man, and apparently he was enjoying himself. She could have been pushing at a stone wall.

When he tried to part her lips and jabbed his tongue between them, Dory resisted in earnest. "Grant, please stop!" she said when she finally managed to disengage herself long enough to use her voice.

"What's wrong?" he asked thickly. His arms reached for her. "Oh, Dory, you're so delicious and womanly. Let me kiss you again. You're the kind of woman a man wants to bury himself inside."

"No, really!" She yanked at the seat belt, cursing the thing. He might as well have her tied up in a straitjacket.

"Dory . . ."

"Grant, I think we've both made a mistake here—or rather, I have. It's my fault, really. You're a very nice man and I like you, but I don't like you this much.'' Finally she heard the seat belt click and mercifully it loosened.

"I'm sorry if I've been too..."

"No, I'm the one who's sorry. It's all my fault.'' She pushed open the door and swung her legs toward the pavement. "I have to be going now. Good night. But I did enjoy the evening. I really did.''

"Dory, wait!''

He snatched at her coat, but she managed to elude him. Awkward in her dressy evening shoes, she clattered across the sidewalk and up the steps to her door, where she began fishing frantically for her keys. Of course they were lost somewhere in the bottom of her purse.

She heard the car door slam and, glancing back, saw that he was coming after her. At that moment her hand closed around the key and she jammed it into the lock. "Grant, really, I don't want to talk about it.''

"Dory, we can't say goodbye like this. What about Virginia?''

"I don't think so.'' Just as he reached the top step, she propelled herself through the door and slammed it behind her.

"But, Dory...''

Through the wood, his voice was faint but insistent.

"Grant, I'm sorry. Good night.''

He rang the doorbell, but she ignored it. Weakly she leaned against the barrier and waited to hear the sound of his departing footsteps. At last she did, and then the Volvo's engine roared to life. Shaking like a leaf in a gale, Dory tottered to the window and peered out. The street was blessedly empty. He was gone.

"Oh, my God,'' she moaned. "That was awful, just awful.''

Shivering with reaction, flushing hot and then cold, she clutched at her stomach and moaned again. She'd never felt more ashamed of herself or more like a total fool in her entire life.

Okay, he'd been a little pushy, but surely she could have put him off more gracefully. She should never have let herself be talked into going out with him in the first place. But she'd like the man, for heaven's sake. She couldn't have known she'd have such a visceral reaction to his kiss. She'd hated it!

What I need now is a nice hot cup of tea, Dory told herself. Still shaky, she made her way down the hall. Could she call the man and apologize for running away from him like that, she wondered. But, no, she didn't want to see him again and that would just drag things out. Maybe she could write him a note.

In the kitchen Dory spotted Beth's message on the refrigerator. "Jim Gordon stopped by to see you," it read. "He looks cuter than ever, and I think he was jealous that you were out with someone else."

Dory took the sheet of paper out from under the magnet and stared down at it. Jim. If only she'd been here. She glanced at the phone, overwhelmed by the urge to dial his number just so she could hear his voice. Slowly she began to reach for the receiver. But just as her fingers closed around it, the thing started to ring.

Dory was so unnerved by the sudden noise in the dark and silent kitchen that she jerked back, knocking the receiver to the floor.

"Oh, my God," she mumbled as she scrambled for it. Who could it be at this hour? Could Grant be calling her to try to renew his pursuit? Reluctantly Dory put her ear to the receiver. "Hello?"

But the anxious voice on the other end of the line belonged to a woman. "Dory, is that you?"

"Yes."

"What happened? What was that loud noise?"

"I dropped the phone. Who is this? Katie?"

"Yes, it's your everlovin' little sister."

"Do you realize what time it is?"

"Yes, it's early. Only eleven and the night is young."

"Where are you calling from? Are you all right?"

"I'm in my apartment in New York, and of course I'm all right. Listen, I know it's late by your provincial standards, but I had to call you. I was too excited to wait until tomorrow."

Wearily Dory rubbed her temple. "What are you talking about?"

"I just got home from a dinner meeting that's going to change your dull little life. First of all, I received your Christmas gift, and fortunately it arrived unbroken."

"Oh, really? Katie, as I recall, I wrote 'Do not open until Xmas' in red all over the package."

"You didn't really expect me to pay any attention to that, did you? Anyhow, I opened it right away. And you can thank your lucky stars I did."

"Why should I thank *my* lucky stars? The gift is for you, not me."

"And a beautiful gift it is. The moment I took the tissue paper off it, I just loved it. I'm really serious, Dory. Your pottery is getting better and better. This canister set is really gorgeous. So gorgeous, in fact, that when I saw it I packed it and the other pottery items you've sent me and carted the lot down to Helen Priestly."

"Who's that?"

"She's the buyer for the Kitchen Boutique section in my department store."

Dory's eyebrows lifted. "Oh?"

"Yes, and she was crazy about them. So crazy that she's ready to stock them."

"She is?"

"Yes! She's going to put in an order with you. For starters, what do you say to a dozen canister sets, another dozen colanders, three dozen spoon rests and twenty mixing bowl sets?"

Dory put her hand over her fluttering heart. "You're kidding."

"I'm not kidding. This is for real. Aren't you excited?"

Dory clutched the phone. "Oh, yes. Oh, yes! I'm very excited. Oh, Katie, thank you! It's like a dream come true!"

CHAPTER FOURTEEN

"OH, NOT AGAIN!" Dory muttered. Swallowing her irritation, she rinsed her hands and hurried upstairs from her makeshift studio in the basement. Not more than a quarter of an hour earlier she'd finished an awkward phone conversation with Grant in which they'd both apologized for the disastrous finale to their date and agreed not to press their luck by trying again.

And now this was the second time the doorbell had rung this morning. Normally Dory wouldn't have minded the interruption. But she'd gone to a lot of trouble negotiating with Lorraine so that she could get two days off to work on this wonderful department store order of Katie's, and time was precious.

"Neal!" When she flung open the door Dory couldn't have been more surprised if Rudolph the Red-nosed Reindeer had been standing there. Her ex-husband never dropped in casually. When he wanted to talk to her he almost always came to the office. Otherwise she saw him only when he picked up Beth.

"I had a little free time this morning, so I thought I'd drop around and talk to you."

"Oh, well—come in. Can I, er, can I fix you a cup of coffee?"

"That sounds good."

As he followed her into the kitchen, he looked her over critically, his blue eyes traveling over her worn jeans and flannel shirt. "I suppose you're dressed like that because you're making pots or something."

"Yes, I've been working in my studio downstairs. And there's not much point in putting on makeup if you're going to be covered with clay, anyway." She didn't explain to him about her order from New York. Neal had always been patronizing about her hobby, and she didn't feel like sharing her hopes about this exciting new possibility with him.

"You're looking good," she said, glancing over her shoulder as she filled the coffee maker. As always, it was the truth. Neal was impeccably dressed in a gray wool suit, striped shirt and paisley silk tie. Over the suit he wore a double-breasted trench coat, left undone, which gave him a slightly roguish air, as if he'd just stepped off the Orient Express after successfully completing a dangerous mission.

Then she noticed that his expression didn't quite match his power-broker turnout. Lines of strain tightened the corners of his mouth and he seemed rather pale. "Are you okay?" Dory asked.

"Yes, no, oh, I don't know. Things have been rough lately."

She turned to face him. "Are you here because there's some problem you need to discuss with me?"

"It's next weekend." He dropped down into one of the kitchen chairs. "My plans have changed."

"They have?" She cocked her head. "I thought you and Deanna were spending Christmas in Aruba."

"We were. But that's fallen through."

"Oh?" Though Neal looked as if he were expecting sympathy, Dory decided not to be hypocritical and say she was sorry. In all the years they'd been married Neal had never taken her on a Caribbean vacation. They'd always gone to visit his folks in Connecticut. "I suppose you're both too busy to get away from the office for that long."

"It's not that." Abruptly Neal got up and began pacing back and forth. "Deanna left."

"Left?"

"Just up and left."

Dory blinked. "I don't understand."

"She was offered a cushy job in San Francisco and given only a week to make the decision. Well, good old Deanna didn't even take the week. She decided right away. Yesterday, after leaving a message on my answering machine, she boarded a jet for the coast." As he spoke, Neal's face turned red and his handsome features became distorted with anger. "Pffft. No more Deanna."

"I . . . I see." Nonplussed, Dory tried to think of an appropriate response. "That does seem a bit—"

"Cruel, heartless, hard-boiled?" Neal spit. "Yeah, well, I've learned my lesson. No more armor-plated women like Deanna Ingram for me."

"Hmm." Dory busied herself getting mugs and filling them with freshly perked coffee. As she worked, Neal came up and stood next to her.

"That smells delicious."

"Thank you."

"You always were a good cook. I've never been able to beat your morning coffee."

When he laid a hand on her shoulder, Dory flinched, thrust a mug at him and then moved so that the kitchen table was between them. "Well, I certainly tried."

As Neal regarded her, a calculating gleam came into his eyes. "Beth tells me you don't fix those big dinners anymore that you used to like to cook for me. She says the two of you live on salad and soup."

"That's more or less true." She had never enjoyed slaving in the kitchen over huge meals and had only done it because she'd been brainwashed to think it was her duty.

"Well, I have to congratulate you. Whatever you're doing, it's really paid off. Beth looks a hundred percent better. You know, it was getting so that I was ashamed to introduce her as my daughter. But now she looks great."

Incensed that he would actually admit to ever being ashamed of Beth because she'd been a few pounds over-weight, Dory turned away. "Beth's the one you should be congratulating, not me," she said coldly. "Beth's the one who's learned to control her appetite, and that's the hard part."

"Yeah, though I'm not too sure about her self-control. A funny thing happened the last time she spent the night in my place. You know I keep several varieties of gourmet ice cream in my freezer. Well, Sunday after I dropped her off back here I felt in the mood for a dish of chocolate chunk crunch. But it was all gone, and so was the carton of rocky road, which I hadn't even touched."

Frowning, Dory swiveled back to face him. "You think Beth ate them without telling you?"

"It must have been her. But . . ." He shrugged. "I guess it doesn't matter. If she pigged out, it sure doesn't show. The kid looks great. Now her figure's almost as good as yours." Neal set down his coffee cup and crossed to the spot next to the microwave, where Dory had retreated.

"You know, Dor, I've been thinking about you a lot lately."

"You have?"

"We had some good times together."

"Did we?"

"Of course we did—despite everything. I've been think-ing about how lonely you must be here with no one to talk to but Beth, and she's not even around half the time."

"Well, I do have a job, Neal. And I'm going to school. Then there's my pottery."

"Oh, but that's just . . . I mean, you can't really take that seriously."

"I do, though. I take it very seriously."

He stopped in front of her and put his hands out so that they rested on her shoulders, weighing her down. "You don't have to pretend with me, Dor. You don't have to put up a brave front. I know how hard it was on you when I left. Lately I've been thinking about the way I treated you and feeling pretty guilty about it, let me tell you. You're a young, healthy, beautiful woman. Yes, you are, Dor—don't try to deny it. You've always been too self-effacing. Maybe you're not beautiful in the way that a knockout like Deanna is—but in your own way you're damned attractive. And here you are, all alone for two years with no man to appreciate you. It's not right."

"Really, Neal, it hasn't been so bad." Dory tried to wriggle out of his grasp, but he had her pinned against the edge of the counter.

"I have a proposition for you, Dor."

"What's that?"

"Why don't we give it another try? In fact, why don't we conduct a little experiment here and now?" He glanced toward the staircase in the hall. "You're here all alone. Beth's in school, and I've got the morning free. How about it?"

"How about what?" Dory asked, even though she knew exactly what Neal had in mind.

"How about seeing if we can find an ember or two and breathe some life back into them?" As he spoke, he started to lower his head, his lips seeking hers.

Horrified, Dory ducked. "Neal, really, I'm not interested in breathing life into dead embers. Let's just let all that rest in peace."

"C'mon Dory, don't play hard to get. You need a man. I know you do."

"No, I don't." As he grabbed for her chin, Dory felt a surge of anger. She shoved hard at his shoulders and twisted away. "I don't need anything from you, Neal. I've already got a man," she said defiantly.

"What?" He looked thunderstruck.

It was the last thing Dory had planned to say, but now that the words were out she had no intention of taking them back. Her chin went up and her blue eyes met her ex-husband's squarely. "You heard me. I'm seeing someone. I'm involved with someone."

"Involved?" Once again Neal began to turn an angry red. "Involved? You mean you're actually sleeping with someone."

"Yes, I am," Dory lied. Her brief love affair with Jim was now past tense, but she wasn't going to let Neal in on that fact.

"Where? Here?" His outraged glance swept the kitchen as if he were picturing Dory entwined with a lover on top of the stove.

Suddenly the idea appealed to her. "Yes," she informed him calmly. "Everywhere. On the kitchen floor, on the rug in front of the fireplace, in the bathtub, on the staircase. Once we even did it in a closet. We can't get enough of each other. Half the time when we're together we're so aroused that we can't even make it to the bedroom."

Neal's eyes bulged. "Have you lost your mind?" he sputtered. "Who is this sex maniac?" His brows snapped together. "Is it that guy who changed your tire? The one who's seeing Lucas?"

Dory had forgotten that Jim and Neal had met. She took a step backward. "It's none of your business who he is."

"It's him, isn't it? You're carrying on like this with a guy who's some kind of a nut."

"Jim Gordon is not a nut. He's one of the sanest men I've ever met—a lot saner than you."

"Aha! So it is him. And I suppose you're going to tell me you're in love with him."

"Yes, I'm in love with him," Dory answered between her teeth. "I'm so in love with him that I ache whenever I think about him. At night he's in my dreams. During the day he's constantly in my thoughts. Beside him other men seem dull and gray and totally uninteresting, and I realize that he's the only one I'll ever want. So you see, Neal, it's no use trying to breathe life into our embers. Whatever we had, it's dead and gone."

Neal glared at her. Bristling, he started to stalk toward the door. "I feel sorry for you," he hissed. "You haven't changed a bit. You're as dumb as you ever were. You're letting this guy take you for whatever he can get."

Dory, who had followed him out into the hall, watched as Neal yanked open the front door. "And when he's tired of you, he's going to be gone, just like me. Gone, you hear!" Neal snapped, and then slammed the door behind him so hard that it rattled.

For a long moment, Dory stared at it. Finally she sank down onto the bottom step of the staircase, covered her face with her hands and started to cry. Rivers of tears gushed out of her eyes and sobs racked her throat and chest.

Deep within the storm of emotion that had seized her, she knew exactly why she was crying. It wasn't because of what Neal had said. No, it was because of what he'd made her say. In the heat of her anger, she'd put into words what she'd been trying to keep hidden from herself. She was in love with Jim Gordon—deeply in love. And it was all no use because she'd already lost him.

After a while Dory's crying stopped. She wiped her face on her sleeve, then got up and went into the kitchen. Sniff-

ing into a tissue, she heated some water for tea and swallowed an aspirin. When the tea was ready she carried it
down to her studio. *I don't have time to sit around crying
over lost causes,* she told herself sternly. *I have too much
work to do.*

EARLY THAT AFTERNOON Jim knocked at Bill Perkins's office. The door was open, but his colleague was nowhere in
sight. Jim stood out in the corridor a minute or two more,
then walked in and sat down. While he waited he studied
one of the many charts pinned up on Perkins's bulletin
board and thought of his conversation with Beth. All
morning it had nagged at him.

"Sorry I'm late," Perkins said, bustling in with a stack of
periodicals. "To tell you the truth, I'd forgotten we set this
up."

"It's nothing crucial." Jim smiled up at the other physi-
cian. "It's just that you handled a case of Lyme disease recently, and I wanted to discuss it with you."

"That's right. You're heading up this new task force."
Perkins pulled out the chair behind his desk and settled into
it. "Well, it was an interesting case," he said, and began to
describe it.

While he talked, Jim took careful notes and asked a
question from time to time. But all the while his gaze kept
being drawn back to the chart behind Bill Perkins's head.

When they'd finished discussing the Lyme disease case,
Jim pointed at the chart. "I'd forgotten that you did a study
last year on bulimia and anorexia."

"Yes. Surprised the hell out of me, and depressed the hell
out of me, too."

"What do you mean?"

"Oh, when I began the study I was aware that eating disorders were epidemic among teenage girls. But I hadn't realized just how prevalent they were in Howard County."

"Really?"

Perkins, a balding little man with intelligent shoe-button eyes, grimaced. "It's a phenomenon that's skyrocketed in the eighties. A survey in '83 by one of the big women's magazines indicated that fully twenty percent of women under twenty had purged for weight control. Now it's got to be much higher. I tell you, these kids are going crazy trying to live up to the body images they see in the television ads. Last year there were cases in the county of girls who died, literally starved themselves to death. Who knows how many are out there now destroying their health."

"Who knows?" Jim repeated with a frown. "Actually, I'm not that familiar with the syndrome. What's the most common hazard of bulimia?"

"Mineral imbalance, which, as you know, can lead to heart palpitations, hair and tooth loss, glucose intolerance, atherosclerosis, pernicious anemia, coronary thrombosis, blood clots in the heart and brain, calcium deposits in the kidneys..."

Jim held up a hand. "Okay, I get the picture."

"Listen, if you're interested, I can dig out my report and some of my research materials for you."

"I'd appreciate that," Jim told him. "I'd like to look them over."

Much later that day in his own office, Jim finished scanning the sheaf of papers Perkins had bestowed on him and laid them on his desk. He was frowning, deeply disturbed by what he'd read. What could be more tragic, he reflected, than healthy young bodies literally wasting away in a misguided attempt to be thought beautiful? Something terrible was going on, a secret horror that remained undercover until, in many cases, it was too late to be corrected.

Again he found himself thinking about Beth Barker. Perkins's report had mentioned that teens involved in body-conscious activities like ballet, modeling and certain sports were more likely to develop these types of problems. Figure skating certainly fell into that category. But really, he had no good reason to think she might have an eating disorder—except for the conviction that he'd seen her in French Fry Heaven recently, and she hadn't been eating a salad.

He shook his head. No, he had to be wrong. Just because she'd dieted off quite a bit of weight lately didn't mean she wasn't perfectly healthy. And so what if she did go crazy on fast food occasionally? A little bit wouldn't hurt.

Nevertheless Jim got up and began to pace back and forth. Doing all this reading about the problems of teenagers had made him restless. It had taken him back to his own boyhood, made him remember things that were long buried.

He pulled the slats of the venetian blind apart and glanced through them. The day outside was crisp and sunny, and the rest of his afternoon was free. He could leave now if he wanted. With sudden decision, he reached for his parka and then, after depositing a message with his receptionist, walked out.

He drove his car north of Baltimore and then exited off the beltway onto a road leading to an area that was still rural and unspoiled. As he sped along the two-lane highway, he glanced from right to left, taking in the patchwork of rolling, stubbled fields interspersed with fenced-in pastures where horses and cattle still grazed. It was a relief to see that the developers hadn't made their way out here yet.

So many years had passed since his last visit that he'd been worried he might not remember the road. But he recognized the turnoff he wanted the moment he saw it. It looked almost eerily the same, as if he were traveling back in time. Twenty minutes later, when he slowed in front of a square farmhouse and stopped the car on the opposite side of the road, the illusion was shattered.

The house, which had once belonged to his grandfather, had long since been sold. The new owners had covered the white clapboard exterior, which Jim had remembered fondly, with barn-red aluminum siding. That and other "improvements" made the place almost unrecognizable.

After a moment, Jim cruised down the road until he found a gravel area where he could pull off out of sight of the house. It wasn't the house he'd come to visit, anyway. When the car was parked, he got out, climbed over a low barbed wire fence and melted into the forest. As he made his way through the trees, he again had the sensation of traveling back to a less complicated time in his life. During the summers of his youth, he and his brother, Tom, had played in these woods. They'd pretended to be Indians and trappers and hidden from their sister, Maggie, when she'd tried to summon them for chores or intrude on their camaraderie.

He paused to stare at a large clump of wild laurel. Those bushes had to be at least thirty years old. When he and Tom were nine and ten they'd used this spot as a rendezvous point.

After a moment's contemplation, Jim stepped over a fallen log and proceeded down the slope. The thick carpet of dead leaves crunched under his shoes. In summer you wouldn't know about the river until you were practically on top of it. But now, with the trees bare, he could see it already. A few yards farther on he stopped to look down at it—a thin line of cold dark water moving sluggishly, now hardly more than a creek.

In spring, however, it would swell into a respectable body of water big enough for a pair of boys to take their grandfather's boat out into. For a second or two, Jim could almost hear the sound of boyish laughter. For several minutes he stood as still as a statue, gazing out over the water, lost in memories.

"THEY'RE HERE NOW, Mom. I'm going."

"Okay," Dory shouted up from her studio, where she'd been working throughout the day. "Have fun, and don't stay up all night."

"I won't," Beth promised.

To Dory's surprise, she heard Beth's feet on the stairs to the basement. An instant later Beth came up behind her stool and threw her arms around her neck.

"I just wanted to give you a kiss goodbye," Beth said.

"Why, thank you, honey," Dory replied, pleased and startled. "I'd like to give you a hug, but as you can see, I'm up to my elbows in clay."

"That's okay." Beth pressed her lips to her mother's cheek. "You really are a nice mom, you know, and I really do love you a lot."

"I love you, too   with all my heart."

Beth drew back. "Well, I've gotta go." She turned and ran back up the stairs.

Dory stared at the staircase until she heard the sound of the front door slamming. She was surprised by her daughter's display of affection. Beth didn't often do that sort of thing anymore. She considered herself much too adult. But every now and then she'd forget all her newly acquired sophistication and revert for a moment or two to the affectionate little girl she'd once been.

Smiling, Dory shook her head and glanced at the clock on the wall. Her back ached and her hands were beginning to feel numb from exhaustion, but if she could do just two more pots she'd have all the flour canisters.

After arranging a large lump of clay in the center of her wheel and wetting it down, she started the wheel rotating. For a second or two her hands hovered over the shapeless clay, which spun lopsidedly. Then her thumbs came down, instinctively found the center of the gray material and started the process of imbuing it with form and symmetry.

Since Neal's visit early that morning, Dory hadn't allowed herself to think of anything but the work she needed to do to fill the order from New York. It was wonderful, she kept telling herself—the opportunity of a lifetime. It was as if a fairy godmother had magically appeared with a wand. Except, of course, that instead of a ball gown and glass slippers Dory wore clay-stained jeans. To protect her hair, she'd covered it with a garish bandanna and her arms were literally coated with liquid clay.

Now, with singleness of purpose, Dory bent over her wheel and concentrated on the object she intended to shape. Long ago she learned that you couldn't throw a pot and think about other things. Her mind was so completely focused on her task that when the doorbell once again rang upstairs, the summons seemed to come from another world.

"Oh, for crying out loud!" At first she wanted to ignore it. Who could it be? Not Neal again. Probably a neighbor collecting for a charity or wanting her to sign a petition—neither of which she was in the mood for. But when the doorbell rang again and again, she gave up, stopped the wheel, covered the pot she'd been working on with a damp cloth, wiped her hands on a paper towel and clumped upstairs.

As she opened the door, she smeared traces of clay still left on her hands onto the brass doorknob. She was frowning about that when she looked up into the face of the man standing on the other side of the threshold.

"Jim!"

"Yes, it's me. I was about to go. I thought maybe you weren't home and had just left a light on in the living room to scare away burglars."

"I was down in the basement working." She stared at him. He was wearing the parka she'd found so attractive on him the last time they'd been together. Outside it had started to snow. Fat white flakes drifted down in the circle of light cast by her porch lamp, coating the wrought iron railing on the porch and dusting the stoop. They'd also begun to collect in Jim's dark hair, where they seemed to glisten like diamonds. He looked wonderful, more wonderful even than she'd remembered, and at the sight of him the admission of love she'd made to Neal echoed in her mind and her heart turned over.

Jim stamped his feet. "It's cold out here," he said. "Can I come in?"

"Uh, yes, of course." A little dazed, she stood aside. As he walked past her, she noticed he was carrying a bottle of champagne. In his other hand he held a small plastic sack.

"It's good to see you, Dory," he said, turning to face her.

"Why, uh, thanks."

"I stopped by a couple of nights ago. I guess Beth told you?"

"Yes."

"This is for you," he said, proffering the bag. "A little Christmas gift."

"Oh, Jim!" Dory exclaimed as she accepted the bag. "I didn't expect anything like this. I'm afraid I don't have anything to give you in return."

"I just bought it on impulse. I saw it and it seemed right for you."

Dory reached into the bag and withdrew a small box wrapped in silver paper. "Do you want me to open it now or put it under the tree?"

"Your choice."

"Then if it's all right with you, I think I'll put it under the tree. It's so nice to have things to open Christmas morning."

He watched as she walked into the living room and slipped the silver box among the other presents. When she returned to the hall he said, "I've been thinking about you and wanting to talk to you. There's a lot I have to say. But it looks as if I haven't picked the best of times," he added, letting his gaze sweep slowly over her.

It was then that she realized how she must look in her dirty old clothes, her hair tied back. Doubtless there were even spatters of clay on her face.

"I'm sorry I'm such a mess," she said. "I've been working in my studio all day."

"I didn't know you had a studio."

"It's nothing fancy, just a place in the basement I cleared the junk away from so I could set up a pottery wheel."

"Oh, really? Could I see it?"

"Yes, I guess so, if you really want to."

"I do."

She glanced at the bottle he held. "Did you want me to do something with that?"

"Could I just leave it in the kitchen for the time being?"

"Sure." What had he brought it for, Dory wondered. Despite her curiosity, she decided not to ask. What was it about this day? For two years there'd been almost no men in her life. Yet in the past twenty-four hours she'd had to beat off two, and now here was Jim—the man she now knew she loved, even if she had no intention of ever admitting it to him.

Downstairs, he walked around the small work area she'd laid out for herself. "You seem to be very busy," he said, pointing at the row of almost identical flour canisters she'd spent the day throwing. "Those can't all be Christmas presents."

"No, they're not intended for Christmas." Haltingly Dory explained what she'd been doing and why.

"That's wonderful," he said, "a terrific opportunity." He looked at her searchingly. "It worried me when I found out that you weren't teaching another class. I was afraid you'd given up something you love because you didn't want to have to deal with me anymore."

"Oh, no," Dory said quickly. "That wasn't the reason. I just felt I needed a break." As she spoke, she realized with disgust that she was doing something she was beginning to hate in herself—compromising her integrity in order to spare someone else's feelings. It was true that she'd needed a break. But Jim *was* part of the reason she'd opted not to teach that class. She'd been afraid that if he'd signed up again she'd find herself drawn into his orbit, and wind up in his bed once more. And that, she was still convinced, could only end in more pain for her.

"You're wondering what I'm doing here, aren't you?" Jim said quietly.

"You said you wanted to talk to me?"

"Yes, but I can see that you're busy and that I've interrupted you."

"It's okay. I needed a break." That much was true.

"Really?"

"Yes." She wanted to know what was on his mind. If he left without telling her, her curiosity would drive her crazy, and she wouldn't be able to work anymore, anyway.

"Actually, there's something I felt like celebrating, and I wanted to celebrate it with you."

"Oh? You've finished your therapy with Sam?"

"Yes, but that's not it. In the past two or three days I've been doing some therapy of my own, and I'd like to tell you about it." He glanced over his shoulder. "Could we go back upstairs?"

"Sure."

"Where's Beth?" he asked as they returned to the upper floor.

"Oh, school let out for Christmas vacation today. She's gone to a pajama party with some girls from her high school. I'm so glad she's finally making new friends that I said it was okay."

"Do they live around here?"

"Not far. I've only met one or two of them. But they seem nice enough. They have a name, actually."

"Oh?"

"Yes, they call themselves the Golden Susans."

"Golden Susans?" Jim frowned, as if he'd just had a troubling thought.

"Can I offer you some coffee or tea?" Dory asked politely.

"No, thanks." He paused, glancing around the hall. "Could we sit in the living room?"

"Why, yes."

But once they were in the living room, Jim looked around with a faintly dissatisfied expression.

Again Dory wondered what he had in mind. "Can I take your coat?" she asked.

"Thanks." He shrugged it off, and gave it to her. Underneath he wore gray slacks and a thick cream-colored fisherman's knit sweater. The casual combination set off his dark coloring and rangy build. As Dory reached to take the coat, her fingers brushed the springy wool of the sweater. A pang of longing shot through her. Quickly she turned away and hurried to the closet opposite the front door.

"I see wood in your fireplace but no ashes. Don't you have fires very often?" Jim asked.

"Not very often," she admitted as she returned to the living room. "It's not that I don't like them. It's just that I'm not much good at building them."

"Well, I'm an ex-Boy Scout. Fire construction happens to be one of my accomplishments. Do you mind if I build a small one for us?"

Dory's eyebrows lifted. What was this all about? "Not at all," she said. She glanced out the window, where snow hissed against the dark panes. "It's a perfect night for a fire."

While Jim arranged pieces of wood on the hearth, Dory pulled the drapes, then switched on the Christmas tree lights. While his back was still turned, she seized the moment to glance into the oval mirror over the Sheraton desk. Instantly she yanked the bandanna off her head and jabbed at her flattened curls.

"Beth told me you were out on a date," Jim said.

"Yes." She swiveled around, relieved to see he was still bent over the hearth and hadn't seen her desperate attempt to primp. She heard the scratch of a match and then flame flared up as he applied the match to one of the screws of twisted paper he'd wedged beneath the wood.

"I know it's none of my business, Dory. But I can't stop myself from asking. How was it?"

"How was my date?"

"Yes." Still bent on one knee, he turned and gazed across the room at her. "Do you intend to see him again?"

"Well, no, actually," she admitted. "I don't think I do."

Jim's shoulders seemed to slump and suddenly she realized how tense he'd been, waiting for her answer.

"Jim," she said as she crossed the room toward him. "What is it? What are you here for?"

"I'm here because I want to tell you some things about me, Dory. I want to see if I can make you understand some things I don't think either of us understood before. And," he added in a lower, more strained tone, "I want to tell you how much, how very much, I've missed you."

CHAPTER FIFTEEN

TOO SURPRISED TO ANSWER immediately, Dory dropped down on the couch and folded her hands in her lap. "I've missed you, too," she finally managed.

"Have you?"

"Yes, I really have."

"Dory, I haven't just missed you. I've been miserable without you. When you walked out on me that day and then started doing everything you could to avoid me, I desperately wanted to come see you and make you change your mind."

"Why didn't you?"

"Because of Lucas. He pointed out how unfair that would be to you, given my situation, and advised me to leave you alone for a while. He suggested I ought to test my feelings for you by seeing other women."

"Oh?" Without knowing any more about it, Dory felt a spurt of irritation—even though she knew Sam's suggestion made sense. "And did you?"

"Yes." Jim sat down cross-legged in front of the hearth and rested his forearms on his knees. "My sister, Maggie, was only too happy to arrange several blind dates."

While Dory listened wide-eyed, he began to describe them, ending the narrative with a heavily edited version of his evening with Jessica Burch.

"All these young women your sister rounded up for you sound wonderful. But this Jessica—a Ph.D. in electrical engineering and she's going to administer government research in Antarctica? My goodness!"

A wicked gleam lit Jim's dark eyes. "She ought to be arriving at the South Pole any day now. What a wonderful Christmas bonus for the guys who've been stationed there. I bet some of them haven't seen a woman in months. Wait until they catch Jessica's act."

"You already caught her act. What did you think?" Privately Dory thought there was no way she could compete with the woman he'd described—no way in the world.

"That's just the point, Dory. I thought she was fabulous. I thought she was one hell of an impressive woman. But I still didn't want her. When I was with her, all I could think of was you."

He turned to poke the fire. A moment earlier he'd pushed the sleeves of his sweater up to his elbows. Dory stared at the way the firelight bathed his skin in a warm, reddish glow and made the short dark hairs covering his forearms gleam.

"There's something else I want to tell you," he continued. "It happened after I left Jessica's apartment building and because I was driving my sister's fancy car."

Calmly, almost tonelessly, he described his encounter with the young thug who'd pulled a knife on him.

When he finished, Dory shivered. "The police were right. You shouldn't have taken such an awful chance. You should have just let him get away."

"I know, but I'm not sorry I did what I did, because it freed me from a fear I've been harboring."

"A fear?"

He stared into the flames. "When I came back from overseas I was a wreck—not just physically, but emotionally, too. There was such a violent anger inside me. It scared me. I was afraid that if I ever let it out—"

"I can imagine," Dory said softly.

Jim shook his head. "No, I don't think you've ever felt as if there were a live bomb ticking away inside of you. But the bomb isn't there anymore, Dory. It exploded—harmlessly, thank God—all over that poor unfortunate kid. For a split second I was angry enough to tear him apart. But I didn't. And now I know I'll never have to worry about myself in that regard again."

Dory longed to reach out and touch his shoulder. Instead she contented herself with saying, "You're really a very gentle person, Jim. I've always known that about you. You've had some terrible experiences, that's all. And you feel things deeply—more deeply than any of the other men I've known."

"From what I've seen of your ex-husband, that's not saying much," Jim commented.

Remembering her morning encounter with Neal, Dory had to smile. "He's never going to win the Nobel Prize for emotional depth," she conceded.

"I don't understand how you could have stayed married to him for so long."

"Neither do I." She shrugged. "But I've changed a lot in the past two years, grown a lot."

"Has he?"

"No, but my guess is that he's about to." Dory thought about Deanna Ingram's flight west. "I suspect the time has come for Neal to do some reevaluating."

Jim stirred the logs, sending a shower of sparks dancing upward like a miniature fireworks display. Outside, the falling snow spit against the windows.

When he turned back toward her his eyes were shadowed. "I don't really want to talk about him. Thinking about the way the man treated you makes me too angry." He hesitated. "There's something I want to tell you, Dory.

Except for Lucas, you'll be the only person I've ever told this to."

Dory felt her shoulders tighten. Slowly she sat forward. "What is it?"

"It's about what happened just before Tom and I were kidnapped—and about why we were kidnapped in the first place."

Stunned and feeling totally unprepared, Dory swallowed and said nothing.

"I think I already explained to you that most of the time we weren't in Afghanistan itself, but just across the Pakistan border near Peshawar."

"Yes."

"There were about two hundred doctors, nurses, medics and hangers-on living in Peshawar those days. They represented close to fifty humanitarian organizations. Some of those people were soldiers-of-fortune-style ultraconservatives who saw themselves battling on the ramparts of freedom. My brother got to be a little like that."

Dory was surprised. "I thought you said he volunteered to go there for strictly humanitarian reasons."

"Yes, but as time went on, he changed. We all did, I guess. We saw and heard so many terrible things, and it affected each of us differently. Anyway, since our group was funded by an American organization we were forbidden from going into Afghanistan because it would directly link the U.S. government to the guerrilla war against the Soviets. We could only treat the refugees who streamed in and train young Afghans as medics, then send them back across the border.

"But we knew that as bad as things were in Peshawar, they were much worse in Afghanistan. Because of the lack of trained medical personnel there, people were dying from even minor wounds. Knowing that drove Tom crazy."

"What happened?"

"He decided to slip across the border so he could see for himself what was going on, and because I was afraid he would be killed if he went on his own, I decided to go with him."

"That was very brave of you."

"Brave or stupid, I'm not sure which. It's hard to explain the situation we faced. The territory around the border was, is, a pretty wild place. It wasn't just the Afghans and Soviets we had to worry about. There are outlaw tribes in the area who had initiated their own terrorist attacks because the Pakistani army had bulldozed their heroin labs up on the Khyber Pass. The year before they had kidnapped an Australian couple and held them for ransom. Everyone knew they'd love to get their hands on some Americans, who might be worth even more money to them."

"And they were the ones who captured you?"

"Yes, but that's not the part of the story I want to tell you, Dory. I want to tell you how it happened."

Suddenly the back of Dory's neck prickled with apprehension. "How did it?"

"We borrowed a jeep and drove through the mountains, past fortified villages of feuding Pathan tribes, toward Terri Mangal on the Afghan border. It was the center of perpetual opium-heroin wars between outlaw tribes, bloody Sunni-Shiite conflicts and roving terror squads."

"My God, Jim! You're making my blood run cold."

"We were pretty nervous ourselves. But I think we might have made it, except—"

"Except what?"

He sighed. "In situations of extreme danger, people feel close to each other, sometimes so close they get confessional. It affected Tom like that."

"What do you mean? You mean he confessed some-thing?"

"He told me about Lauren and him."

"Your wife?"

"My ex-wife. We'd already been divorced for over a year. She'd already remarried. I'd never really understood what had driven us apart, why things had gone sour. Tom ex-plained to me that before the divorce he and Lauren had had a brief affair. They'd both felt too guilty to continue it for long. Nevertheless, though I never knew, it was the begin-ning of the end of our marriage. Nothing was ever right be-tween us after that."

"Oh, Jim. Oh, I *am* sorry." Dory leaped off the couch so that she could kneel on the floor next to him and offer her hand, which he immediately seized. "That must have been a horrible thing for you to hear."

"Yes," he replied gruffly. "It really hurt like hell—the two people I loved and trusted the most. Normally my brother was a very sensitive guy. But telling me like that was a serious miscalculation, one he paid for with his life."

Dory felt his grip on her fingers tighten, as if she were a lifeline to a place of safety. "What do you mean?"

"Though we didn't know it at the time, our jeep was creeping past an encampment of Pathan bandits. I was driving." Jim swallowed. "After Tom told me about Lau-ren, I suddenly couldn't stand to sit next to him. I turned off the engine, jumped out of the jeep and started walking back in the direction from which we'd come. I wasn't thinking straight at all."

"Of course you weren't. That was a very natural reac-tion."

"Given the circumstances, it was an extremely stupid re-action. Tom caught up with me, and we started to argue. We started to shout at each other. Then I took a swing at him.

That's how we were taken, by having a fight practically in the middle of a band of cutthroat drug dealers."

"And all this time you've been feeling guilty about this? Oh, Jim!" Dory put her arm around his shoulder and looked deep into his eyes. "You shouldn't. It was just hideous bad luck."

Jim shook his head. "And hideous bad judgment on both our parts. Dory, in my mind I know it wasn't really my fault, that somehow everything just came together wrong. But my emotions have been telling me something else. For months after Tom died I was in torment, racked with guilt. That's why I went into therapy—to try to work it out of my system somehow."

"And have you?"

"Yes, I think so. I know I have. You remember that picture I bought for my living room? Today I went back to my grandfather's place, back to that creek I told you about where my brother and I used to play. And as I stood there remembering how we were together in those days, I knew it was going to be all right. I knew that that was what I would always keep of Tom, and that I could just let the rest, the painful part, go."

"Oh, Jim, I'm so glad!"

He brought his hands up to her face, cupping it in his palms so that he could gaze deep into her wide blue eyes. "Knowing you has helped. I see you wanting to shake your head, but it's true, Dory. Knowing you, holding you in my arms has helped to heal that wound."

"Jim...I..."

"There's something sweet and wonderful and magic about you, Dory. Magic," he repeated with a groan, and then, still cupping her face, he lowered his head. And suddenly, at the touch of his lips, she felt the magic, too, and it

was all around them. A shimmering web of feeling seemed
to envelop them in the darkened room.

"Oh, Jim," Dory murmured against his mouth, "Oh,
Jim..."

"I want you so much," he whispered fiercely. His hand
slipped down to cradle her back.

"I want you, too," she answered as he lowered her to the
rug. It didn't matter, she told herself as he kissed her again
with an unleashed passion that left her clinging to him, taut
with her own urgent need. Nothing mattered but this gold-
en moment packed with a sweetness that defied reason. Tomorrow she would deal with the consequences.

Tenderly he undressed her, stripping away the flannel shirt
and jeans, then caressing her quivering body with his lips
and hands. Soon his clothing lay abandoned next to hers on
the carpet. Firelight played over their bodies, turning their
flesh to a glowing luster. Sighs and moans of mutual pleasure punctuated by the intimate crackle of the logs filled the
darkened living room.

"Oh, Jim, when you touch me like that..."

"I wish I could touch you like this forever. You're so
lovely, Dory! I can't get enough of you."

As their bodies merged, the fire that bathed them with
radiance seemed to come from within. It sprang high and
hot, consuming them with its feverish brilliance. When at
last it died down, they clung to each other, kissing and caressing, uttering sighs of longing and satisfaction.

"Don't move, Dory. Just let me hold you like this. I feel
as if I have everything in the world I ever wanted in my
arms."

"I have no intention of moving." She clung to him more
tightly, drawing warmth and comfort. At last, her cheek
resting against his shoulder, she opened her eyes so that she
could gaze at the long lean length of his flank and muscled

upper leg. She allowed her hand to stroke along the plane of his chest and down to the indentation of his waist. "Your body is beautiful now."

"Not as beautiful as yours." His hand found her breast and cupped it.

"Yes, just different," she insisted, and then moved so that she could tangle her legs with his and run her toe along the hair-crisped ridge of his calf.

"I don't know why that should be so sexy," he growled, "but it is," and rolled her over on her back so that he could make ardent, demanding love to her all over again.

When at last they were both spent, they lay close, stroking each other idly and gazing into the fire. "I should put another log on," Jim said.

"Oh, but that means you'll have to move."

"Yes, but it can't be helped. We wouldn't want the fire to die on us."

"Certainly not. Then we'd have to breathe new life into its embers," Dory commented with a giggle. Once again she was thinking back to her encounter with Neal. Only that morning she'd brazenly claimed to have made love with Jim in front of the fireplace. Then it had been a lie, but now it was the truth. She'd have to keep the other spots around the house in mind, she thought a little giddily.

Jim sat up, wedged another log in the fire and stirred the ashes. "What's so funny? You're grinning like the Cheshire cat."

"Oh, nothing."

"A moment ago you were praising the way I look in my birthday suit. Now it amuses you?"

"I wasn't laughing at you." She sat up next to him, kissed his shoulder and then reached for her shirt.

"You're not going to get dressed, are you?"

"I think I'd better. Now that all that blazing passion has finally died down, it's a wee bit chilly in here."

He sighed. "I suppose you're right, but I'm not going to pretend to like it."

Dory leered roguishly. "I liked it very much, no pretense involved."

He gave her a playful pinch on the cheek, and then, laughing at each other, they dressed. Jim helped her tuck in her shirt and zip up her jeans and Dory, between joking remarks, did the same for him.

When they were once again fully clothed, Jim went to the window, parted the curtains and peered out. "Wow. It's really coming down out there. If I'm not careful I'll be snowed in and you'll be stuck with me all night."

"I wouldn't mind that."

He looked back at her over his shoulder and smiled. "Me, neither, but I think I'd better not. What if Beth came home unexpectedly?"

"It's unlikely, but I suppose you have a point. You don't have to leave right away, do you?"

He shook his head. "No, that cheap little car of mine has front-wheel drive, so I should be okay here for a while. How about your car? Is the Plum good in snow? You're not going to have to get up and drive Beth to skating practice, are you?"

Dory came and stood next to him by the window. "One of the girls' mothers at this party has a four-wheel-drive vehicle. She's going to drop Beth off at the rink. By morning the snow plows will have been out, so it should be okay."

Jim put his arm around her. "Does Beth like circuses?"

"I guess so. I mean, doesn't everybody? Why do you ask?"

He reached into his pocket and pulled out three tickets. "These were one of my peace offerings. The Moscow Circus is going to be at the Patriot Center Christmas week. You know, dancing bears, Russian acrobats, Cossack trick riding. I was hoping to persuade the two of you to go with me on the twenty-fourth.''

Dory gave a small squeal of delight. ''Oh, Jim, that's a wonderful idea. What a perfect way to spend Christmas Eve. Beth will love it. And so will I.''

''Then it's a date? You're not going to tell me you don't want to get involved with me because I'm such a risky prospect?'' He looked at her anxiously, his gaze searching.

As she realized how important her answer was to him, her heart melted a little more. ''No, I'm feeling a little braver these days, so I'm not going to tell you that. It's definitely a date.''

He tightened his arm around her. Then he ruffled her hair. ''That's all I was hoping for when I came here, you know. I just wanted to persuade you to go on seeing me, to give us a chance. I didn't expect what just happened between us in front of the fireplace.''

''Neither did I,'' Dory replied. ''But I'm not sorry.''

He took her in his arms and held her for a moment. Then he stood back and grinned down at her. ''I think all this agreement calls for a celebration. Why don't we crack open that bottle of champagne I brought?''

''Excellent idea. You open the bottle, and I'll see if I can find some munchies to go with it. Do you like mixed nuts?''

''Love them. That would be just the ticket.''

Arm in arm, they crossed the hall into the kitchen. After Dory flicked on the light, she found a dish towel for Jim to hold around the champagne bottle, then stood back and watched while he pried the cork up. After it exploded with a satisfying little pop, she cheered and got out two of her best crystal glasses. As he filled them, she started to look for the nuts.

"Your glass brimmeth over, *madame*."

"Oh, yes, just a minute," Dory replied as she rooted through her pantry. "I know there's a tin of fancy mixed nuts here. I always keep one around for special occasions."

He came up behind her. "Where do you usually store it?"

"In this corner here by the baking supplies. But I don't see it." Standing on her tiptoes, she began sorting through the boxes and cans on a top shelf. "In fact—that's funny."

"What's funny?"

"It's a good thing I haven't felt like baking lately. I don't see the coconut or the brown sugar, either. And the Karo Syrup is missing." She put her hands on her hips and gazed up at the shelf in obvious exasperation.

As Jim watched her, a thoughtful expression came into his eyes and his brows drew together. "Does this happen very often?"

"Does what happen?"

"Do you find large quantities of food missing?"

She turned around. "Well, when you have a teenager, there's bound to be a certain amount of that."

"Do you think Beth might have taken the nuts?"

"She might have. In fact, she probably did. Neal was complaining to me today about ice cream being missing from his freezer after the last time she was over."

"How about your freezer? Does ice cream disappear out of it?"

"I don't often keep the stuff around. But on the rare occasions when I do, it has a way of vanishing pronto. And I'm never the one who ate it." Dory's brow wrinkled. "Why do you ask? What's on your mind?"

Jim fingered the stem of the champagne glass, then set it down next to the toaster. He wished they hadn't gotten on this subject. It was definitely going to put a damper on their celebration. But he had to tell Dory his suspicions.

"When I dropped around the other night and you weren't here, I spent a little time talking to Beth."

"Yes."

"She's lost quite a bit of weight in a very short amount of time."

Dory nodded. "Yes, I'm very proud of her. That shows a lot of self-control for someone her age and with her sweet tooth."

Jim indicated the open pantry. "If she's making off with tins of nuts and eating whole boxes of brown sugar and coconut, she's not displaying an awful lot of self-control."

"Oh, but I can't be sure about the baking supplies. I haven't done any baking in months. And the nuts—she could have eaten those before she started dieting. I must have bought them well over a month ago."

"What about the missing ice cream your husband complained of?"

Dory looked perplexed. "Well, I suppose she must have had a relapse and gone on a little binge. But she's been so good lately, I really can't make too big a fuss about her raiding Neal's freezer. Truthfully, I think she may have taken off one or two pounds too many. A little ice cream won't hurt her."

"Aren't you concerned about her nutrition?"

Dory had been concerned. It had seemed to her that Beth was slimming down much too quickly. But Jim's question put her in a defensive mode. "No, why should I be? I know what she's eating at home. The meals I feed her are light, but very well balanced and nutritious. I've seen her eating my healthful salads and wholesome soups."

"And I've seen her gulping down shakes and bags of fries at that fast food place up the street."

"What?" Dory's eyebrows rose. "What are you talking about?"

Jim raked a hand through his hair. "This isn't the time I would have picked for this discussion. Maybe we should just drop it."

Dory walked around so that she could confront him. "Oh, no, we can't drop it now. I want to know what's bugging you."

He drummed his fingers against the countertop. "Okay. At the clinic I have access to a lot of facts and figures that you don't. Recently I read a study dealing with eating disorders in adolescent girls."

"Eating disorders!" Dory's hand flew to her heart.

"It's much more widespread than you might imagine. In fact, in our decade it's turning into an epidemic—an extremely dangerous one."

Dory tensed. "You can't be suggesting that Beth might be anorexic. I know that's not true. I watch what she eats, remember? I know that her nutrition is good. Besides, anorexics don't raid the pantry and refrigerator."

"Anorexia isn't the only form that eating disorders can take."

"What are you saying?"

"Morbid obesity is another."

"That's certainly not Beth's problem."

"There's also bulimia."

"Bulimia!" Dory's hand jerked up to her throat and under the kitchen's fluorescent light she turned paper white. "You can't be seriously suggesting that Beth—no, you can't possibly mean that! Jim, that's a terrible thing to say!"

Dory looked so horrified as she stared up at him that he put his hands on her forearms to steady her. But, as if his touch were offensive, she took a step back and shook him off.

"Dory, I'm not telling you that Beth is bulimic. I'm just alerting you to the possibility."

"What in the world would make you think that it was even a possibility?"

"These days, whenever you see a young girl lose weight so swiftly it's something to consider."

"But why would you accuse Beth of such a dreadful thing?"

"I'm not accusing her. Dory, this isn't an accusation. It's just that some of the facts about her weight loss don't quite add up. There's the suddenness of it, and we both know that it started just after she'd experienced a tremendous disappointment."

"South Atlantics, you mean. But she recovered from that," Dory argued. "She's working toward next year. Even though she was attending this pajama party tonight, she insisted on going to skating practice early tomorrow morning."

"It's not just that. It's the binges you've been describing and the way Beth talked when I saw her. When she got on the subject of her weight, she sounded almost fanatic."

"A lot of women are fanatic on that subject. I'm a little that way myself."

"But your skin isn't flaky, and your hair hasn't lost its sheen."

Dory's eyes widened. "All right, I have noticed that her skin has been dry. In fact, last night I gave her some cream. But it's the weather, I'm sure. We have a humidifier, but I don't think it's been working properly. I've been meaning to replace it."

"Fine, that's probably all it is then—just lack of humidity and your cream will do the trick. Look, let's drop it, okay?" He picked up his glass. "Why don't we forget I ever mentioned the subject and go back into the living room and drink our champagne?"

"I don't think so."

"Dory..."

"Jim, I don't feel like drinking champagne now. I'm much too upset."

"Dory, I'm sorry. I didn't mean to distress you. That's the last thing I wanted to do."

"But you have, and now I don't feel like drinking champagne, or...or talking anymore."

Once again he set down his glass. "You want me to leave, is that it?"

"Yes, I think I do."

"Dory..." He gave her an anguished look. Then he shrugged and said heavily, "All right, maybe I'd better."

AFTER HE WAS GONE and she'd heard the muffled sound of his car driving away in the snow, Dory wandered into the living room. Plopping down on the couch, she stared into the dying fire. It was warm in the living room, yet she sat with her knees pressed together, twisting her hands and shivering.

It was hard to believe that less than an hour earlier she'd felt so relaxed and happy. She glanced toward the tree, where Jim's silver-wrapped gift still nestled among the other presents. She'd been so pleased when he'd given it to her. How she felt like hurling it into the fire.

What he'd suggested couldn't possibly have any basis in fact—oh, surely not! Bulimia, that was something movie stars and models with crazy life-styles and twisted values did. She wasn't even sure what it involved and couldn't imagine it going on under her own roof.

Jerkily she stood and closed the glass doors on the fireplace. Then she switched off the tree lights and, ignoring the uncorked bottle of champagne going flat on the kitchen counter, trudged upstairs.

Somehow needing to cleanse herself, she spent fifteen minutes under a hot shower, then slipped into a freshly laundered flannel nightgown. Though it was now after eleven, she didn't feel like going to bed. Nevertheless she got under the blankets and picked up the novel she'd been reading. But she couldn't make it past the open page and after a few minutes tossed it aside.

Restlessly she yanked off the comforter, stuck her feet into slippers and reached for her robe. For a moment she stood staring uncertainly at her door. Then she threw it open and walked down the hall to the bathroom Beth used.

She wasn't really sure what she was looking for, yet when the light was on, her hand went immediately to the mirrored door of the medicine cabinet. The shelves were filled with prescription medicines, some of them badly out of date and needing to be thrown away. There was a little brown bottle that had been in one cabinet or another since Beth was young. It was a substance that all mothers kept around in case of accidental poisoning. But when Dory looked for the bottle she couldn't find it.

Her heart thumping heavily in her rib cage, she closed the cabinet, left the hall bathroom and went into her daughter's bedroom. Dory believed that her daughter was old enough to deserve privacy. But now there didn't seem to be much choice.

The room was in its customary state of disarray, the bed haphazardly made, magazines, books, record jackets and clothes strewn around. Beth had obviously left for this party in a fluster. Dory picked up a pile of sweaters and began to fold them and put them in drawers. While she worked she glanced around, studying the objects cluttering all available surfaces—photographs, ticket stubs, perfume and makeup bottles, half-used lipsticks, buttons and safety pins. When she opened Beth's drawers, she felt around carefully, looking for anything that might give her a clue as to whether Jim's notion had any foundation.

Other than a stash of candy bars, she found nothing incriminating. The candy bars gave her a jolt, though. They were hidden beneath Beth's underwear. Had Beth been eating them recently, or were they left over from before she'd started her diet? Disquieted, Dory began poking around in the corners of Beth's closet.

Much to her relief, she found nothing but dirty laundry and a few overdue library books. It was then that she turned to the wastebasket. It brimmed with paper, much of which was discarded candy wrappers. "Oh, Beth," Dory groaned when she realized how many. Maybe they were left over from before, Dory tried to tell herself. She hadn't really been enforcing room cleanup lately. She sniffed one of the wrappers. The residue of chocolate in the creases smelled fresh.

The discovery sent a surge of panic through Dory. Decisively she tipped the overflowing wastebasket over and began pawing through its contents. Hidden inside a paper bag she discovered the little brown bottle that had been missing from the medicine cabinet. Ipecac Syrup, the label read. And it was empty.

Dazed, horrified, Dory left her daughter's room. For many minutes she paced aimlessly up and down the hall while she tried to assimilate the implications of what she'd found. Finally she wandered back into her bedroom, shut the door and pulled a chair up to the window. With the light off, she could see the snow falling through the darkness, coating the world in a blanket of purity.

Somewhere out in that whiteness Beth was probably still awake, laughing with her new friends. *Should I call her now,* Dory wondered, *make her come home so I can talk to her about this?* But, no, it was too late. She'd have to wait until

Beth came back from her practice. Then she would confront her.

But what good was that going to do? *I need to have a plan,* Dory thought. *Just talking won't solve this problem.*

She went downstairs, got paper and pencil out of the Sheraton desk and took them back up to her room. There, in front of the window, shielded from the outside world by a curtain of snow, she began making a list: Call Sam Lucas and set up an appointment; set up an appointment for a medical exam; speak to Beth's counselor at school; see Neal and have a <u>serious</u> discussion with him about this situation; set up an appointment with a nutritionist.

Beth had to be made to understand that what she was doing could ruin her health. *If she is so committed to being thin, maybe I should look into professional weight control programs,* Dory thought. Maybe they could help her go at this in a constructive way. She went back downstairs for the phone book, then started writing down names and numbers of organizations in the Yellow Pages.

Dory was up half that night, alternately pacing back and forth thinking, or writing lists of things to do, things to think about, places to call for help and information. By four o'clock in the morning, however, she was so exhausted that she finally fell asleep in her chair.

When gray light began filtering through the window, she woke up. The first thing she saw was a list. With a groan, she glanced at her watch, then stumbled to her feet and headed for the bathroom, where she took another shower. In another hour she could drive to the rink and pick Beth up.

Dory was downstairs snatching a last cup of coffee before setting off, when the phone rang.

"Dory?"

"Yes." Dory's stomach clenched as she recognized the voice of Peggy Schrion, Beth's coach.

"It's Peggy. I'm at the rink."

"Why are you calling? Has something happened?"

"I'm afraid so."

"It's Beth, isn't it?" Dory's fingers strangled the telephone cord.

"Dory, she collapsed a few minutes ago."

"Collapsed!"

"I don't know what happened. One minute she seemed okay, a little pale and tired, maybe, but nothing seriously wrong. Then she just fell down on the ice, and we couldn't get her to come to."

"Oh, my God!"

"I called an ambulance. They're taking her to emergency now. Maybe you'd better meet us there."

CHAPTER SIXTEEN

"DORY?"

She looked up from the plastic chair where she huddled in the Emergency waiting room. "Jim!"

She'd been gazing at the floor for what seemed like hours, so lost in her thoughts that she hadn't even noticed when he'd come in. Now he stood directly in front of her, looking different in his white doctor's coat, more distant and official somehow.

"It's going to be all right." He dropped down into the chair next to hers, and suddenly he was the Jim she knew. "Don't look that way. It's going to be all right."

When she'd arrived at Emergency and they'd asked for the name of Beth's doctor, she'd given Jim's. As soon as he'd received the call he'd rearranged his other appointments and rushed over.

"Is she awake now?" Dory's lips felt stiff.

"Yes, though she's a little groggy. We've put some drugs into her and they're affecting her."

"Drugs?"

"Nothing dangerous, just something to put her chemistry back on an even keel."

Dory's knuckles were white. "Can I go to her now?"

After filling out the proper forms, and before Jim had arrived, they'd allowed her to look in on Beth briefly. But at that time the teenager had still been unconscious. Seeing her daughter lying in the Emergency ward so pale and still, hooked up to an IV unit, had scared the life out of Dory.

"Yes, you can see her. But first I want to talk to you." He glanced around. "Let's go to the cafeteria. It should be nearly empty this time of the morning, and we can have a little privacy."

With a short, silent nod Dory agreed. Then, shakily, she stood and allowed him to guide her through a maze of green-tiled corridors and into a small, brightly lit eating area. Jim was right. Only a few people sat at the Formica tables. She and Jim were able to find an isolated spot in the corner.

"Do you want something to drink?"

Dory shook her head, but he ignored that. "You look like a ghost. I'm going to get coffee."

He strode to one of the machines, returning a few minutes later with a steaming Styrofoam cup of coffee which he placed directly in front of her. She wrapped her cold hands around it and held on as though it were the only source of heat on an iceberg at the North Pole.

"Tell me the truth, Jim. Why did this happen? Has she been... has she been...?" Dory's eyes pleaded with him.

"Beth is bulimic."

"Oh, God!"

"Before you get any more upset than you already are, she's only been this way for a few weeks. All her tests aren't in yet, but she's young, and basically as healthy as a horse. Since the time in which she's been abusing herself is so short, I don't believe any serious damage has been done. My guess is that she'll be out of here and back home with you in twenty-four hours."

Was he just humoring her, Dory wondered. "If it's not so serious, why did she black out like that?"

"Beth is an athlete. According to her couch, she was trying to complete a difficult triple jump. Chemical imbalances are likely to make themselves known in a body upon which physical demands are being made sooner than in the average person's. It's a lucky thing, actually."

"Lucky!"

"Yes, because it's going to give us the chance to nip this business in the bud."

"Oh, God, if only we can." Haltingly Dory described the way she'd searched Beth's room and what she'd found.

"Ipecac." He nodded. "That fits in with everything else she told me."

"You've actually talked to her about this?"

"Not in any detail. But when she came to, I had to ask her some pretty pointed questions. It was important to my diagnosis."

"Of course."

"At first she didn't want to answer those questions. But when she realized I already had an idea what was going on, she broke down. I suspect she's been wanting to tell someone, but she was just too ashamed and guilty to confess on her own."

"And I've been too blind to see it."

"Don't berate yourself over this, Dory." Jim's dark eyes gazed straight into hers. "There are girls who go on this way for many months without their parents ever suspecting. And when they do find out, the habit is so ingrained that it's almost impossible to break. Fortunately that's not going to be the case with Beth."

"You sound so sure."

"I am sure." He took Dory's hand. "Listen to me. Beth knows that what she's been doing is wrong, and she's filled with guilt and remorse. I honestly don't think it will take much to translate that guilt and remorse into positive action. But we have to think carefully about this."

Dory stared at him, suddenly aware through her misery of the surprising attitude Jim seemed to be taking. He was talking about the situation almost as if he were Beth's father. "Why, yes, of course," she said. "I can't think about anything else."

He leaned toward her. "You should know that Beth didn't start this business on her own. She got involved in it through a set of girls at school—the Golden Susans."

Dory's jaw dropped. "Oh, no. She spent the night with those girls."

"Yes, that's what probably brought on her blackout this morning."

"Their parents need to be told."

"Yes, but we can talk about this some more after you've seen Beth and after her test results are in."

"And after we've both had a little more time to think."

He nodded, then consulted his watch. Dory could see from his grim expression that his mind was on the things he planned to do next. "Why don't you see Beth now? Then I think we should meet again and make some decisions."

"Yes," she said, still feeling both surprised and comforted by the degree to which he was involving himself.

"I can't stay at the hospital much longer. I have to go back to my office and take care of some of my other appointments. How about getting together this afternoon around three?"

"Anything you say." She took her hands off the still-warm coffee cup, which she hadn't drunk out of, and started to get up.

Jim stood too, then put his hand on her shoulder. "Dory, after you've seen Beth, go home and get some sleep. You look like the walking dead."

"Oh, Jim, I don't know if I can."

"Take a sleeping pill if you have to. I'll write you a prescription. Believe me, you're going to need your strength."

IT TOOK ALL Dory's strength to walk into her daughter's hospital room and not cry. "Beth?"

"Mom?" Beth turned her face away from the wall. Her cheeks were tracked with tears. When she saw her mother, fresh moisture began to leak from the corners of her reddened eyes. "Oh, Mom."

Dory hurried to her side and, careful not to disturb the needles attached to Beth's arms, kissed her and hugged her gently. "How are you doing, baby?"

"Terrible. Do you ... do you know?"

Dory didn't need to ask for clarification. "Yes, Jim told me all about it."

Beth squeezed her teary eyes shut. "I feel so awful. I know you must hate me."

"Of course not!" Once again Dory hugged and kissed her daughter. "I love you. I love you very much."

"I don't see how you can."

"That's because you're not a mother. Wait until you have a daughter of your own." Through the mist in her eyes, Dory tried to smile.

Beth sniffed. "Does Dad know?"

"Not yet." Dory hadn't even given Neal a thought. The realization made her feel guilty. She supposed she should have called him right away. Instead she'd thought only about calling Jim.

"Does Dad have to know?" Beth's gaze was anguished.

"I'm afraid he does, honey."

"Couldn't you wait a little bit?"

"How can I do that? He's your father. It wouldn't be right not to tell him as soon as possible."

Beth moaned. "I can just imagine what he's going to say."

Dory could, too—and she wasn't looking forward to hearing it.

An hour later, when she finally left Beth and the hospital, her exhaustion was so overpowering that she could barely stumble out to the parking lot. Nevertheless she stopped on the way home to fill Jim's prescription. She knew that if she didn't, she'd lie wide-awake in her bed, her mind seething until she made herself sick. And he'd been right. She *was* going to need every ounce of strength she possessed.

Once back in her town house, Dory called Neal's office, only to be told that he would be in court until late that afternoon. Part of her was relieved she wouldn't have to deal with his anger and recriminations until she'd gotten some sleep.

Her alarm went off in time so that she had a few minutes to make herself presentable before Jim arrived. When she opened the door to him, she thought he looked pale. But there was a hard-edged determination about him. It was expressed in the way he held himself, the set of his features, even the brisk manner in which he strode past her into the living room.

As she followed him, it occurred to her that she was seeing a different side of the man who'd become such an important part of her life. This Jim bore little resemblance to the person she'd first met, the one who'd been uncertain about himself and his future. On the contrary, this was a man who, once he decided on a course of action, wouldn't be balked. And somehow she got the feeling he'd made a number of decisions.

"Beth's tests are in," he said as he unbuttoned his jacket. "I was right. She should be coming home sometime tomorrow."

"Thank goodness." Dory sagged into the nearest chair.

He sat down opposite. "Yes, but I've been consulting some experts on the bulimia syndrome. I'm afraid the battle isn't over. In fact, it's just began."

"I know that." Dory got up to hand him the lists she'd made the night before. "These are some of the things I was thinking about doing to help Beth."

Frowning thoughtfully, he studied them. While he read, Dory paced back and forth in front of the fireplace. She was feeling a lot less crushed than she had last night and this morning. Her mind had begun to work more efficiently. She shot a grateful glance at Jim. Just the knowledge that she wasn't alone in this, that she had an ally, made all the difference.

"Most of the ideas in these lists are good, Dory. But before implementing them, there are some things that need to be done first."

"It feels as if there are a million things that need to be done. I haven't even gotten in touch with Neal yet."

Over the top of the sheets of paper she'd given him, he looked at her intently. "Would you mind if I went to see him?"

The suggestion startled her. "That's my job. I should tell him before anyone else does."

"Yes, but after you've done that. I'd like to talk to him personally. In fact, if you'd write down his address, I'd like to stop by his place on my way home from the office tonight. Do I have your permission?"

Dory gazed at him, nonplussed. What did he have in mind? But, she reminded herself, Jim was Beth's doctor now. Maybe it made sense. "All right. But what do you suggest I do with the rest of this afternoon?"

"Beth's school should be informed about what's going on."

"I can't attend to that until tomorrow."

"There's a very unpleasant job that needs doing. As soon as possible, someone has to talk to the parents of these Golden Susans."

Dory blanched. He was right to describe the task as unpleasant. Ghastly was more like it. But he was also correct about it having to be done. She took a breath. "Okay. While you're speaking with Neal, I'll go see each of them."

"That's not necessary, Dory."

"I think it is. This is just too important for a phone call."

He grimaced. "You're making it hard on yourself, but maybe you're right. Good luck." He stood and they faced each other, their eyes saying more than either was ready to put into words. "I'll get in touch with you again tonight."

"Thanks. I appreciate that." She held out her hand. "I really do mean it, Jim. I'm not sure why you're going to all this trouble, doing all this, but I'm very, very grateful."

He stared at her. "You really don't know why I'm doing this?"

"I...no..." She shook her head.

"Then I'll have to explain it to you, won't I? I'll do that as soon as I get the chance. And when I do, I'll make very certain that you understand."

GETTING UP to Neal Barker's fancy condo was more complicated than Jim had anticipated. Neal lived in Harbor Court, an elegant new brick building overlooking Baltimore's renovated Inner Harbor.

Besides an astronomical price tag, Harbor Court condominiums featured an iron-clad security system. "Sign in here, please," the man at the desk said, "and I'll call up to see if Mr. Barker can receive you."

While Jim scribbled his name in the leather-bound book, he watched with interest as the guard picked up a phone and pushed a complicated set of buttons. The conversation between him and the person on the other end of the line was terse.

"Mr. Barker will see you," the man finally said, but as Jim stepped into the chrome-and-black-marble elevator that whisked him to the nineteenth floor, he had the distinct impression he hadn't squeaked past with any hospitality to spare.

Jim was in no mood to be impressed by anything about Dory's ex-husband, but he had to admit that the guy wasn't exactly toughing it out in a hovel. Neal Barker's green marble foyer opened into an expansive living room with nine-foot ceilings and a view so spectacular it would stop any visitor in his tracks. Through the floor-to-ceiling windows the harbor, now carpeted with lights, spread itself out like a satellite photograph.

"Nice place you have here," Jim said, gazing down at the way the setting sun made the water look like wrinkled black silk. Next he took a quick survey of his surroundings, eyeing the glossy antique reproductions, which had that inimitable hundred-dollar-an hour decorator touch and which fairly screamed "affluent bachelor on the make."

It was impossible not to contrast Dory's homey little town house with all this self-conscious luxury and wonder how she and Neal Barker had managed to live together for ten years. On the other hand, no wonder Beth adored spending the weekend with her father. Riding up the elevator to this cushy tower castle must make her feel like a princess.

"Somehow I don't think you're here to admire the decor," Neal muttered with palpable hostility. "Just what did you come for?"

"Dory didn't call you about Beth?"

"I've been in court all day. I didn't get in until ten minutes ago."

The phone on an inlaid, marble-topped desk rang and Neal picked it up. Jim knew after only a few words had been exchanged that it was Dory on the other end of the line. He also knew the exact moment when she told her ex his daughter's problem.

"W-w-what?" Neal spluttered, clearly flabbergasted. His mouth dropped open, destroying the perfect symmetry of his Boy Scout profile. A few minutes later he hung up with a crash and whirled to confront Jim. "Well, now, at least I have some clue as to why you've showed up at my doorstep."

"I'm here to talk to you about Beth."

"Because Dory's made you her doctor and you think that gives you some kind of authority? We'll see about that!"

Neal, flushed and clearly upset, hotfooted it to the small bar on the mirrored wall next to the window and began pouring himself a stiff drink. Though he didn't offer one to Jim, Jim felt almost sorry for the man. Neal didn't look like someone who'd had a good day.

"That clears up the mystery of the missing ice cream," he muttered as he raised his glass to his lips. He took a long, thirsty swallow and grimaced. "When I think of the money I've spent on that kid, and now this! She's really let me down."

Jim lost all his sympathy. "If Beth's let you down, it's because you've let her down, and badly."

"Hey!" Neal set his half-empty glass down with a clank. "What are you getting at?"

"Barker, I wanted to see you like this because I can say things to you that Dory can't."

"Such as?"

"Beth talked to me in the hospital. She was upset enough to come out with things that Dory hasn't heard and that I don't want her to hear. Do you love your daughter?"

Neal's neck began to redden. "Of course I love my daughter. You've got a hell of a nerve! What makes you think you have the right to ask such a question of me?"

"I'm asking it because I want Beth to get past this potentially ruinous eating disorder she's developed, and I'm convinced that her relationship with you is behind a lot of her problem."

"Her relationship with me? What have I got to do with it? What about her relationship with her mother? Beth sees a lot more of Dory than she does me."

"That's part of the dilemma. Beth adores you. When you divorced her mother, she felt you'd rejected her, too. Right now your love and approval are worth more to her than anyone else's and she thinks she has to be perfect to win them.''

"Well, she certainly has a funny way of showing it.''

"What do you mean?''

"Screwing up at South Atlantics, turning into a teenage blimp and then choosing this way to get thin. None of it is very appealing—or perfect,'' Neal spit.

Jim scowled, and then in a slow, dangerous prowl crossed the room to the younger man. "Don't you dare say anything like that to her.''

"What?'' Neal stiffened.

"You have to make her believe that you love and accept her no matter what she does—that you'll never be judgmental of her the way you've been of her mother. And if you don't really feel that it's the truth, then you're going to have to do some Oscar-winning acting.''

"Are you threatening me?''

"You bet I am. Do you have any idea what sort of dangers bulimics face? Bulimia isn't just an unappealing way of controlling weight. It can kill.'' One by one Jim ticked off every item on the deadly list of consequences he'd now committed to memory.

By the time Jim had finished, Neal Barker was ashen. He stumbled to a chair and sank into it. "I didn't realize. I'd never want anything like that to happen to Beth. I do love her. Of course I love my little girl. If I can't get back together with Dory, she's the only thing I've got really.''

Jim's eyes narrowed. "That's why I came here. You need to realize the dangers and take them seriously. And you need to know that you're the key to the problem.''

"I still don't understand what you think I should do.'' Neal shook his head.

"Just offer her all the love and support you can. Don't let her feel that you've abandoned her, or that you find her repulsive in some way.''

"Repulsive? I never felt anything like that."

Jim shrugged. "Her secret fear is that you do. I've treated girls Beth's age, so I know they can get some very strange ideas into their heads—ideas they're not equipped to deal with constructively."

"I'll say. I could never find my own daughter repulsive."

"Convince her of that."

Neal sighed and then glanced longingly at the drink he'd abandoned. "All right. You have my word on it that I'll try." Under his brows he shot Jim a suspicious look. "But you'll never convince me that you came over here just to talk about Beth. There's something else on your mind, isn't there?"

"You're right," Jim conceded. "There is something else."

"What?"

"A minute ago you mentioned the possibility of getting back together with Dory." Jim planted his feet wide apart, put his hands on his hips and shook his head. "I want to let you know, Barker, that if I have anything to say about it, that will never happen. I'm in love with your ex-wife. I'm crazy about Dory, and if I can convince her to have me, I want to marry her."

A FEW DAYS LATER Jim sped north in his car with Dory and Beth along the Washington beltway, headed back home from the Patriot Center in Fairfax, where they had just been spectators at the Moscow Circus.

"That was sooo wonderful!" Beth exclaimed.

"Yes, it really was," Dory agreed.

Jim chuckled. "That makes it unanimous. I thought it was the best entertainment I've seen in years." He checked the rearview mirror to make sure Beth's expression matched the enthusiasm in her voice. It did.

"I wonder how they get bears to juggle that way," the girl questioned.

Dory turned toward the back seat. "I suppose they train them from the time they're cubs. They *were* cute."

"Oh, yes! And those seventeen Sumatran tigers jumping through fiery hoops! What a blast!"

"For my money, the Cossack trick riders were the most impressive," Jim interjected.

All the way home they debated the merits of the various acts. Every now and then, Jim and Dory shot each other pleased glances. Since this was only the fourth day since Beth had come home from the hospital, they hadn't decided until the last minute whether they could actually take her to the circus. But her recovery had been so swift and she'd been so excited when she'd heard about the tickets that they'd finally agreed to risk it.

Obviously it had been the right thing to do. Beth fairly glowed. And she seemed to particularly enjoy an outing with them, almost as if being part of something that resembled a family unit was reassuring to her.

When they arrived back at the town house, the clock on the mantel read past ten and the teenager began to droop. Dory lit the Christmas tree lights and after Jim made a small fire, they had cups of hot cider together on the couch. Soon, however, Beth wished them both good-night and a Merry Christmas and went upstairs to her room.

After Jim and Dory were sure she was out of earshot, they gave each other long looks.

"Well, what do you think?" he questioned.

"I think those tickets were a godsend. It was the perfect thing to do with her on Christmas Eve. Thank you for thinking of it and for taking us."

"You know how welcome you are, but I didn't mean that. What do you think about Beth? How's she doing?"

Dory studied the soft pink glow a Christmas tree light cast on an adjacent angel-shaped ornament. Then she sighed. "As you can imagine, I've been watching her like a hawk, so I know she's all right so far. I'm keeping an inventory of what's in the pantry and refrigerator. There's no ipecac in this house, and no candy or rich foods to stuff on, either. For a while there I was worried because she didn't seem to want to eat anything at all."

"That's not a surprising reaction."

"But the past couple of days she's been eating more normally. We've had several long talks about it. She's very sorry and embarrassed about what happened and says she wants to establish sensible habits. We're going to work together to do that over the holidays before she starts back to school."

"Not the best of times for that."

"No, but this holiday isn't going to be like any other. Neal is going to help, so I think we might just manage to do it. I mean, it made such a difference in Beth's attitude when he came over here to see her and asked her to spend Christmas Day with him. He's agreed to take responsibility for cutting down her allowance so she won't be able to afford to eat out. And he promised me there wouldn't be any ice cream in his freezer."

"He'll have to do more than that. What about the rich restaurant dinners he's always liked to feed her?"

"Jim, he talked to me about it, and I believe he's really sincere. He's going to have their Christmas meals catered. They're going to be eating all low calorie foods—lean meats, salads, Jell-O."

"Hmm." Jim rubbed his chin. "Quite a sacrifice for him, I imagine."

"It is. Neal loves his rich foods. When we were married Christmas dinner had to be a banquet fit for Henry VIII. Now he's really being supportive, and I'm very grateful."

Speculatively Jim eyed the woman next to him. In honor of the season, she was wearing a red wool dress. Its long loosely pleated skirt flared around her hips and fell softly to her knees. The fitted bodice molded the fullness of her breasts. Between them tiny gold buttons marched to the dress's rounded neckline and set off the halo of golden curls around her face.

As Jim remembered the silken texture of those curls and the rounded beauty of those breasts, he swallowed and looked away. He hadn't told Dory the details of his conversation with her ex-husband. But, judging from Neal's about-face, it had paid off—*maybe more handsomely than I'd bargained for,* Jim suddenly thought. What if Dory decided Neal Barker wasn't such a bad guy, after all?

Frowning, Jim cleared his throat. "Because of the holidays, it hasn't been so easy getting appointments at the clinic. But I've got Beth set up with an excellent nutritionist for next Tuesday."

"Great! And she's already seeing Sam. As a favor to me, he rearranged his schedule and they had a session together yesterday."

"Wonderful. I can testify that he's a good man." Jim tapped the handle of his cup. "Have you heard anything more from the parents of the Golden Susans?"

"Not since I went to see them all. Oh, Jim, that was so awful!"

"I can imagine."

"No." Dory's eyes clouded. "It's like when you told me about your terrible experiences in Afghanistan. I sympathized and said I could imagine what it must have been like, and you answered that it was impossible to imagine. You had to be there. Well, telling these people about their daughters was like that. You had to be there."

"None of them had suspected?"

"No. They'd all been completely fooled. Such a thing hadn't even entered their heads, just like me. So you can understand their shock." Dory grimaced. "In fact, I'm not even sure they all believed me and will act on what I told them. One woman, Melissa Fairbanks's mother, practically chased me out of her house. I know she thought I was just a crazy alarmist."

"For her daughter's sake, I hope you're wrong. Have you considered that it's going to be pretty tough for Beth to go back to that school?"

"Not just tough, impossible," Dory answered emphatically. "When Neal came over, we discussed this. We agreed that Beth can't return to that environment. We're going to send her to the high school in her old neighborhood. That way she'll be with Gracie Prentice and the other kids she grew up with."

"It may not be so easy to arrange with the school board. They can be sticky about that sort of thing."

"Oh, Neal can do it," Dory stated confidently. "He's not a top-notch lawyer for nothing. When he wants something, he gets it."

"You ought to know," Jim muttered. *Neal again,* he thought, trying to keep the frown out of his eyes. When Dory mentioned her ex-husband's name, it was in an entirely different tone of voice. Had he outsmarted himself by talking some sense into the guy? The notion sent an arrow of alarm plunging into Jim. He decided to shift the conversation onto a different track. "Did you know that Howard County has an eating disorder support group?"

"Really?" Dory looked surprised. "You mean like Alcoholics Anonymous?"

"Something along those lines. It was formed fairly recently. I don't think Beth's quite ready for it yet, but maybe later."

"Yes! Something like that would be good for her. Who's in it?"

"Mostly girls Beth's age or older. In fact, remember Janice from your ceramics course?"

"Of course I do. You're not going to tell me that she was bulimic." Dory's eyes widened in amazement.

"Anorexic. Apparently that's why she was taking pottery with her mother. It was part of her therapy—family togetherness."

"Well, it must have worked. She looked fine to me."

"Yes, she did." Jim set his cider cup down on the coffee table, then reached over and took Dory's hand. "Kids do recover from this sort of thing. It's never easy, but they have a lot of resilience and they do make it."

"Oh, I know they do."

Tears came to Dory's eyes, tears Jim felt an overwhelming urge to kiss away because it hurt him to see her unhappy or in pain.

"I know Beth will get over this," she whispered earnestly. "I know a year from now she'll be fine and this will all be in the past. I have to believe that. I can't believe anything else."

Jim tightened his fingers on hers, but he made no move to take her into his arms and comfort her with his hands and lips. So much had happened since they'd made love in front of this fireplace that it seemed aeons ago. It wasn't just the trauma of Beth's collapse that had changed things. It was also the new understanding Dory seemed to have reached with her ex-husband.

Though Jim had seen her and frequently talked to her on the phone during the past few days, their conversations had centered around Beth. They'd been professional in tone, almost as if their previous intimacy had been pushed aside and forgotten. Now Jim felt unsure how she would respond to a physical overture from him, and he didn't want to press her in a way that might alienate her. Carefully he said, "You mentioned that Beth was going to be spending Christmas Day with her father. What about you? Will you be joining them?"

Dory gave a quick little shake of her head. "Oh, no, I don't think so. There's a lot of work to be done around here and in my studio. I still have that department store order to fill, you know."

"I see." Jim considered her. "It's a big job. I guess I thought that with all that's happened, you might have decided to give it up."

Dory thrust out her chin defiantly. "Definitely not. I want to have a business of my own. It's very important to me."

"I can see that it is—and I'm glad." He hesitated. "Still, making pots by yourself . . . that doesn't sound like much of a Christmas."

"If I get lonely or bored, I can always drop in on the Prentices."

That brought a smile to his lips and he shook his head. "You're not the type who just drops in on people. You need an invitation."

She lowered her eyes. "You know me too well."

"I'd like to know you even better, Dory. I'd like to know you better than anyone else in the world." The little silence that fell between them was interrupted by the sharp crack of a burning log. Jim cleared his throat. "Here's an invitation I wish you'd consider. How about spending Christmas with me?"

She looked up, her lips slightly parted. "You're not going to your sister's place?"

"Fond as I am of Maggie, I'd much rather be with you."

"I—I'm flattered. But we haven't made any plans. I mean I haven't shopped for a Christmas dinner or anything. What would we do?"

"I don't know, but we could eat at a restaurant, and after that I'm sure we could find some mutually pleasant way to pass the time." He thought he saw her cheeks pinken, though it was hard to tell in the light from the Christmas tree.

"Yes, I suppose we could. All right," she murmured.

"All right, it's a date?"

"Yes." She looked away. "Would you like more cider? There's plenty left on the stove."

He rested his hands on his knees. "Actually, what I'd like now is that champagne toast we started last week but never finished. You remember, don't you?"

Her gaze darted back to his, and now he was sure that her cheeks had gone a shade darker. "Of course I remember. But I'm afraid that bottle went flat and I emptied it into the sink."

"I have another bottle in the car."

"You do?"

"Yes, I didn't bring it in because I wasn't sure whether you'd be receptive."

She cocked her head. "Didn't you? Well, I am receptive. Very. Hadn't you better get it before it freezes and explodes all over your upholstery?"

He answered her sparkling smile with a grin that lit his eyes. "Yes, I think maybe I had."

By the time Jim had returned, Dory had placed two crystal glasses on the coffee table in front of the fire. With flushed cheeks, she watched while he pried off the champagne cork, which flew up to the ceiling with a satisfying pop.

"What kind of a toast do you want to propose?" she asked as he filled the glasses. "Do you want to drink to Beth's recovery?"

"That's not a bad idea, but it's not what I had in mind." He gazed down at the bubbling glasses and then across the coffee table at Dory. "I'd like to drink to us, and to the many Christmases I hope we'll share in the future."

She blinked as she absorbed his words, then repeated questioningly. "To us and our *many* Christmases?"

It was too late to turn back now, so Jim decided to forge ahead. "A few days ago you came out with something that surprised me, and hurt me a little. You thanked me for helping Beth. Then you said you weren't sure why I was getting so involved."

"That hurt you? I'm sorry, I didn't mean..."

"Dory," he said in a low voice that suddenly quivered with tension, "don't you understand that I want to be involved with every aspect of your life? Don't you understand that I'm in love with you?"

Her jaw dropped. "I...you never said...you said you just wanted—"

"Oh, Lord, I said a lot of stupid things. And there are a lot of things I want in this life. But a casual affair with you isn't one of them. I'm in love with you, and I've felt that way for a long time."

"You have?"

"Why do you think I went rushing up to Philadelphia? You were the magnet that drew me, that drew me from the first moment I laid eyes on you. I kept telling myself that you weren't my type."

"I thought the same thing."

"At first I was afraid that it was just—"

Her hands flew to her throat. "So was I!"

"But since I've met you, no other woman holds the slightest appeal. When we're apart, you're all I think of. If I should lose you, it would be far worse than anything I've ever endured. I love you, Dory. I love everything about you, and I want to share your problems and your joys. I want to make my life with you."

Forgetting the champagne, forgetting everything but Dory, he rounded the table and gathered her into his arms. He met with no resistance. She threw her arms around his neck and gladly lifted her face to his.

"Oh, Dory," he murmured before covering her lips and sating himself with their sweetness.

As the kiss went on, they held each other tightly. And when they had breath enough and space, they murmured incoherent assurances and endearments.

"I was so afraid," Jim whispered against her cheek.

"Afraid of what?"

"The way you talked about Neal. I was afraid that you'd decided to go back to him."

"Never. How could I do that after knowing you? I love you, Jim. Every wonderful thing you just said about me, that's how I feel about you, only doubled."

"Impossible. There isn't room enough in the universe," he declared before kissing her yet again.

At last they parted long enough to pick up their neglected champagne glasses and drink to the toast he had proposed.

"To us and the many Christmases I hope we'll share," Dory said, raising her glass and gazing into his dark eyes. Hungrily they kissed again and again, feeding from each other's lips. But at last they drew apart and sat together on the couch, their arms around each other.

"Were you really afraid I might go back to Neal?" Dory asked as she snuggled against Jim's shoulder.

"Very. You were married to him for ten years, after all. And now this situation with Beth is bound to bring you together."

"Yes, but I would never want to be his wife again. I've changed too much. I'm a different person. Even when I thought there wasn't any hope for us, I knew I had to go on alone—that I could never go back to Neal."

He stroked her hair. "You don't know how happy that makes me feel."

She grinned up at him. "What else would make you happy?"

"I think you can guess." He kissed the tip of her nose. "But with Beth upstairs, it's impossible."

"We have all day tomorrow."

"I haven't looked forward to Christmas so much since I was a kid."

She laughed, but then a frown puckered her brow. "I feel guilty that I haven't got a gift for you. I meant to buy something special, but with all that's been happening there's been no chance."

"You haven't opened my present yet. How do you know it's not a box of paper clips or a ninety-eight-cent bottle of cologne?" He pointed to the small silver-wrapped box, still tucked under the tree.

"It wouldn't matter if it was. But I'm certain it's not."

"Maybe you'd better open it just to be sure."

"Do you want me to?"

When he nodded, she plucked the box out of its resting place and undid the shimmering bow. "Oh, Jim!" she exclaimed after she opened the small white box. "What a beautiful ring!" She held the intricately worked silver circlet up against the firelight. "It's exquisite. Such beautiful blue stones!"

"They reminded me of the color of your eyes."

"I love it," she declared, and slipped the ring onto the middle finger of her right hand.

They both gazed down at the ornament and then Jim took her other hand in his. "Would you like a different kind of ring? Would you like a diamond?"

Dory drew in a sharp breath. "Oh, Jim!"

"Because if you would, we could pick one out together."

Slowly she exhaled. "I don't think so."

"No?" He looked at her searchingly.

"Jim, I'm just not ready yet. So much has happened. So much is going on. I need time to sort things out." Her gaze searched his. "Do you understand?"

Swallowing his disappointment, he nodded. "Yes."

"Do you really?"

"Yes. But I'm going to ask again. And I'm going to keep asking."

She offered him her lips. "I love persistent men."

"And I love you, Dory Barker." Slowly he lowered his mouth toward hers. "I love you."

EPILOGUE

DORY STOOD BACK as Jim inserted the key into their motel room door. "I don't know if I'm going to be able to bear watching it," she said.

"There's no way you can get out of being a terrified on-looker when Junior Ladies compete in freestyle tomorrow. So steel yourself." He stood aside so that she could walk past him into the room. It wasn't the same one they'd first made love in a year earlier, but very similar with its nondescript furnishings and queen-size bed. After all the time they'd spent together at the rink, watching Beth once again come in fifth in figures, Dory had been chilled. Now something inside her warmed. Jim was being so wonderfully supportive, and she loved him so much!

"I suppose you're right. I'll just have to be strong." She began to unbutton her alpaca coat, one of the many small luxuries she'd been able to purchase from the proceeds of her booming pottery business. Dory no longer worked as a receptionist for Sam Lucas. Filling the orders that had begun flooding in for her handmade wares once they started appearing in a major department store was far too time-consuming and far too rewarding.

"Dory, sweetheart, relax. Beth isn't the mixed up kid she was last year. She can handle this whole scene a lot better."

"I know, but can I?"

Jim crossed the room, slipped his arms under hers and drew her toward him. "You don't know it, but you're made of very sturdy stuff, sweetheart," he said. "Stop underestimating yourself. You can handle just about anything that comes along."

As Jim's warm lips settled on hers, Dory felt some of the tension that had been winding tight in her all afternoon loosen. It was always that way with the two of them, she reflected. Even after all this time, when Jim touched her everything else seemed to fade into the background.

"Mmm," she murmured, when his mouth finally lifted from hers and he began dropping tiny kisses along her hairline. "Mmmmm, that's nice."

"See," he said as he nuzzled her ear. "I was right."

"Right about what?"

"About us." Sensuously he ran his hand down the length of her backbone. It was a moment before she realized that he was dragging the zipper of her dress open with it. "I was right to bully you into marrying me last month."

"You didn't bully me. I said 'I do' in front of that justice of the peace very, very willingly."

"Only after you spent most of the year testing our compatibility in just about every way you could think of," he growled. His fingers were now slipping open the hooks on her bra.

Her blue eyes twinkled up at him. "Don't tell me that you didn't enjoy some of those tests?"

"I enjoyed all of them, my sweet Dory. I enjoy everything about you, and I always will." Effortlessly he lifted her up into his arms and carried her to the bed.

And then they were in each other's arms, coming together with the same feverish need and desire that never seemed to abate between them. This time as they eagerly removed each other's clothing there was no talk of protection. Since their marriage they'd given up any thought of birth control. Dory had acknowledged that she'd like another child, and Jim had been ecstatic at the idea.

"I love you, Mrs. Gordon," he whispered much later when their union was complete and they cuddled under the blankets.

"It's mutual, sir," she whispered back. As she spoke, a secret smile played around her lips and one of her hands went to the slight round of her belly. She hadn't told Jim yet, but for a week now she'd suspected that she might be pregnant. The prospect brought a dreamy look to her eyes and she pressed her lips to her husband's shoulder. If she was right, what would the child she carried be like, she wondered—a little girl with her father's gypsy looks? Or perhaps the baby was a boy with blue eyes and black curls.

With a thrill of happiness, Dory hugged the thought to her. She longed for another child, a child of Jim's. Yet she didn't kid herself about the awesome responsibilities of parenthood. After what she—and Jim—had been through together this year, that was quite impossible.

The notion brought her worries about Beth back into focus. "Do you think we should look in on the girls again before we go to sleep?" she whispered into Jim's ear. "I know Beth and Gracie promised to go to bed early tonight, but you know how they are when they get together."

He was already half-asleep. "Um, no," he muttered. "Beth's going to be okay, Dory. Now let's get some sleep ourselves. We have to be fresh so we can cheer her on to victory tomorrow."

"Or console her."

"Or console her," he agreed calmly. "Disappointments are part of life."

THE NEXT MORNING Dory and Jim met the girls for breakfast. Beth, clearly nervous, ate a hearty but healthy breakfast of juice and oatmeal. She didn't talk much about the freestyle event scheduled for that evening, but she had a look of resolve. During the year she'd gained back five of the fifteen pounds she'd dropped during her illness, but she was trim and fit. And she was here because she wanted to be. Not even her father had been able to talk her out of coming back to try her skill once again at this nerve-racking competition.

"I have to, Mom," she'd told Dory. "I'd never be able to live with myself if I didn't. But," she'd added, leaning forward to give Dory a kiss on the cheek, "thanks for not wanting me to. I know you and Jim love me and that you don't want me to get hurt again the way I was last year."

Despite Beth's reassurances, Dory's tension mounted throughout the day. How could she not worry, she asked herself. The atmosphere at an event like this fairly crackled with the adrenaline of young athletes preparing to pit themselves against one another. And she could never forget what had happened the last time her daughter had been one of them.

"Well, this is it," Jim said at eight o'clock that evening as the crowd gathered to watch the Junior Ladies competition. Jim and Dory had just come back from dinner with the Prentices. Beth had stayed at the rink to take advantage of an extra practice session. Now she was on the ice, receiving last-minute instructions from Peggy Schrion.

"Beth looks good, doesn't she?" Dory commented. During the year the teenager had grown, become leggier. Tall and more solidly built then Dory, she would never be small and skinny like some of her competitors. But her body was firm and muscular and the womanliness of her maturing physique held an undeniable appeal.

"She looks great," Lydia said. "I love that snazzy new haircut she's got. And that yellow chiffon dress is beautiful on her. I don't know how you found time to make it, what with running your own business and taking care of that big old house you and Jim just moved into."

"Dory is a wonder." Jim put his arm around his new wife's waist. "Last week I came home to find that on top of everything else, she'd wallpapered all the bathrooms."

Dory laughed. "Well, I knew that the only reason you married me was that you wanted your own personal interior decorator."

Warmly they grinned at each other, sharing the private joke.

A few minutes later the announcer began reading off the names of the first flight of competitors. As the audience quieted to listen, Dory glanced at a nearby bleacher where her ex-husband and his new ladyfriend watched. Neal had been upset when Dory had married Jim and she knew that things between them would always be slightly awkward. During the year when they'd had to spend so much time coordinating their efforts to put Beth back on a healthy track, he'd tried on several occasions to reestablish a more intimate relationship.

But Dory had no interest in an intimate relationship with anyone but Jim and had rejected Neal's overtures firmly. Now that he saw how happy she was with her new husband and knew that there was no further hope of ever getting her back, he seemed reconciled. Dory hoped so, and honestly wished he'd find happiness with one of the many pretty women he continued to squire around town. Much to Dory's relief, Beth no longer appeared to worry about comparing herself with her father's girlfriends—maybe because she was so comfortable with the secure new family unit Dory and Jim had established.

"This is Beth's flight coming up," Jim said.

Dory nodded and, too anxious to speak, watched as her daughter and the other girls came out to warm up. Again she found herself thinking that Beth looked good, really good. There was a confidence about her, a sureness. And as Dory acknowledged this, some of her anxiety drained away.

When the warm-up was over, the other four girls left the ice and Beth took up her starting pose.

"Miss Beth Barker, Columbia Figure Skating Club," the announcer's voice boomed over the loudspeaker.

After a few seconds' hiatus, the music started and Beth went into her first move, a graceful series of double threes ending in a breathtaking lay-back spin.

When it was over and Beth was flying across the ice in preparation for her first double jump, Dory started to smile. For suddenly she knew that it was going to be all right. Probably Beth wouldn't win, but she was going to skate well enough to be proud of herself. And even if she took a tumble, she wouldn't be devastated by it. She would pick herself up and keep trying—which, as Dory had learned, was all that really mattered.

Jim took her hand. "It's going to be okay," he whispered as Beth landed the difficult maneuver.

"Yes," Dory whispered back, returning the pressure of his fingers and shooting him a look radiant with love. "Yes, it's going to be just fine."

Harlequin Superromance

COMING NEXT MONTH

Indulge a Little, Give a Lot

To receive your free gift send us the required number of proofs-of-purchase from any specially marked "Indulge A Little" Harlequin or Silhouette book with the Offer Certificate properly completed, plus a cheque or money order (do not send cash) to cover postage and handling payable to Harlequin/Silhouette "Indulge A Little, Give A Lot" Offer. We will send you the specified gift.

Mail-in-Offer

OFFER CERTIFICATE

Item:	A. Collector's Doll	B. Soaps in a Basket	C. Potpourri Sachet	D. Scented Hangers
# of Proofs-of-Purchase	18	12	6	4
Postage & Handling	$3.25	$2.75	$2.25	$2.00
Check One				

Name _____

Address _____ Apt. # _____

City _____ State _____ Zip _____

ONE PROOF OF PURCHASE

To collect your free gift by mail you must include the necessary number of proofs-of-purchase plus postage and handling with offer certificate.

HS-1

Harlequin®/Silhouette®

Mail this certificate, designated number of proofs-of-purchase and check or money order for postage and handling to:

INDULGE A LITTLE
P.O. Box 9055 Buffalo, N.Y. 14269-9055

NOTE THIS IMPORTANT OFFER'S TERMS

Offer available in the United States and Canada.